RIPPLES THROUGH TIME

Christina Courtenay

REVIEW

Copyright © Christina Courtenay 2025

The right of Christina Courtenay to be identified as the
Author of the Work has been asserted by her in accordance with the
Copyright, Designs and Patents Act 1988.

Chapter header illustration © AMarc/iStockphoto

First published in 2025 by Headline Review
An imprint of Headline Publishing Group Limited

1

Apart from any use permitted under UK copyright law, this publication
may only be reproduced, stored, or transmitted, in any form, or by any
means, with prior permission in writing of the publishers or, in the
case of reprographic production, in accordance with the terms
of licences issued by the Copyright Licensing Agency.

Cataloguing in Publication Data is available from the British Library

Paperback ISBN 978 1 0354 1863 3

Typeset in 11/14 pt Minion Pro
by Six Red Marbles UK, Thetford, Norfolk

Printed and bound in Great Britain by Clays Ltd, Elcograf S.p.A.

Headline's policy is to use papers that are natural, renewable and
recyclable products and made from wood grown in well-managed
forests and other controlled sources. The logging and manufacturing
processes are expected to conform to the environmental
regulations of the country of origin.

Headline Publishing Group Limited
An Hachette UK Company
Carmelite House
50 Victoria Embankment
London EC4Y 0DZ

The authorised representative in the EEA is Hachette Ireland, 8 Castlecourt
Centre, Dublin 15, D15 XTP3, Ireland (email: info@hbgi.ie)

www.headline.co.uk
www.hachette.co.uk

**Acclaim for Christina Courtenay's enthralling
time slip and dual time romances**

'The Queen of Time Slip Romance has done it again! A romantic
and compelling read – a total page turner'
Sandy Barker

'A brilliantly written time slip that combines mystery and
romance into a compelling and vividly imagined story'
Nicola Cornick

'Christina Courtenay is guaranteed to carry me off to another place
and time in a way that no other author succeeds in doing'
Sue Moorcroft

'A wonderful dual timeline story with captivating characters
and full of vivid historical detail bringing the Viking
world alive, I didn't want it to end!'
Clare Marchant

'Seals Christina Courtenay's crown as the Queen of Viking Romance.
This sweeping tale . . . will leave you wanting more'
Catherine Miller

'An absorbing story, fast-paced and vividly imagined,
which really brought the Viking world to life'
Pamela Hartshorne

'A love story and an adventure, all rolled up inside a huge amount of
intricately detailed, well-researched history. Thoroughly enjoyable'
Kathleen McGurl

'Prepare to be swept along in this treasure of an adventure!
With a smart, courageous heroine and hunky, honourable
hero at the helm, what's not to like?'
Kate Ryder

'Christina Courtenay's particular talent is to entice
you into her world and capture you'
Alison Morton

'I was totally captivated by this story of love and adventure which
had me racing through the pages . . . I was drawn into the
Viking world so easily which felt authentic and real'
Sue Fortin

'Brought the 9th century world alive to me and made
me desperate to read more about it'
Gill Stewart

Christina Courtenay is an award-winning author of historical romance and time slip (dual time) stories. She started writing so that she could be a stay-at-home mum to her two daughters, but didn't get published until daughter number one left home aged twenty-one, so that didn't quite go to plan! Since then, however, she's made up for it by having twenty novels published and winning the RNA's Romantic Novel of the Year Award for Best Historical Romantic Novel twice with *Highland Storms* (2012) and *The Gilded Fan* (2014), and once for Best Fantasy Romantic Novel with *Echoes of the Runes* (2021).

Christina is half Swedish and grew up in that country. She has also lived in Japan and Switzerland, but is now based in Herefordshire, close to the Welsh border. She's a keen amateur genealogist and loves history and archaeology (the armchair variety).

To find out more, visit **christinacourtenay.com**, find her on Facebook **/Christinacourtenayauthor** or follow her on X **@PiaCCourtenay** and Instagram **@christinacourtenayauthor**.

By Christina Courtenay

Standalones	*The Runes novels*
Trade Winds	Echoes of the Runes
Highland Storms	The Runes of Destiny
Monsoon Mists	Whispers of the Runes
The Scarlet Kimono	Tempted by the Runes
The Gilded Fan	Promises of the Runes
The Jade Lioness	Legacy of the Runes
The Silent Touch of Shadows	
The Secret Kiss of Darkness	
The Soft Whisper of Dreams	
The Velvet Cloak of Moonlight	
Hidden in the Mists	
Shadows in the Ashes	
Shadows in the Spring	
Ripples Through Time	

To Bucky and Lillie, my lovely 'grand-birds', who kept me company when I wrote this novel – thank you!

Prologue

The longship glided through the water with a muted hiss, the gaping mouth of its dragon's-head prow parting the veils of early-morning mist that draped the river. The motley crew of men sitting on their travelling kists along the sides dipped the oars in unison, making only the smallest of splashing noises. Anyone listening would have assumed it was a fish slapping its tail fin above the surface, nothing more.

No one spoke. They all knew what to do and looked to their leader for a signal. He stood in the stern, manning the steering oar while scanning the riverbank for the right place to beach his ship. A collection of roofs came into view, looming in the distance, a few curls of smoke beginning to float up into the sky through the thatch. The inhabitants were stirring, but they'd be sleepy and unprepared when the attack came.

One of the crewmen momentarily closed his eyes. He didn't want to be here. Had tired of this game of cat-and-mouse they'd been engaged in for years. But loyalty and honour forbade him from rebelling and kept him seated, wordlessly working his oar with the rest of them. When the time came, he would jump over the gunwale, sword in one hand, shield in the other, and sprint towards their unsuspecting victims. Surprise was the key. If your enemy *didn't know you were coming, you always had the upper hand. And by the time they realised what was happening, it would already be too late.*

The campaign of terror and plunder would carry on until his uncle had had enough. And that would not be any time soon, if ever, because the man was insatiable.

Chapter One

West Mercia, spring AD 873

'Hurry, you're wanted in the hall!'

Merewen looked up from the cough mixture she was preparing in the small hut she used for such tasks. Her younger sister, Aelfwynn, had pulled the door open and stuck her head inside, panting slightly. She'd clearly run as fast as she could, and the obvious urgency of her mission made Merewen's stomach muscles clench.

'Why? What's the matter? Has someone hurt themselves?'

As the settlement's healer, it fell to her to see to any injuries. It would help to know what she'd be dealing with so that she could bring the right supplies.

'No. Father wants a word, is all.'

'Oh.' That still sounded ominous, but Merewen knew it was best not to keep him waiting. If she was in for a scolding, that would only make matters worse. 'Very well, I'm coming.'

She abandoned the cough mixture and wiped her hands on a cloth before leaving. While walking quickly in the direction of the main building, she made sure her hair was tidy, smoothing down the curly wisps that always seemed to escape despite her best efforts to tame them.

'What do you think I've done this time, Sceadu?' she whispered to the shaggy hound who had been waiting for her outside the hut. He was a huge, hairy grey beast, the size of a small calf, and her constant shadow and guardian, but he couldn't protect her from reprimands. He padded along next to her, giving silent support.

For the life of her she couldn't remember any possible transgressions, but no doubt she'd soon find out what she had done wrong. Her older sister, Burghild, who effectively ran the household since their mother's passing, was good at blaming Merewen for anything that went awry. The two sisters had never seen eye to eye, and Burghild appeared to delight in making Merewen's life difficult. And unfortunately, their father, Beorthric, believed his oldest daughter more often than not because she was a very convincing liar.

As she entered the hall, Merewen halted momentarily, taken aback by the sight of her betrothed, Oslac, sitting next to her father. She hadn't realised he was due to visit today or she would have made more of an effort with her appearance. He was the son and heir of their closest neighbour, and she was set to marry him this summer. It was a good match, and she was excited by the prospect of finally having her own household and escaping her sister's machinations. It didn't hurt that Oslac was handsome, with dark hair and hazel eyes. She knew he was admired by all the local women, and she felt very lucky to be the one he had chosen.

She frowned as she registered that Burghild was sitting next to him looking smug. Never a good sign. In contrast, Oslac kept his gaze fixed on the floor. That was strange. Normally he couldn't seem to take his eyes off Merewen. What on earth was going on? She walked over to the group and stopped in front of them.

'Father? Is there something amiss?'

'Not as such.' Beorthric cleared his throat before launching into speech. 'I merely wished to inform you that I have decided your sister will make a better match for Oslac than you.' He indicated the now smirking Burghild. 'As you know, her betrothed was recently killed by the heathens, although why he felt the need to go off and fight them I'll never know. Be that as it may, she is my eldest child, and whomsoever she marries will inherit this settlement since I have not been blessed with any sons. Oslac will take over his own father's domains in due course, and as Burghild's husband he can eventually merge the two properties into a larger one. That will create a very rich holding and increase our families' standing in the area. So from this moment on, I declare your betrothal to Oslac at an end. He and Burghild will be wed at midsummer.'

Merewen was speechless and simply stared at him for a moment. Her sister's husband-to-be getting himself killed fighting the so-called Heathen Army that was rampaging around the country had been a blow. Naturally Merewen had felt for Burghild and had wished for her to find happiness with someone else. But not at her own expense. Not with *her* man.

'You're giving my betrothed to Burghild?' she asked, anger stirring inside her. 'And what about me? Am I to be palmed off to that old widower with six children instead?' Godric, a man almost her father's age, was currently the only other marriage prospect in these parts, as most of the younger men had gone off to fight the heathens and hadn't come back. At least not yet.

'Do not be impertinent. I have other plans for you.' Beorthric scowled at her, although she could see him squirming slightly, as if he was fully aware of the fact that he was hurting her.

'And what, pray tell, might those be?' She wasn't convinced she wanted to hear them, and his next words proved her right.

'I have it in mind to send you to the nuns at Hreopandune. I have heard they are in need of healers, and you have the necessary skills. Your dowry isn't large, as I have to provide for your two younger sisters as well, but it should be enough to secure you a place with them. Once there, you can pray daily for the souls of everyone in our family. You might even rise to the rank of abbess one day. They wield a lot of power, or so I'm told, and that could benefit us as well.'

'You're banishing me to a monastery?'

Merewen could not believe what she was hearing. That morning she'd had a bright future, but now all her dreams had been dashed in one fell swoop. She was to live a solitary life dedicated to God. No husband, no children, no household to run. It could be viewed as an honour to serve the Lord, but to her it sounded more like a prison sentence. And it was all to benefit her sister, who in Merewen's opinion did not deserve it.

'Do not be so dramatic. It is a good life, and you know as well as I do that there is a dearth of young men in these parts. All over the country, in fact, what with the constant fighting. And what's more, you can help defeat the enemy with prayers.'

She snorted in disbelief. As if prayers had any effect on the Norsemen. Fury made her clench her fists and fix her erstwhile betrothed with a glare. 'And you are amenable to this change, Oslac? Am I to take it that all the sweet words you've been plying me with were a lie? You no longer prefer me over Burghild, as you've said time and time again?'

That last sentence made her sister's superior expression disappear. They both knew that Merewen was the prettier of the two. She wasn't vain and didn't consider herself anything special, but poor Burghild had inherited their father's large nose and prominent chin, an unfortunate combination. Merewen was convinced this was at least partly to blame for the enmity Burghild bore her, but her appearance wasn't something she could do anything about. And Oslac had told her repeatedly how attractive he found her. How he couldn't wait to make her his in every way.

She saw him flinch, and he raised his gaze to hers at last. There was guilt and conflicted emotions in the depths of his eyes, but he squared his shoulders and stared back, swallowing hard. 'You know I meant what I said, um, at the time, but . . . circumstances change. Your father's arrangements make sense. Had Burghild not already been betrothed, I would have asked for her hand in marriage instead of yours from the beginning.'

A huff of incredulous laughter escaped before she could stop it. 'Is that so?' she scoffed. It wasn't true. He'd mentioned on several occasions that he had always had his eye on Merewen and wanted no one but her. The loathsome liar. 'Well then, I wish you well and I hope you don't live to regret your decision. Forgive me if I don't pray for your future happiness and prosperity. I shall concentrate my efforts solely on the Norsemen.'

'Merewen!' her father barked, but for once his outrage did not scare her, and she paid him no heed.

She turned on her heel and stormed out of the hall, slamming the door behind her. Sceadu was waiting for her outside, and he followed without hesitation as she ran back to her hut. Once inside, she sank down onto the floor and allowed her emotions free rein. For a long time she wept with great big hiccoughing sobs while hugging her dog's neck. He leaned his head against hers, giving her the occasional lick to show his sympathy.

'Oh Sceadu, what am I to do? I don't want to become a nun! And what will happen to you? I doubt they allow animals in the monastery.' The thought of having to leave him behind made her sob even harder.

Eventually she calmed down and tried to accept her fate. Perhaps God had never meant for her to have a husband and family.

He might have intended her for His service all along. She'd have to make the best of it, but until such time as she left this settlement, she would only speak to her father or sister when strictly necessary. And as for that lying toad Oslac, he could rot in hell.

London, April, present day

'How long do we have to keep sneaking around like this? Can't we just tell her and get it over with?'

Alix Howell stopped abruptly at the sound of her younger sister's voice. It was coming from the mud room beyond the kitchen in their parents' house, and although Autumn was whispering, the words were still perfectly audible.

'Patience, baby.' The voice replying belonged to Alix's fiancé, Sean, and hearing it made her freeze in shock. 'We have to wait until the mortgage application for the flat has been approved,' he continued. 'You know we need Alix to cover the down payment. It's not like we can afford it ourselves. Once all the paperwork is signed, it won't matter so much, and I'll pay her back when I can. Or you can pay her rent so she can go and live somewhere else. I doubt she'll want to share with us, even though there are two bedrooms.'

A muffled giggle was the answer to that statement. *What the hell?* The pain of betrayal hit Alix right in the middle of the sternum, knocking all the air out of her. She clutched her stomach and tried to breathe while processing what she'd just heard. Her sister was having an affair with Sean? Since when? No. This couldn't be true. Alix hadn't noticed him acting any different recently. There had been quite a few late nights in the office and some outings with his mates that he'd claimed were for boys only, but no other red flags. He'd acted as loving as normal. *What a consummate liar!* She hadn't suspected a thing.

And what was this about the down payment? Was he seriously planning to use Alix's life savings, combined with his own meagre contribution, to obtain a mortgage for the flat they were buying together, then dump her? A flat that apparently she was never going to live in. *The utter bastard!*

So not happening.

After the week she'd had at work – although she didn't want to think about that right now – this was the last straw. She marched over to the door that separated the mud room from the kitchen and threw it open.

'No need to wait. I won't be signing any of those papers now, or providing any money, so you can go ahead and make your relationship official,' she announced, pulling off the cheap zirconia ring Sean had bought her instead of a diamond one and throwing it at him. It was supposed to have been temporary until he could afford something better, since they'd needed the money for the flat. So much for that.

'I wouldn't have been able to afford the mortgage payments anyway, as I quit my job yesterday,' she added. She hadn't had a chance to tell anyone yet, and now it probably didn't matter. It might even be a blessing in disguise.

Autumn and Sean's stunned expressions and gaping mouths would have been hilarious if the cause hadn't been so hurtful. Alix didn't intend to stick around and wait for them to recover, however. No doubt they'd try and come up with some excuse as to why they were perfect for each other. Judging by previous experience, it would involve a variation on the theme of Alix being too serious or boring, compared to her uber-glamorous sister. Autumn was the 'fun one' of the two, according to most of their friends. The one with the natural charm and a gift for socialising and hogging the limelight. Whereas Alix was shy and introverted, more interested in reading than partying.

Being less than a year apart, most people had mistaken them for twins when they were children. They did look fairly similar when in their natural state, but Alix always felt overshadowed by her sister. Autumn was a beautician and knew how to enhance her looks; from chemical hair-straightening and lip fillers to a year-round spray tan and hours spent with a personal trainer each week, nothing was left to chance. And it would seem that Sean preferred this improved version of what the gods had given them.

He was welcome to it.

'Alix, wait! I can explain! Stop for a minute . . .'

She ignored the increasingly anxious pleas from behind her and swore that this was the last time she'd allow Autumn to steal anything that belonged to her. Her sister had been doing it more or less from birth, and mostly getting away with it too. She had been the golden child for as long as Alix could remember. The one who could do no wrong. As soon as she'd been born, Alix had been effectively sidelined. Autumn had been a beautiful, contented baby, by all accounts, whereas Alix had been colicky and difficult. The new baby was able to charm their parents in a way that Alix had never mastered, and later she had lying down to a fine art as well. More times than she cared to count, Alix had been blamed for every misdemeanour, despite any lack of evidence. It was enough that Autumn turned her limpid gaze on their parents and shed a few theatrical tears. They fell for it every time. There was no competing with her. She always got her way.

Well, enough was enough.

Sweeping past their astonished parents, and assorted other relatives who had come over for Sunday lunch, Alix grabbed her handbag and jacket and slammed her way out of the house. Thank goodness she hadn't completed the flat purchase with Sean yet. She was still sharing a loft apartment with two friends, but that would have to change too. Now that she'd left the job that tied her to the capital, it was time to move somewhere far from London. Anywhere her sister wasn't living would be fine.

Vindictively, she hoped it would be many years before Sean and Autumn could afford to buy a flat. Her own nest egg would be used to purchase a property that was all hers.

Chapter Two

Hreopandune/Repton, Mercia, April/Einmánuðr AD 874

'Have we not accumulated all the treasure we need by now? We've been campaigning for years, and I for one am sick of it!' Eirik Ormsson glared at his uncle Hastein, but received only a disdainful glance in return.

'We have nowhere near enough, boy! There is much more plunder to be had in these lands. Why give up so soon? Are you a coward that you don't wish to fight for more? You wouldn't want to end up like your father, would you, dying in his bed like an old man?'

The slur on his father's character stung, but Eirik knew from long acquaintance with his uncle that it was useless to defend him.

'I've amply demonstrated my courage these past twelve years or more,' he growled. 'But unlike you, I have no aspirations to live like a king. I'd be perfectly content with a prosperous property of my own to settle in. Preferably before I'm too old or irrevocably maimed.'

Hastein snorted. 'Want to till the soil like a thrall, do you?

Why aim so low when you can just take what you want? No. I say we head west from here and don't stop until our horses are weighed down with silver and gold.'

Eirik gave up. There was no reasoning with the man at the moment. In theory, he could have headed north by himself with some of Jarl Halfdan Hvitserk's men when they left in a week or two. They were bound for Northumbria, where Halfdan had promised to allocate lands to those who wished to settle there. The insult to Eirik's honour did not permit this course of action, however. Hastein was all the family he had now, and Eirik's loyalty to the man who had taken care of him since his father's death ran deep.

'One more summer of plundering, then I'll persuade him to stop,' he muttered to himself. Surely even Hastein had some limit as to how much loot he needed in order to live out his days in luxury.

Then again, maybe not. The man's avarice knew no bounds.

Agitated beyond measure, Eirik left the perimeter of the encampment to walk off his frustration. The thousands-strong force of Norsemen that the Vestrsaxar called the Heathen Army had overwintered at Hreopandune in the heart of the Mercian kingdom after overpowering the former ruler the previous autumn. It had been a stronghold and sacred site of the Mercian royal family for centuries, and contained a church with adjoining mausoleum. This had been filled with the bones of Mercian kings, but Eirik knew some of his comrades had plundered the caskets for treasure and strewn the bones haphazardly around the small crypt. Those bones would never again be pieced together to form a whole skeleton.

Once ensconced at Hreopandune, the warbands had set about fortifying the area, and created a small secure enclosure where their leaders stayed. During the winter, one of them, Halfdan

Hvitserk, had had the remains of his brother, Ivar the Boneless, transferred here, and a large grave mound had been constructed to house them. This now dominated the area and signalled Norse power to anyone contemplating it.

'Ivar was a formidable fighter, by all accounts, taking what he wanted,' Hastein had told Eirik, implying that this was the kind of man he should aspire to become. Yet Eirik couldn't find it in himself to want more than a peaceful existence. He'd been part of a warband since the age of eleven. Now he had seen twenty-four winters, and it felt as though he had taken part in enough bloodshed to last for several lifetimes. His uncle had claimed it was necessary to wage war on the inhabitants of this large island, but Eirik was beginning to doubt it was true any longer.

The Heathen Army's initial intent had been to accumulate enough riches for those taking part to gain status in their homelands. Their backgrounds varied, as the men came from all over the northern lands, as well as Írland, Frisia and elsewhere. The leaders appeared to have a different agenda, however, aiming to take over the various kingdoms here one by one and settle there. So far the East Angles, Northumbrians and Mercians had been defeated. Surely that was enough for the three- or four-thousand-strong force? There would be plenty of land to go around.

But some men, like Hastein, had become used to a life without toil, where all they had to do was grab what they wanted. Who was the lazy one in this scenario? Eirik wondered sourly. He knew the life of a farmer was hard, but it would be more satisfying than taking what others had strived for. More peaceful. And surely more honourable. Also, they had enough silver now to pay an army of people to till the land for them. It wasn't as though they would become thralls overnight.

With a sigh, he carried on walking. After a while, he reached the place where the greater part of the army was camped, east of

Hreopandune, on a hillside overlooking the river. Longships lined the banks nearby, some of them in the process of being repaired or overhauled, causing much noise and bustle. A veritable forest of tents covered the hill itself, grouped together in clusters. Each warband – virtual brotherhoods that stuck together under one leader and were bound by their oaths to him – made up a separate zone of the camp. Their tents had been set up to leave an open space in the centre, where there were trestle tables and a hearth for communal cooking and warmth.

The tents themselves were simple triangular timber frames covered with canvas. This did not afford much in the way of protection from the winter cold, but they were lined with blankets and furs, which helped. Each one slept five or six men, their gear stowed inside, while shields and spears leaned against the outside. In the evenings, the groups would gather round their own fires, sharing the steaming-hot broth or stew that someone's woman had cooked, drinking ale, telling tall tales or playing board games. Quite often this evolved into fights as men bored with this sedentary existence released their pent-up frustrations. They couldn't wait for spring, when they'd be off on new adventures.

Eirik passed some of these tent groupings and continued towards the other side of the camp, where traders and craftsmen had set up their booths. Some were warriors during the fighting season and plied a trade during the winter, while others were craftsmen full-time. Eirik himself had learned the trade of a comb-maker to pass the time, but he didn't have his own stall. Instead, another man – Haldor – sold whatever he made and in return took a small cut of the profit for himself. It was an arrangement that suited them both.

Eirik stopped by Reidulf the silversmith's booth. The man looked up and smiled when he caught sight of him. 'Ah, there you are. Your items are all ready for collection.' He went to rummage in a chest that had been kept locked for safety, and brought out a bundle wrapped in a woollen cloth, which he unrolled and proffered to Eirik. 'Here, will this do?'

'Perfect. My thanks!'

The metalworker had taken all the items Eirik had brought him from the previous year's campaign and melted them down. Some he'd fashioned into thick armbands of various shapes and forms – plain circles, twisted strands or flat surfaces with decorative punchwork – others into small ingots that were easily portable. What had formerly been goblets and platters looted from churches and monasteries were now much more useful items. The kind of wealth Eirik could bring with him anywhere and use as payment if necessary, but also as ornaments to show off his riches.

'You've done brilliant work,' he commented, threading the bands onto his arms, where they joined a multitude of others from previous seasons. Unlike some of his warrior brothers, he hadn't squandered his gains on gaming, bets or camp women. He didn't bother nicking the silver to check for purity, as he trusted Reidulf implicitly. They'd been friends for years now, and he knew the man wouldn't cheat him like some of the other metalworkers were wont to do.

'I'm glad you're pleased.' Reidulf invited Eirik to sit down on a stool for a chat. 'I gather you'll be leaving soon, so I guess I'll see you in the autumn.'

'Yes, probably.' Eirik heaved a sigh and told his friend about the argument with his uncle. 'I'm beginning to think he'll never settle anywhere. I'm stuck raiding with him until the day he dies.'

'Hmm, yes, it does sound like it. I'm sorry. I suppose he'd be furious if you decided to go your own way.'

'He would see it as the ultimate betrayal. I can't do that. I owe him for looking after me and my mother when Father died. He could have left us on that stinking island in Frisia, but he didn't.'

Eirik and his parents had been living on an island not far from Dorestad, the main trading town in Frisia, when his father had died of a sudden illness. Eirik had only hazy memories from that time of a larger-than-life uncle sweeping in to save his mother from having to become a camp follower. Since Hastein didn't have children of his own, he'd more or less adopted Eirik, spending time each day teaching him battle skills. How could Eirik possibly leave the man now? He owed him everything.

But he could still dream of a future where he had his own domains, and a wife and family to come home to at night. With the help of the gods, perhaps one day he'd get there. He only hoped it would be sooner rather than later.

Chapter Three

Hereford, May, present day

'So where were you on the twenty-eighth of March, Mr Vaughan?'

The police officer scowled at Noah and he glared back, refusing to be intimidated.

'Probably in the lambing barn. Hang on a second.' He pulled up the calendar on his phone and checked the relevant date. 'Yep. The last four lambs were born that day. I remember the third one got stuck. Took hours to come out. Thought I'd lose the ewe, but luckily she managed to give birth successfully in the end.'

Officer Jones wrinkled his nose, as if he didn't want to hear the nitty-gritty about birthing lambs. Too bad. He was the one who'd asked.

'And where were your sister and her boyfriend at this time?'

Noah shrugged. 'How should I know? Niamh is an adult. I don't keep tabs on her twenty-four seven. As for Reece, hopefully he was far away from my farm.'

Chance would be a fine thing.

He'd suspected for some time that Reece, his sister's good-for-nothing boyfriend, had had a hand in the sheep rustling that had happened the previous autumn. It had stopped when he'd told the guy he was going to install security cameras in all his fields. He hadn't, since there were no funds for such an extravagance, but Reece didn't know that and was too stupid – or too lazy – to check. It did seem a bit of a coincidence that there hadn't been any more thefts after that, though.

'He wasn't,' Officer Jones said. 'He claimed you had given him permission to use a metal detector to search your fields, and that was the day he found the Viking hoard.'

'I gave *Niamh* permission, not him. I should have guessed he was in on it too, but I didn't think to ask. It was her metal detector – I gave it to her for Christmas.' Noah ground his teeth together. He wished he'd never bought the damned thing now. It had caused nothing but trouble.

'Your sister says she wasn't with Mr Watkins that day and that he was out in the fields on his own. You're sure she wasn't helping you with the lambing?'

Noah snorted. 'Yeah, right. As if!' At the officer's raised eyebrow, he elaborated. 'She hates farm work and only helps out if I force her. She's much too squeamish and wouldn't be caught dead near the back end of a sheep, especially not one that's giving birth. The property belongs to me and the animals are my responsibility. Niamh just lives there while she's studying sociology at uni, long-distance.'

He wished she'd go and study at an actual university, but she'd tried it for one term and hated it. The realisation that she would have to live off her student loan and not have her room and board paid for by him, the way she did at home, probably had a lot to do with it. At the moment, she didn't contribute a penny towards the household costs and used most of her student loan for frivolous things like clothes and clubbing. She seemed to take it for granted that he'd foot the bill for everything else, although she'd occasionally do a grocery run and pay for that.

'Letting me stay here and paying for my food is the least you can do after you got your big inheritance,' she'd told him when she moved back home without even asking if he was OK with that.

The fact that he'd inherited the farm and everything in it from his late uncle had been a huge bone of contention between them. But it was *his* uncle, not hers, brother to Noah's dad. Niamh was only his half-sister; they had the same mother, but different fathers. Neither man was in the picture – Noah's father was deceased, and God only knew where Niamh's was – so when their mum had died, Uncle Ifan and Aunt Jane had kindly taken both siblings into their home. Niamh should have been grateful to be included, since she wasn't actually their relative, but instead she'd resented having to live 'out in the sticks', as she'd termed it, and on a 'smelly farm' instead of in London. Granted, she'd been a stroppy teenager at the time, only fourteen when they moved in, but she ought to have matured a bit since then. Sadly, that hadn't happened.

Uncle Ifan had stated in his will that he wished the property to stay in the family, as it had done for centuries, and he knew Noah would take good care of it. If Niamh had ever lifted a finger around the place to help out, he might have given her a share, but he didn't deem her worthy of receiving anything. She disagreed.

'I'm family too, even if it's not by blood. Part of it should have been mine.' She had been furious, but the will was legal and watertight. Nothing she could do about it.

Except punish Noah by staying on and scrounging off him every chance she got.

Officer Jones jolted him back to the present and started off in a new direction. 'The items we've recovered from the hoard so far were sold via your laptop. How do you explain that?'

With a sigh, Noah closed his eyes and prayed for patience. 'It's not my private laptop as such, it's the farm computer. It's used for things like ordering feed and keeping up to date with our breeding programme. It's old and doesn't even have a password. Anyone could have had access to it, as long as they were in the house.'

Knowing Reece and Niamh, they'd used it while he was fast asleep. After a day spent working hard around the place, Noah slept like the dead. He wouldn't have heard a thing.

But what had they been thinking?

One – or both? – of them had apparently found a Viking hoard on his land with the help of that accursed metal detector. Instead of declaring it to the authorities and paying him half the value, as he'd told Niamh she would have to do if she came across anything of note, they had sold some of the artefacts online. Illegally. Someone had noticed and alerted the police, who had swept in and arrested first Noah, then Reece and Niamh. Noah had been let go almost immediately, although he was still brought in for questioning from time to time, like today. Niamh had also been allowed home when Reece told officers she hadn't been part of the crime. Reece himself had been arrested, as he'd been dumb enough to keep a few items from the hoard at his home, thus incriminating himself.

Noah didn't believe for a moment that Niamh hadn't been part of the illicit venture. She was besotted with her thug of a boyfriend. But did he really want her to end up in jail, like Reece? With all their other relatives gone, and him the older sibling, he still felt responsible for her despite everything. Taking the fall for the crime while not implicating Niamh was possibly the only good thing her useless partner had ever done for her. Noah wasn't going to argue with that unless he had to.

'Did Mr Watkins stay over at the farm often?' the police officer queried.

'Yes.'

Way too often, if you asked Noah. The man had practically lived there, and he was another freeloader who never offered to pay for any of the food or drink he consumed. Noah really should have put his foot down ages ago.

'So you're saying he could have had access to your laptop when you were asleep?'

'To the farm laptop, yes. Look, I'm not very computer savvy. Ask anyone. I wouldn't know where to even begin to sell anything online. I buy feed for my livestock and I look up things like auction times. That's it. And if I'd found gold on my land, I would have gone straight to the authorities. I'm an honest man.'

The officer bit his lip as though he wasn't convinced, but finally he nodded. 'Very well. You may go for now, but we might need to question you again. Mr Watkins is refusing to say where the rest of the treasure is. Until we've found it all, we won't give up.'

'How do you know there was more?'

So far about twenty items had been recovered – all the objects Reece had attempted to sell online, plus the few he'd kept for himself. A gold ring, a couple of bracelets of some sort, a pendant and an assortment of coins. Most from the mid to late ninth century or thereabouts. Noah hadn't known there were others.

'Because we found photos on his phone of the treasure *in situ* as he uncovered it. There looked to be hundreds of coins and possibly other items as well, like silver ingots. Also, he apparently bragged to some of his mates that he'd found a huge pile of gold and silver that was going to make him rich.' Officer Jones rolled his eyes. 'What he's sold so far is valuable, but nowhere near a fortune. Whenever we try to get him to reveal the whereabouts of the rest, however, he clams up, although he has this really shifty look on his face.'

Yes, Noah was very familiar with that particular expression

and could well believe Reece was holding something back. The only problem was that if it was true, Niamh probably knew where he'd stashed his finds. She wasn't telling, though. And Noah had no way of making Reece talk either. The man couldn't be reasoned with and physical intimidation was out of the question, even if Noah had been so inclined, which he wasn't. The authorities had acted unusually fast and Reece had already been tried, found guilty and sentenced to a ten-year prison sentence. He was safely behind bars and if he wasn't talking to the police, he'd never divulge anything to Noah even if he went to visit him. It was a hopeless situation.

'I see. Well, I hope you do find it, Officer. Bye for now.'

He left the police station with a crushing weight on his shoulders. It was bad enough that his sister's boyfriend was in jail, but the thought that she was in danger of being prosecuted as well was awful. She'd been difficult for as long as he could remember, and hadn't made life easy for the kind people who had taken them both in, but he'd never thought of her as a criminal. As a teenager, he hadn't exactly been a saint himself, at least not while they lived in London. Coming to the farm, where he was expected to work hard if he wanted to stay, had been his salvation.

Niamh was a different matter, and when Aunt Jane had died of COVID, things had gone from bad to worse. Poor Uncle Ifan couldn't control Niamh and didn't understand girls. He'd never had children of his own, and dealing with a rebellious teen was beyond him. His way of coping had been to ignore her, leaving her free to go her own way. That mostly entailed her getting into trouble, which Noah then had to bail her out of.

He sighed again as he headed for his battered Land Rover. Niamh was twenty-three now. Wasn't it past time for her to grow up and take some responsibility for her life? But egged on by the likes of Reece, that was never going to happen. Noah needed to be firmer with her. Tell her she was only welcome to stay at the farm until her last semester was over. After that, she needed to stand on her own two feet.

He wasn't looking forward to that conversation one bit.

Driving past his fields, Noah kept an eye out for anything unusual, as always. Sheep could get themselves into all sorts of trouble, like getting their heads stuck in the fence or somehow wandering out onto the road. It was second nature to him now to check as he went by.

The sheep were fine, but there was a small electric-blue car parked at the entrance to one of the neighbour's fields that abutted his own. The two fields shared an access area, and his happened to contain a Neolithic stone cairn. The very cairn where Reece claimed to have found his Viking hoard, although he had so far refused to pinpoint the exact spot. The local archaeologists had been out to check, but the thief had covered his tracks well. Since the treasure was gone, and it had rained heavily since, they'd been unable to say for sure where it had been hidden. They weren't best pleased about that, muttering something about 'context' and 'layers' in the soil, which Noah hadn't understood.

He braked and parked next to the little Fiat 500, which looked dinky next to his much larger car. Did it belong to one of the archaeologists? This was private land, and no one had asked his permission to come and take another look. The cairn was a listed monument, and he'd been thinking of allowing the public access to it, but it was something Uncle Ifan had vehemently opposed, so he hadn't decided yet. At the moment, however, it was off limits to everyone. Perhaps the intruder was one of the nosy newspaper reporters who had tried to get him to comment – without success. They weren't very good at taking no for an answer.

He got out and scanned the neighbour's field first, but it was empty, so he headed into his own, vaulting the gate instead of opening it. At first, he didn't see anyone there either, but then he spotted movement by the cairn, which was situated on top of a small hill in the far corner. Taking long strides, he made his way towards the stones and saw that it was a woman, perhaps in her mid to late twenties. She was standing staring at the cairn, obviously deep in thought, but she looked very out of place in the bucolic setting. She was wearing a pencil skirt and tights, with sensible flattish shoes and a short windbreaker, her long dark hair pulled into a tight bun at the back of her neck and secured with a large clip. Definitely not an archaeologist. Journalist then?

'This is private land. You're trespassing,' he said, his voice a little gruffer than he'd intended.

Her eyes widened in consternation, and he registered their unusual colour – a clear grey that seemed like brilliant quicksilver in the spring sunshine.

'I'm so sorry. I just . . .' Her cheeks turned pink and she lowered her gaze. 'It sounds really silly, but I wanted to see the place where it was found. The hoard, I mean.'

'Why? Are you writing about it?' He stuck his hands in his pockets, planting himself firmly in front of her. If he gave off an unfriendly vibe, too bad. She had no business being here.

'Writing? I suppose you could say that, but really I was just curious.'

'Sure you were. Well, I'd appreciate it if you'd leave now. As I said, this is my land. There's no public footpath anywhere near here.' He frowned at her.

Some of her hair had come loose from the bun and was blowing around in the breeze. It caressed her smooth cheeks, which had gone an even deeper shade of pink, obscuring the smattering of freckles that spread across them and her nose. She tucked a curly strand behind her ear, but it immediately escaped again, buffeted by the spring wind. The gesture was curiously endearing, and he couldn't help but notice that she was very pretty in a nerdy kind of way. She had delicate features and fine bone structure, and combined with those gorgeous eyes, the sight of her packed quite a punch. He tried to ignore the way his body reacted with sudden interest.

'I'm s-sorry,' she stammered. 'I didn't realise . . . You're right. I should have asked permission. I'll, um, get going now.'

'Good.'

She set off towards the gate and he followed close behind her. The silence between them felt awkward, and he wondered if he was being too harsh. A part of him would love an excuse to see this gorgeous woman again, but he didn't really have time to date.

They had reached the gate now, and he opened it for her, to speed up her departure.

She passed through with a quick thank you, then bolted for her toy-sized car, throwing him one last uncertain look over her shoulder before climbing in. Those clear grey eyes made him want to follow her and apologise for his rudeness, but there was no point. He refused to talk to journalists, and they wouldn't meet again. He watched as she drove off, then hopped into his own car.

Time to get back to a reality that would never include a lovely woman like that.

Chapter Four

West Mercia, May/Gaukmánuðr AD 874

'Are you ever going to forgive me, Merewen? I did what I had to do, and you know I would have much preferred to marry you. Your sister is a shrew and cannot hold a candle to you in terms of beauty.'

Merewen ignored Oslac, who had followed her into the barn, where she was about to milk the goats. He had shut the door so that they were alone in the semi-darkness, which was way too intimate for her liking. Not to mention inappropriate. She was tempted to run out of there, but it was time she stood her ground. He'd been hounding her for weeks, months even. Ever since Burghild had become with child, Oslac had turned his attention to Merewen, albeit in secret. Several times now he'd cornered her somewhere, trying to persuade her to allow him liberties.

That was not going to happen.

'There's no reason why we cannot still be friends,' he continued, grabbing a milking stool to sink down next to her. He reached out and put a hand on her knee, his thumb rubbing circles on top of her skirts as his voice grew husky. 'More even, since you'll never have another man in your life. I can show you what you'll be missing before you go off to the nuns. Where's the harm?'

Sceadu, who was lying on the floor on her other side, growled low in his throat and Oslac sent him an irritated glance. Merewen yanked her knee to one side, dislodging his fingers. 'Go away and leave me alone, or I'll tell Burghild and Father,' she hissed. 'You chose her and you can't have it both ways.'

'Merewen.' He sighed and pushed his fingers through his hair in an exasperated gesture. 'I didn't want your sister, but for the sake of my family and yours I was forced to wed her. It made sense to combine the two properties. You must see that?'

'There was no force involved, and your father's domains were plenty big enough. What I saw was a man who betrayed his promises to me. A man who was swayed by greed. One who lied.' Her eyes bored into his with a fierce glare. 'Do you seriously believe I'll give myself to you outside of wedlock? I am not a whore.'

'I never said you were. It merely seems like such a waste, you going off to that monastery without ever having felt a man's touch. You should live a little before being sequestered for life. Have something to remember. I can give you that. You'll enjoy it, I promise.'

She sent him another scathing gaze. 'Believe me, even if I wanted to make such memories, it wouldn't be with you. And how do you think the nuns would receive me if I arrived with a belly big with child? Now leave this barn before I scream at the top of my voice.'

He sighed. 'Very well. I can see there's no reasoning with you today, but at least think about it. I care for you. I hate to see your youth and beauty wasted this way.'

'*Go!*' She pointed at the door. 'And get it through your thick skull that I want nothing to do with you! You made your bed, now lie in it. Without me.'

He finally stomped out of the barn like a sulky child, and she breathed a sigh of relief. It probably wasn't the last she'd hear on this matter, but for now she was safe. Hopefully she'd remain out of his reach until such time as she left for the monastery. When that would be, she wasn't certain as her father's plans had been derailed by the Heathen Army for over a year now, but it couldn't be long. Perhaps it would be a blessing after all if it took her away from Oslac.

'Curse those Mercians! They've cut our brotherhood down to half the size – I can't believe it!'

Hastein was beside himself, and Eirik contemplated the fury and devastation on his uncle's face. They'd been steadily making their way west towards Bretland, raiding as they went. As usual, they relied on surprise attacks, and had mostly aimed at anything that looked like Christian buildings or more prosperous settlements. Sweeping in quickly to take what they wanted with minimum bloodshed on either side, they'd had a few successes. Not enough for his uncle's greed, though. Hastein had apparently envisaged much more loot, and that morning, impatient with the lack of suitable targets, he'd decided to swoop down on what looked like a cluster of small farms.

That had been a mistake.

Despite it being just before dawn and still semi-dark, someone must have seen them coming and raised the alarm. By the time Hastein's warband descended on them, the inhabitants were ready for them and fought with quiet desperation to protect their possessions. Although Hastein and his men had come away with a goodly amount of provisions – though next to no treasure – almost half his warriors had been slain in the process. What made it even more ignominious was that they'd been killed with pitchforks and other ordinary implements, as well as anything the women of the community had to hand. In the face of such fierce determination, Eirik had only participated half-heartedly in the raid, although thankfully Hastein hadn't noticed. Eirik mourned his fallen comrades, of course, but he couldn't help but admire the courage of the locals.

'It's a disaster,' Hastein continued, pacing the makeshift camp they'd set up as far from the settlement as they could go that day. 'How are we supposed to proceed now? We don't have the numbers needed to overpower most targets.'

'Perhaps we should head back?' Eirik suggested. 'It's not too late to catch up with either Halfdan's men in the north or the others who went south. I'm sure we can find them.'

There had been some sort of disagreement between the leaders of the Heathen Army and most of them had gone south-east, the jarls Guthrum, Anwend and Oscetel among them. Halfdan's brother Ubba had a mind of his own and no one knew where he'd been headed, but it should be easy enough to pick up the trail of the rest.

'No!' Hastein swung around and glared at his nephew. 'I'm tired of following others. I want to be in charge now. Be the *hringdrifi*, not forever the recipient. Decide where to go and when. And not have to share my gains with anyone except my men.' He shook his head. 'There must be a way.'

Hringdrifi was what the Norsemen called leaders who were strong enough to gather so much treasure that they were able to bestow gifts on anyone who followed them and swore allegiance. In other words, Hastein wanted to be a jarl.

After some more pacing, the man stopped again. 'Perhaps we can join another smaller band for a while, then lure some of them into coming with us.'

'Who? We were the only ones heading west.' Irritation coursed through Eirik, and he wanted to shake his uncle. He hadn't seen anyone else foolhardy enough to venture deeper into Mercian territory without the rest of the warbands to back them up.

'Yes, but don't you remember that ship we spotted on the river yesterday? They didn't see us, but it might be worth our while seeking them out. We can pretend to go along with them, swear allegiance, then get rid of their leader and I'll take over. I've never owned a ship, but it would be better than having to travel on horseback everywhere. I hate riding. It's so uncomfortable.'

'What? That's a dishonourable plan,' Eirik protested. It was common for warbands to come together from time to time to create a stronger force momentarily, but to plot a takeover beforehand in this way did not seem right. Still, rivalry between petty chieftains was commonplace, so he shouldn't have been surprised at Hastein's plans.

'Pish!' his uncle sneered. 'Who cares? Now let's bury our dead and tomorrow we'll go in search of the river raiders. We'll bribe them with a tiny amount of our loot. The rest we'll hide for now.'

The ancient stone monument rose up before them, wreathed in swirls of mist and damp from a recent rainstorm. Set at the top of a small hill not far from the river the locals called Wye, it consisted of massive stone slabs that had somehow been perfectly balanced one on top of another. An impressive construction, it was nevertheless an eerie place, the souls of those long departed making their presence felt. There was a distinct chill in the air here, as if to warn off intruders, but the four warriors approaching the cairn were undaunted. They feared nothing, not even *draugar*, vengeful spirits.

'Look, the perfect place! Easy to remember and with no dwellings nearby,' Hastein proclaimed. 'Start digging, but be quiet and make haste.'

He and his two most trusted men, together with Eirik, had snuck off from the rest to bury their loot. They carried a shovel each and a sack filled with plunder. Mostly gold and silver coins and ingots, as well as armbands and other jewellery, but Eirik knew his uncle had also kept some old sword pommels set with garnets and quite a few objects looted from churches and monasteries. Hastein liked to look at his ill-gotten gains and hadn't had as much melted down as his nephew had. It seemed foolish to Eirik, but transporting it wasn't his problem. He'd kept a few of his arm rings and some coins, but would be burying the greater part of his treasure. He definitely didn't want the river raiders to steal it from him – his uncle was right about that.

They chose hiding places in a field surrounding the cairn site – far enough from the stone structure not to disturb the dead, yet within sight of it in a place that would be easy to find. Working with silent efficiency, they swiftly scooped out enough soil to hide their riches. Eirik surreptitiously observed the others, marking the spots they'd chosen and committing this information to memory. Everyone else was focused on their own task, wanting to leave this place as soon as possible. But just in case they were paying attention, he pretended to bury all his loot in one place near the others. In reality, he only placed a couple of things there, then loitered near the stone structure itself where he hurriedly dug the greater part of his treasure into a spot on the other side of the monument, where Hastein and his comrades couldn't see him. Although these men were supposedly his blood brothers, he wasn't taking any chances.

'We will return here when we are ready to depart Mercia for good,' Hastein declared once he'd replaced the square of grass that hid the hole he had dug and the treasure beneath. 'For now, we keep this site to ourselves. No need for everyone in our group to know.'

Eirik very much hoped they would live long enough to retrieve their possessions, and that his uncle actually intended to leave.

That was by no means certain. He sent up a silent prayer to Odin to keep the site – and him – safe.

As it turned out, the river raiders had recently suffered setbacks and losses as well, and after some initial posturing and a hefty bribe, they accepted Hastein and his men into their group. There was strength in numbers. The horses were sold at the nearest market, where the Norsemen pretended to be civilised traders, and then their adventures on the river began.

Or so they thought, except unfortunately their first raid went horribly wrong.

It was a Sunnudagr – the one day a week when the locals appeared to worship the White Christ more than any other – and also some sort of special feast day. The raiders knew it was easier to take their victims by surprise when they were busy praying and celebrating their god, but they hadn't reckoned with the fact that their reputation preceded them and a lookout had been posted.

The skirmish, which should have been swift and seamless, turned into fierce fighting as local men poured out of their little church armed and ready. Eirik was beginning to think he wouldn't make it through another summer at this rate. His uncle and the others had obviously severely miscalculated the resistance they'd encounter in this part of the country. Unlike the Angles and Vestrsaxar, who mostly tried to sue for peace by offering large amounts of silver so their enemies would go away, these West Mercians were defending themselves tooth and nail.

It was a gloomy day, with rain drizzling down and making the ground slippery and muddy, which didn't help. Cold drops also found their way inside their clothing and made gripping their weapons more difficult than usual. As he fought with all his might, Eirik was only dimly aware of what was going on around him. There was shouting, cursing, the clang of steel on steel and metal on wood, as well as screams of pain and the gurgling of men in the throes of death. He ignored it all and concentrated on his immediate opponents. The raiders were outnumbered, but the defenders were not trained warriors, and that balanced things out somewhat. Wiping moisture off his face with the sleeve of his tunic, Eirik found himself battling two men at once. Although he was a skilled fighter and light on his feet, it was difficult to guard against both at the same time. And when a third man joined them, he was in serious trouble.

'Die, you Norse swine! You're not having what is ours,' one of them snarled.

Eirik didn't bother to answer, merely thrust and parried with his sword, while keeping his shield up. This trusted accoutrement had been with him for some time now, though, and a particularly vicious blow from an axe sliced it in two. The pieces fell to the ground and he was left holding the iron boss from the middle of the shield, with only a few splinters of wood remaining either side. He slipped on the sodden ground and cursed under his breath. Throwing the heavy metal part at one of the men, he pulled his battleaxe from his belt to use with his left hand.

Too late, he saw the third man jab at him with a spear, the point entering his groin only a hair's breadth away from his most vital parts. The flash of pain as the weapon was pulled out again was like a red-hot fire iron piercing his skin and muscle. He recoiled, hissing out a breath as the damage registered.

'*Skítr!*'

In the heat of the fight, however, the pain disappeared almost instantly, and instead his left leg went numb all the way down. He knew that wouldn't last – it was probably the shock of the sudden stab wound – but he took advantage of the reprieve while he could and launched a counter-attack. Wielding his sword and battleaxe at the same time, howling like a berserker, he whirled on his opponents and cut them down before they had time to regroup. By then, sensation had returned to his leg and groin tenfold, and absolute agony streaked through him. Biting his teeth together, he looked around and noticed the other raiders already fleeing back towards the ship. A sudden attack of dizziness made him fall to the ground. He lay there motionless for a moment, staring at the sky with unblinking eyes while he waited for another wave of excruciating pain to roll over him.

'Back to the ship! Hurry!' He dimly heard Hastein shouting, but it took a while before he could muster the energy to turn his head. Taking a deep breath, he tried to focus and saw his uncle and the others running full tilt towards the river, pursued by the locals. None of them had come to check whether he was alive, or even called out to him. Not even Hastein.

So much for loyalty.

Gathering his remaining strength, he forced himself to stand up, swaying slightly. It occurred to him that this was his only chance to escape; if the defenders found him here when they returned from chasing off the raiders, they'd kill him on the spot. He couldn't let that happen; he had too much to live for. And from now on, he was going to stop listening to his uncle, loyalty oath or not.

A quick glance around told him that all the other men lying on the ground were dead, so he was on his own. Limping badly, he took off towards the nearest stand of trees and bushes. A peek behind him showed that no one was paying attention to him, but that could change at any moment. He carried on, wanting to get as far away from this settlement as possible, but soon realised he wasn't capable of running far. Certainly not at a rapid pace. As he had no way of reaching the ship without being caught, he took the only other alternative – he decided to head inland. There had to be somewhere he could hide while his wound healed.

He only hoped it wasn't mortal.

Chapter Five

Near Hereford, May, present day

'How are you doing, Grandpa? Arthritis OK today?'

Alix's grandfather, Morgan Howell, lived twenty minutes south of Hereford in a flat that was part of a converted former manor house. The entire building had been redesigned with the elderly in mind, and there were carers and other staff on hand to help those who needed assistance. Morgan had bought the flat after he'd become a widower four years earlier, and he seemed content there. There were activities to take part in each day, and he'd made some friends. Alix was very pleased about that, as she often worried about him being lonely, with his only son – Alix's dad – and his family living in London and hardly ever visiting.

Morgan had been a huge part of her decision to move to this part of the country, as she'd long wanted to live closer to him. He and her grandmother had owned a farm south of the city, and when Alix and Autumn were younger they'd spent every summer there. She had many happy memories of those times and had always been grateful for the love and care their grandparents had shown them. Autumn had enjoyed it too at first, but during their teens she'd been desperate to stay in London, deeming the countryside 'boring'. To Alix, however, the farm had always been a peaceful haven.

With his wife gone, and his arthritis increasingly flaring up, it had been impossible for Morgan to continue farming. He hadn't sold the property, though. Someone was renting it at the moment, and Alix hoped they were looking after it.

'I'm fine, dear. Not so painful today. How lovely to see you! Come, sit. It'll be teatime soon. We've been promised Victoria sponge today.' The residents of Pentwyn Place were able to order meals and snacks to be delivered if they weren't capable of cooking for themselves. He leaned closer to her and whispered, 'Although sawdust with cream and a layer of jam might be more accurate.' He chuckled, and Alix laughed with him.

'Hmm, I look forward to that. We'll need lots of tea to wash it down, then.'

When the promised treat had arrived, they went to sit on a small patio that overlooked the large garden. It was just outside Morgan's flat and could be reached via French doors. The former manor house had extensive grounds, including a duck pond, and the rooms were high-ceilinged and grand. It wasn't a bad place to live. Alix knew that Morgan missed his previous life, but he was a practical man and never complained about his lot. If only she could help him, but she couldn't run a farm as well as do her job. She'd been lucky to find a position as a librarian in Hereford, and they were very busy, as a new library had just been constructed and all the books had to be moved, shelved and catalogued properly.

'So how are you settling in?' her grandpa asked, making a face as he chewed his very dry piece of cake.

Alix smiled, and swallowed her own with a large mouthful of sweet tea. 'I'm loving it. It's full-on at the moment, and it's exciting to be part of the move, seeing the new library come together, you know? And there's going to be a special section where that Viking treasure they found near here is displayed. Actually, I went to look at the site the other day. Or tried to.'

She turned her face away to hide the blush that she knew was spreading over her face. That farmer had been quite rude when he'd chased her off his land, but she knew he'd been right so she couldn't complain. She should have asked his permission first, but she'd been driving past her grandpa's fields, which were nearby, and had stopped on impulse when she realised where she was. One of the other librarians had told her all about the find, and the speculation that it had been dug up somewhere near the Neolithic cairn. It was a place Alix was familiar with from her childhood, as she and Autumn had played there occasionally. The cairn was such a mysterious place, and once they'd come across it, they'd sneaked back when they could.

'Oh? Anything to see?' Morgan scraped the last of the cake off his plate.

'No. I don't know why I expected there to be.' Alix laughed. 'It's not like *Time Team*, with trenches all over the place. I guess whoever found the hoard just dug it up and then filled in the hole. I didn't get a chance to look for long, as the owner of the field came to chase me off. He seemed quite fierce, so I legged it.'

'What? How unnecessary,' Morgan grumbled under his breath.

'No, it's fine. It is private land after all. Right next to yours, you know. A shame we never looked for treasure in your fields, eh? Who knows what lies buried there.'

'Hah! I doubt there's anything more. Probably just a lucky find. But you can always buy yourself one of those machines and give it a try. Actually, I was going to talk to you about the farm. I want you to have it.'

'You what?' Alix choked on a crumb of Victoria sponge, and it was a while before she could stop coughing. She stared at her grandfather. 'What did you say?'

'If you're agreeable, I'm going to contact a lawyer and sign the place over to you. Your dad was never interested in it. He couldn't wait to leave for the big city as soon as he was old enough. And your sister made it very clear she'd die of boredom if she had to be buried in the countryside. That just leaves you, my dear. I've no other relatives.'

'But—'

Morgan held up a hand. 'Hear me out. I'm not expecting you to become a farmer – I know books are your world – but now that you've moved to Hereford, I thought you might want to live in the house and maybe rent out the fields to some of the neighbours. The building is old and in desperate need of updating, but it could be a lovely home for you if you fixed it up a bit. It's not so far out of town that you can't commute to work each day. Save on rent, eh?' He shrugged. 'It's just an idea. I'd really like for it to stay in the family, but if you can't see yourself living there, then we'll say no more about it.'

'I would absolutely love to! But it's too much, Grandpa. You can't just give it to me. What about the rest of the family?'

'Oh, don't worry about them. If you decide you want it, the farm will be your part of the inheritance, and I'll tell them so. I have plenty of other assets, not least this flat, which wasn't cheap, you know. Plus life insurance and Premium Bonds and various investments. The others will just have to wait a bit longer for theirs, and of course you'd have to sign a document to say you'd already received your share.'

'I see. Honestly, I don't know what to say.' Alix felt love for this old man well up inside her. He'd always been so kind to her, and they had a very special bond.

Morgan patted her hand. 'No need to say anything. I'll amend my will to take this into account, and everyone will get their fair share. Your father might have been expecting to inherit the farm one day, but he'd only sell it. He has no emotional attachment to it. And if there's even the slightest chance that someone in our family can keep the land, I'll be happy. You and your sister are the last of the Howells – our branch anyway – and from what you've told me, Autumn would never want to live here.' He frowned. 'After what she just did to you, I'm not sure she deserves to be given anything, but fair is fair and I won't cheat her out of her due. Still, you're the only one who's kept in touch with me on a regular basis. The only one who actually cares. Will you promise me to at least keep the farm for a few years if I sign it over to you? I wouldn't want you to make any hasty decisions, but naturally you'd be free to sell it in the future if you so wish.'

'Of course I will! I'm just... This is a bit overwhelming, Grandpa. I never expected anything like this.' Alix swallowed down the lump of emotion that clogged her throat. 'Thank you. I'm stunned and grateful, but please, think it over for a bit longer. It's a big step.'

Morgan smiled at her and winked. 'No need. I've been mulling it over for ages and I've checked the value. The farm is almost exactly a quarter of what my estate is worth at the moment. Your father will receive half and Autumn the other quarter. Perfect, eh? I'll call that lawyer tomorrow.'

There was nothing she could say other than to thank him again, and give him a big hug.

'What's for dinner?'

The question was lobbed at Noah the moment he stepped inside the back door. He kicked off his mud-encrusted wellies and looked at his sister, who was sitting at the kitchen table scrolling on her phone. Irritation zinged through him and he scowled at her, but she was engrossed in whatever she was reading and didn't notice.

'Dinner is whatever you've cooked,' he told her, entering the room closely followed by his sheepdog, Shadow. 'I'm not your maid and I've just worked hard outside all day.'

She finally put the phone in her pocket and stood up, glancing at him. 'Jeez, someone's in a bad mood. Sheep misbehaving?'

'No, only little sisters,' he shot back. Heading for the fridge, he rummaged around but found nothing more interesting than cheese and ham. He sighed. Toasted cheese sandwiches again then. He really should do some cooking at some point, but he was always too tired.

'Not this again. I have as much right as you to—'

'*Enough!*' Noah surprised himself with how loudly the word came out as he cut Niamh off. 'I've had it with you and your entitlement.' He dropped the cheese and ham on the counter with a thump and strode towards her, stopping right in front of her. She blinked and took a step back, looking up at him in confusion as he continued his rant. 'You're an adult, Niamh, and family or not, I don't have any obligation whatsoever to feed and house you. I would be within my rights to kick you out of this house at any time and you know it. The only reason I haven't is because I promised Mum I'd look after you, but even she would probably agree that I've done my duty by now. More than.'

'But—'

He held up a hand to stop her protest again. 'No! I'm not listening to any more of your bullshit. Either you start helping out around here or you can find somewhere else to live. I refuse to continue to support your lazy lifestyle. I'm working my butt off on this farm, and contrary to what you believe, I'm not rolling in money. Farming barely pays the bills these days and I'd be a lot better off if I didn't have to feed you and your good-for-nothing boyfriend when he's around. When was the last time you did any cooking, cleaning or laundry in exchange for your room and board? Like I said, I'm not your maid or your mother, and from now on you're living here on my terms or not at all. Do I make myself clear?'

She sent him a mutinous glare. 'And where do you suppose I could live if not here? This is my home.'

'Really? A shame you've never treated it as such. The place is a pigsty, and that's not my doing. I even found a pair of your knickers in the living room the other day, for goodness' sake! Tomorrow you'll be doing some tidying up, hoovering and dusting. And the next time you leave dirty dishes in the sink for me to wash, I'll be dumping them in your room.'

'Dramatic much?' she mumbled, still staring at him with defiance.

He shook his head. 'No, just fed up. I'm too tired to deal with a child after a long day of work. Grow up or get out. Go stay at Reece's place for all I care. It's not like he'll need his room for a while. Now I'm going to make some toasted cheese sandwiches, and I'll do one for you on condition you have a meal ready for me tomorrow night when I come in. Deal?'

Her mouth set in a stubborn line. 'No, thanks. I'm not hungry any more.' She whirled around and stomped out of the kitchen.

'Spoiled brat,' Noah muttered, but he was serious this time. He'd definitely had enough of her behaviour and he wasn't putting up with it any longer. It was time she took responsibility for herself and did some household chores. 'Am I right, Shadow?'

He patted the shaggy dog on his smooth head and received an adoring look and a *woof* in return. Shadow was his constant companion and always had his back. Unlike his sister.

While he waited for his sandwiches to cook under the grill, he wandered into the living room, shaking his head at the mess in there. The coffee table held a collection of used mugs, glasses, plates and takeaway containers. A greasy package with the leftovers of a fish-and-chips meal sat to one side, giving off an unsavoury aroma, while discarded magazines littered the rest of the surfaces. There were chocolate wrappers and other bits and pieces too, as well as items of clothing, unfolded throws, and cushions in a pile at one end of the sofa. Dust coated the nearby bookshelves and the carved wooden Victorian mantelpiece, and there were stains on the rugs.

'Bloody hell,' he muttered, fury coursing through him at the way his sister treated their home. This could not go on.

As he bent to start clearing up, something caught his eye as it glinted under the edge of the sofa. He kneeled on the carpet to check, thinking Niamh must have dropped an earring, but what he found instead was a silver coin. An old one that looked worn and smelled as if someone had tried to polish it recently. It didn't have the name of a country as far as he could see. Instead there was writing around the edge on one side that read *EDELRED REX* in chunky letters, with some sort of drawing of two figures in the middle. On the other side, *MON EDELRED REX* was written vertically in three lines.

'Oh no,' he whispered. He had a horrible feeling he knew exactly where this had come from and how old it was.

Whipping out his mobile, he googled 'coin' and 'Edelred Rex'. His fears were instantly confirmed – it was a silver penny from the reign of King Aethelred I, who had ruled Wessex between AD 865 and 871. He had been King Alfred's older brother and his immediate predecessor.

'Dammit!'

Noah studied the coin some more. As he held it on the palm of his hand, it felt as if the metal gave him a little jolt of electricity, which travelled up his arm. He frowned at it. That wasn't possible, unless it had come into contact with some electrical cord, but there were none nearby. Turning it over, he closed his eyes in despair as the implications became clear – Niamh had most definitely helped Reece find the hoard, and she must still be in possession of at least part of it. It would seem she'd been cleaning the old coins, presumably readying them for sale.

Images suddenly flashed before his closed eyelids. *The Neolithic cairn. Four men digging silently nearby in the half-darkness of a summer's night. Whispers on the wind in a strange language. A sensation of wariness. Frissons of fear. Glances at the surroundings to make sure no one was watching . . .* He shivered and blinked his eyes open.

What on earth was that? And what should he do now?

If he handed in the coin to the police and told them where he'd found it, Niamh would almost certainly be arrested. Did he really want to do that to her? It was possible she'd only kept a few of the coins and wasn't planning on doing anything with them. He could search her room, and if they were there, he could pretend he'd found them somewhere else in the same field, without implicating his sister. Wouldn't that make him a criminal too, though? It was a dilemma and one he needed to mull over some more before he decided what to do.

For now, he carefully stowed the little coin in his wallet, in a corner where it wouldn't fall out. Somehow that felt right.

A while later, he sat down to enjoy his toasted sandwiches in peace and quiet, with Shadow curled up by his feet, having wolfed down his own meal already. Noah's thoughts turned to the farm. It was true what he'd told his sister – he was barely making ends meet. He needed to expand his flock of sheep, but for that he'd require more land. Uncle Ifan had been scraping by for years and had appeared content as long as he wasn't in the red. Noah would prefer to do better than that and actually make a healthy profit. But how?

He'd tried various crops in the fields that were not for grazing, but without much success so far. Sheep were a better bet, especially as quite a few of the ewes had twins or even triplets each year. Perhaps he should take out a mortgage and try to buy more land. His neighbour on one side would never sell, he knew that, but the fields to the east were only rented out at the moment. The old man who used to live there, Morgan Howell, was in a home for the elderly somewhere. Noah wasn't sure what terms he had agreed with his tenant, but it might be worth having a chat with him. If he could persuade Morgan to lease the land to him instead, he could drastically increase his flock. Then maybe the old man would consider selling the fields at a later date.

Yes. Where was the harm in asking, at least?

Chapter Six

West Mercia, May/Gaukmánuðr AD 874

'I'm off to look for herbs and I may be gone some time. We are sadly low on many items after the harsh winter.'

It was early morning and Merewen had found her sister sitting on the edge of the bed she shared with Oslac in their private sleeping chamber. She looked pale and wan. Her pregnancy was beginning to show, and she should have been over the worst stage of the morning sickness by now, but it would seem she still had bad days. Today was clearly one of them.

'Can't it wait? You are needed here,' Burghild protested.

Merewen shrugged and pretended indifference. 'It is up to you, but if someone is hurt or becomes ill and I don't have the necessary herbs to treat them, you'll be responsible.'

Burghild sent her a black look, but finally nodded assent. Even she couldn't dispute the fact that medicinal plants were needed, and as the woman in charge of the household, she could be held accountable if stocks were low. 'Very well, but don't dally. There are plenty of chores to be done.'

Weren't there always? Merewen refrained from rolling her

eyes and instead slipped out into the early-morning sun. It was weak and not particularly warm as yet, but hopefully it would dry the vegetation soon enough after the recent rains.

She hadn't been lying – they were short of just about everything. As healing was her domain – at least until such time as she left for the monastery – she was responsible for obtaining the necessary items. It was possible to buy things from itinerant traders, but it was better if she could gather the herbs herself. The only problem was that it was still very early in the season and she wasn't sure there was anything yet to find. She might have to roam far afield, and to that end she'd brought a basket with a skin of water and some bread and cheese wrapped in cloth. She didn't intend to return until dusk, no matter what her sister said.

She'd also brought Sceadu, her trusted hound. He looked fearsome, but in reality he was as sweet as a lamb unless anyone threatened her, in which case he could turn quite feral.

'Come on, boy. Guard me!'

She knew he would whether she told him to or not, but there was no harm in giving him the command so that he stayed extra alert.

Making her way along old tracks and pathways, through fields and wooded areas, she eventually found herself near the ancient cairn. It had been a part of the landscape for as long as anyone knew, and there were many stories told about it around the hearth of a winter's evening. It was said to house the bones of a long-lost king, whose spirit protected it and the treasure supposedly buried with him. According to legend, if anyone dared to rob him, they'd come to a bad end. This hadn't deterred the many people who had searched anyway, but nothing was ever found, indicating either that the king wasn't giving up his secrets or it was all a lie. Merewen didn't intend to disturb the spirit in any way. She merely wanted a particular herb that sometimes grew nearby.

As she huffed up the hill, Sceadu stopped, lifted one front paw and growled low in his throat. Merewen halted beside him and scanned the area, but couldn't see anything threatening.

'What's the matter? What have you sensed?'

The dog was staring straight at the cairn, on full alert but not barking a warning. He put his head to one side as if he was listening intently, and Merewen did the same. She thought she heard a sound from within the shadowy cave beneath the stones. Sceadu must have done as well, because he began to walk towards them slowly, scenting the air as he went.

Merewen followed, stopping to listen once they were closer. The noise came again. It was a hiss of pain, followed by a moan and what might have been a softly muttered curse. She swallowed hard and debated whether to make a run for it. If someone was hiding under the cairn, they could be a threat, and she was far from any habitation. No one would hear her scream for help if she was attacked. The prudent thing to do would be to leave immediately, but Sceadu didn't have his hackles up and wasn't growling. Instead, he was still tilting his head as if trying to figure out what was happening.

Merewen hesitated. There was another string of curses, louder now and in a tongue that was similar to her own, yet not the same. She recognised it for what it was – Norse – and her insides turned to ice.

'Oh no! Sceadu, let's go,' she ordered, but for once the hound didn't obey. He turned limpid brown eyes on her and whined softly, as if to say, 'You can't leave, someone needs you.'

'Oh, for the love of . . . Fine, we'll take a look, but you'd better protect me or I'll never forgive you,' she whispered. Sceadu took this as assent and walked all the way up to the stones, poking his nose inside.

Another hissed litany of imprecations echoed out as Merewen

followed the hound and crept closer. There was so much anguish in those words, the healer in her couldn't but feel pity for whoever was uttering them. Unsheathing the knife she'd brought for cutting herbs, she held it in one hand while she inched up the hill. She made sure to approach the stones from the side where a large slab blocked the sight of anyone inside the cairn. Once there, she peeked cautiously around it, and had to swallow a gasp.

There was a half-naked man lying on the ground, his head propped on a pile of dried grass and leaves covered by a russet-coloured tunic. A linen shirt had been flung to one side, while he was stretched out on top of a cloak of finest Mercian woollen cloth. She'd recognise the type anywhere, as she helped produce just such a weave. His weapons and a belt with two pouches and a knife had also been discarded. Although he was glistening with perspiration, and clearly burning up with fever, he was shivering so much his teeth were chattering audibly. His face, handsome in an almost unearthly manner, was whiter than the ghost said to roam this place. And his forehead and eyes were scrunched up in extreme pain.

'God and the saints preserve me!' Merewen breathed, lifting a hand to clasp the little silver cross that hung around her neck.

Ever since she'd been a small child, she'd heard tales of the ferocious Norsemen. They were held up as an example of how no honourable person should behave. The ogres of nightmares. 'Keep quiet and go to sleep or the Norsemen will get you,' her nursemaid had often said, after scaring Merewen and her sisters half witless with tales of their misdeeds.

It was well known that they rampaged, looted, killed and raped as they wished, swooping down upon unsuspecting settlements when they least expected it and showing no mercy. Those who weren't killed were dragged off to be sold as slaves, sometimes a fate worse than death. Often, it was said, the raiders left nothing behind but burning buildings and corpses. The mere thought of those fierce marauders struck terror into every man, woman and child.

And now there was one inside the cairn.

Merewen had heard of the recent attack on a nearby settlement, but the raiders hadn't been seen since. Her father had made sure to have a guard posted at all times to warn of any danger, just in case. Was this one of them? It had to be.

The man hadn't noticed her presence. For a while she remained immobile, staring at his chest and broad shoulders almost in a trance. A silver amulet in the shape of a hammer hung around his neck on a leather cord. He had sculpted muscles, smooth skin and a light dusting of hair that covered part of his pectorals and also formed a thin line from his navel into the edge of his trousers. She'd never seen anything like it and couldn't help but take in the sight, enthralled. He had to be incredibly strong when he wasn't laid low with an ague. She hoped he would have the strength to fight whatever ailed him, because for some reason she wanted him to live. Sceadu whined again, obviously of the same mind. The hound had crept closer and was regarding the stranger with a worried expression.

Merewen came to a decision. This man was not a threat to her in his current condition, and as a healer and good Christian, she couldn't leave him to die without trying to help. Her conscience would never allow it. Taking a deep breath, she moved forward to crouch beside him.

'Good morrow. Can I help you?' she said, her voice shaking slightly but brisk and matter-of-fact.

The man jumped and his eyes flew open. Irises of a dusky green shade regarded her warily from under hooded lids. His hair was a golden brown, made darker by the perspiration that coated his brow. Long and slightly wavy, it must have been caught up in a leather cord at some point, but now most of it hung in messy tresses around his shoulders. At first, he didn't reply, merely studying her as if he wasn't sure she was real. If, as she suspected, he was more or less delirious, that was entirely understandable. To put him at ease, she raised her hands, palms facing outwards in a pacifying gesture.

'I mean you no harm,' she murmured.

'Who are you?' he croaked, his voice gravelly.

'Merewen. And you?'

He looked as if he was debating whether to tell her the truth, then closed his eyes in defeat. 'I'm Eirik.'

She would never have guessed him to be a Norseman from his speech, as he had switched to her own language. He was fluent, speaking like a native. Had she not heard his mutterings earlier – or his name – she wouldn't have taken him for a foreigner. Although they would have been able to communicate even if he'd talked to her in Norse, him knowing Mercian made things much easier.

'Where did you learn?' she asked, moving closer to see if she could make out what was wrong with him. If he had an infectious fever, she didn't want to be too near him, but it could be something else. He had various cuts and bruises, but no spots or other marks indicating disease as far as she could see.

'Learn? Oh, your tongue.' He shrugged, then hissed as if even that small movement caused him pain. 'I've been on these shores for a dozen years or more. I picked it up along the way.'

So he'd been raiding her people's lands since he was a mere child, as she judged his age now to be no more than twenty-five. No wonder he'd learned to communicate.

'And who's this?' The man stretched out a hand towards the big hound, who had moved to lie down next to him. He waited until his fingers had been sniffed and given a lick of approval before scratching behind the shaggy ears. The dog's tail thumped on the ground and Eirik received another couple of licks.

'Sceadu. He won't hurt you unless I tell him to.'

Eirik nodded, his hand falling limply to rest on top of his ridged abdomen as if he didn't have the energy to even pet a dog. He was still shivering intermittently.

'What ails you?' she asked, mindful of the fact that she ought to concentrate on that and not her sudden – and unwelcome – fascination with the man.

'Why? Are you going to finish me off?' He managed a lopsided smile that caused her to notice that he had a very enticing mouth currently surrounded by a close-cropped beard and moustache. 'I have to say, I can think of worse ways to go than being killed by a beautiful maiden.'

'What? No! I'm a healer. Tell me what's wrong and perhaps I can help.'

He snorted. 'What's the point? One of your kinsmen will soon find me and all your work would be for naught. If you truly don't wish me harm, then you'd do better to leave and forget you ever saw me. I'll go as soon as I am able.'

She frowned. 'No, I won't let them hurt you.' When she realised that she was defending an enemy, her cheeks heated up. 'I mean, I won't tell anyone you are here. Once you're well enough, you can be on your way. I really don't think one man is a threat to our settlement. Don't you usually hunt in packs?'

The warband that had allegedly attacked the nearby properties a few days ago was said to have consisted of at least twenty or thirty men. Eirik was on his own. She wondered why they hadn't carried him off with them in their sleek ship, but perhaps he'd been left for dead. He certainly looked to be in a bad way now.

'True,' he conceded. 'Very well, little healer, do your worst.' He nodded towards a stain that spread across the top of his thigh and groin area. Merewen hadn't noticed it before as his trousers were black, but when he pointed it out she could see that a substantial amount of blood had soaked through the material. 'I was wounded. Spear. Went in and out, so nothing left inside, but the wound is festering.'

Merewen frowned. Not because she didn't think she could treat him, but because the site of the wound was perilously close to his manly parts. It was a tricky area and would be difficult to bandage. Still, she'd do her best.

'Where exactly is it?' she asked.

A low chuckle made her realise he'd misunderstood and thought her reluctant to take a look. She'd seen men naked before, so she wasn't worried about embarrassment, but he didn't know that.

'I thought healers were used to seeing people's bodies,' he said teasingly. 'And there's no need to worry. I won't molest you if you remove my garments, you have my oath. I'm not really in any condition to hurt a fly.'

His oath. As if that was worth anything from a sworn enemy. And yet she was inclined to believe he meant it. Nothing about him felt threatening, apart from his smile, but that was another matter.

'I'm not worried in the least,' she told him curtly. 'And I have seen worse sights than you. Let's have a look.'

She went into her healer persona and viewed him dispassionately. He was right: all bodies were more or less the same. Although this one, it had to be said, was like nothing she'd ever come across before. Best not to dwell on that. Undoing the drawstring that held his trousers together at the waist, she gently rolled the material downwards on one side. By some judicious manoeuvring, she managed to uncover the wound site without exposing his genitals. As if he was done teasing, he put a hand over them and held the material in place to shield his manhood from view. Merewen ignored him and studied the gash instead.

It was nasty.

The spear had penetrated quite deep, by the look of it, but fortunately it had missed any vital organs or muscles. Because he'd presumably been here for a couple of days now, unable to do anything about it, the wound was red and irritated, with pus and blood oozing sluggishly from the middle, some of it drying round the edges.

'I tried to clean it with water,' he told her, hissing in a breath when she prodded the skin around it. 'But I didn't have any poultices to cleanse it properly.'

'I'll wash it out again, then I'll apply a bandage. I will need to go home to make a proper concoction, though.' Extracting the skin of water she'd brought in her basket, she pulled up her skirts and ripped off a strip of linen from the bottom of her shift. Burghild would have a fit if she knew, but Merewen had no intention of telling her.

She used the linen to clean the wound as she rinsed it out with a gush of water. Something stronger was needed to draw out the infection, but this was the best she could do for now. Dabbing the surrounding area dry, she put the cloth to one side.

'Hold still, please. I won't be a moment. Sceadu, stay!'

Crawling out of the cairn, she went to the nearest hedgerow and began to search for spiderwebs. She evicted several rather angry arachnids, and gathered a small handful of their gauzy creations. Returning to Eirik, she put the webs on the wound, which had been bleeding more after her ministrations, and then tore off another piece of her shift to bind it with.

'There, that should do until I can come back,' she declared, hurriedly pushing his trousers up across that taut stomach with the intriguing trail of hair down the middle that she tried hard not to notice.

'Thank you.' He swallowed audibly. 'I don't suppose you could spare a little more of that water, please?'

'What? Oh! Of course. Here, have it all.' She handed him the skin and watched while he drank as if he hadn't seen water in weeks. The truth was probably that he hadn't had any for several days, and she was ashamed not to have thought of it earlier. 'Would you like something to eat as well?' she asked, taking out the bundle of bread and cheese from her basket.

The smile he gave her was almost blinding. 'I'm beginning to think those angels your people believe in really do exist,' he said. 'Or perhaps you're a Valkyrie, come to take me to Valhalla after you make me stronger again.'

'I'm no such thing. Whatever that is,' she retorted. 'Before you eat, though, you must put your shirt on. Even if you're too hot, you shouldn't be lying around with nothing on.'

He tried to raise his upper body off the ground, but flinched and hissed out another curse. 'Can you help me, please?' he asked, holding out one hand.

Merewen hesitated. Did he truly need her assistance or was it an excuse to touch her? She decided to give him the benefit of the doubt, because he had started trembling yet again. He was obviously sick. She crawled over to him and took his fingers, pulling him halfway up. By wedging her shoulder under his arm, she managed to half lift, half slide him into a sitting position while he ground his teeth together against the pain. A frisson of awareness shot through her at being so close to him, but she ignored it and placed him against an upright stone slab that formed part of the cairn. Once she'd extricated herself from his grip, she inserted his folded tunic behind his back to make him more comfortable.

'Here, let's put this on.' She assisted him in wriggling into his shirt. It took a lot of effort, and he was panting slightly as he finally leaned back against the stone again. 'Now you need to eat.'

He accepted the bread and cheese from her, but divided it in half. 'I won't deprive you of it all. My thanks, Merewen.'

Hearing him say her name caused a strange fluttering inside her that she tried to ignore. He was a Norseman. A heathen. And no doubt incredibly dangerous when he wasn't incapacitated. She'd do well to remember that.

But for now, he was at her mercy and she was going to make the most of it.

Chapter Seven

Hereford, May, present day

'I've finished cleaning every item now. Come and have a look.'

Alix smiled at Eileen, the archaeologist in charge of the Viking hoard and the person she was working with to come up with a suitable way of displaying the find. Eileen was responsible for preservation and cleaning of the items, as well as providing context and historical details about each object. It was then Alix's task to come up with suggestions as to how to turn the relevant information into an interesting display, complete with boards telling the story of the finds and the age in which its owners had lived. It was all very exciting, but nothing beat actually looking at the items themselves.

'Coming.' She followed Eileen into the little back room where she'd been working on the objects under a microscope. Alix had been intrigued to learn that Eileen sometimes used different types of natural thorns for cleaning the items, as they were less likely to scratch the surfaces. The utmost care had to be taken in order not to damage anything.

'Ta-dah!' Eileen spread her arms theatrically and indicated her workbench, on which lay a glittering collection.

'Oh wow, that's fantastic!'

Alix bent to study each part of the treasure in turn. There was a collection of coins – most made of silver, but two of gold – a gold ring, a couple of silver armbands, a small silver ingot and a pendant made of rock crystal in a silver filigree setting. Eileen had told her previously that the coins featured kings from the mid to late ninth century – Aethelwulf, Aethelbald, Aethelberht and Aethelred I of Wessex – a lot of Aethel-somethings! – as well as Beorhtwulf and Burghred of Mercia, plus a couple of Arabic *dirhams*.

'You can touch if you want, but don't tell anyone, and you have to wear gloves.' Eileen grinned, no doubt fully aware of the feeling of awe that swept through Alix as she contemplated the hoard.

'Really? Thank you.'

She put on a pair of disposable gloves and picked up a couple of the coins in turn, marvelling at the fact that you could still read the names of the kings clearly. She studied the ring and the armbands, admiring the craftsmanship. Then she lifted the pendant carefully, holding it by the ornate loop at the top through which a leather cord or a chain must have passed originally. The rock crystal appeared to be a perfect sphere. As she raised it, light from the room's only window illuminated it, showing off the clarity of the transparent quartz.

'It's so pretty!' she whispered with reverence in her voice.

The shafts of light bouncing off the crystal almost made her dizzy, and she had to close her eyes for a moment. When she opened them again, she thought she caught a glimpse of two figures inside the sphere, as if it was a fortune-teller's crystal ball. It was a young couple, and when she blinked, larger but hazy images of them danced across her vision.

The woman had a long plait and she was smiling. The man held up the pendant and fastened it around the woman's neck, his eyes full of love, before nuzzling her cheek and putting his arms around her from behind. Then the scene changed and it was dark. Fear and anxiety flashed through her. She was that woman and she could hear a horse's hooves stamping the ground. Smell it. Then the clang of steel and the grunts and curses of men fighting. There was something in her own hand – a long, lethal-looking knife – and she was trying to defend herself with it . . . The images shifted, and she could feel hard ground beneath her as she kneeled on it, panting, while someone whispered, 'Shh, ást mín, it's over . . .'

'Alix? Are you OK?'

Eileen's voice brought her back to the present, and she blinked at the shafts of sunlight. 'What? Yes, yes, I'm fine. My vision went a bit funny, that's all. It sometimes does that when I'm about to get a migraine.'

'Oh dear. Do you have some tablets you can take?' The archaeologist was peering at her, concern in her eyes.

'Yes, don't worry. I'll swallow a couple of paracetamol straight away and I'll be right as rain.' She returned her gaze to the pendant. 'This is quite magnificent, isn't it? Viking, did you say?'

'Not that one. I think it's probably older. Anglo-Saxon, possibly fifth or sixth century. It could have been an heirloom passed down through the generations that was then looted by the Vikings.'

'I can understand them wanting it.' Alix smiled and put it back on the table, where it was cocooned in soft wool. 'Maybe I should make up a story about how it was given to a woman by her lover. A Viking wooing a local lady, perhaps?' The scene that had invaded her mind earlier lingered in her consciousness. She had no idea where it had come from, but it had felt very real.

'Yes, why not? That will make it more intriguing for visitors.

Maybe we could have a copy made and a couple of life-sized wax dolls dressed in the clothing of the period to display it,' Eileen suggested.

'Excellent idea! I'll have to find out if the budget will stretch to something like that. If not, perhaps we can do some crowdfunding. I'll go and do a bit of research now about the type of garments we'd need. Perhaps reach out to the local re-enactment societies. They should know.'

'You do that. I'd better get this lot stowed away in the safe for now. I'll send you some more notes later.'

'Great. Thank you, Eileen, and thanks again for letting me handle the items. It was very special.'

Just how special, she wouldn't tell her colleague. Eileen would never believe that merely touching the crystal pendant had given her visions or made her see things in its depths. Alix wasn't sure she did either. She must have imagined it, her brain working overtime. Yes, that was surely it. Anything else would be madness.

'Right, that's it, then. All signed and legal once it's been registered. I'll file the paperwork with the correct authorities and will send you both copies.'

The solicitor, Mr Evans, collected up the documents Alix and Morgan had just signed and took his leave. When she'd walked the man to the door and shut it behind him, Alix went over to give her grandpa a big hug. 'Thank you again so much! You're the best and I honestly don't know how to thank you enough.'

He patted her on the back. 'No need to thank me, dear. As long as you look after the place, that's enough for me. I hope you'll be happy there, but I won't hold it against you if you decide it's too isolated and lonely for you. Just give it a few years at least, eh?'

'I promise. I doubt I'll find it lonely. I've never minded being on my own and I'll make sure to have an alarm system installed so I don't have to worry about intruders. Maybe I should get a dog, too?'

Unlike her sister, who was a social butterfly and craved the company of others, Alix enjoyed solitude. She knew she was going to enjoy living at Howell's End. That wouldn't be for a while yet, though. From what her grandfather had told her, she would need to get some builders and decorators in first. Good thing she still had her savings, the money she was supposed to have used to buy a flat with Sean. She'd been renting in Hereford while she looked around for a suitable property, but now there was no need for her to purchase anything.

'I'll tell the rest of your family next time your father gives me a call.' Morgan shook his head. 'That might not be for a while, though. He's always telling me how busy he is. I bet that piece of news will surprise him.' He gave her a mischievous wink that made her laugh.

'Yes, definitely.'

She hoped it wouldn't cause any problems. Her dad had never wanted to return to Herefordshire, but he had probably expected to inherit everything from Morgan since he was an only child. Still, he had a well-paying job in London working in finance, so it wasn't as if he was short of money. And all his possessions would one day be divided between his two daughters – and his wife, if she outlived him – so where was the harm in them receiving a share beforehand? The only difference was that Alix would get hers now, whereas he and Autumn had to wait a while for theirs.

There was a knock on the door and she went to open it, expecting another tea tray with whatever was the dry cake of the day. Instead, she came face to face with the farmer she'd met the previous week. She took a step back and just stared at him for a moment. What on earth was he doing here? Had he tracked her down to berate her some more? Or charge her with trespassing? That seemed a bit extreme.

'Er, hello?' she managed at last. 'Can I help you?'

He looked equally flummoxed, and his eyebrows came down in a frown. 'Sorry, I was looking for Mr Howell. Mr Morgan Howell?' He checked the flat number, which was displayed on the wall outside the door. 'Did I get it wrong?'

'No, he's here. Come in.' She moved aside and gestured for him to pass. Her fists tightened as she wondered whether the man had come to complain to her grandfather about her misdemeanour. But why would he? She was an adult and could take responsibility for her own actions.

He walked into the room somewhat hesitantly, but smiled when he caught sight of Morgan. 'Ah, you're here! Excellent. How are you, Mr Howell? Do you remember me?'

Morgan struggled to his feet and smiled back at the young man. 'Of course I do. Ifan's nephew, right? It's been a while.' He turned to Alix. 'This is Noah Vaughan. Remember Ifan Vaughan, my neighbour? Noah here took over his farm when Ifan passed away. How many years is it now? Four, five?'

'Five. I'm glad to see you looking well, Mr Howell.'

Alix vaguely remembered her grandfather's neighbour and the two teenagers who'd been living with him and his wife. When she had met Noah in the field the previous week, she hadn't realised he was the surly youth she'd come across all those years ago. He'd been older than her and Autumn and not interested in them, so they hadn't interacted much. Back then, he'd given off a bad-boy vibe that terrified and fascinated her in equal measure. How could she have forgotten?

'Please, call me Morgan. No need to be formal. And this is my granddaughter, Alix.' Morgan sank back into his chair, wincing when the arthritis made this difficult, and indicated that his guest should take a seat on the sofa next to Alix. He did, after casting a surreptitious glance at her, which she ignored.

'We've met before,' she informed her grandfather tersely, and had the satisfaction of seeing Noah's cheeks go ruddy.

'Er, yes. You're the journalist, right? I'm, um . . . sorry if I was a bit abrupt last time we met.' He didn't look particularly apologetic, but Alix was more confused by what he'd said.

'Journalist? Where did you get that idea? I'm a librarian.'

'What?' He frowned at her again, nonplussed. 'But you were snooping around the cairn and you said something about writing.'

Alix bristled. 'I wasn't snooping. I wanted to see the site where the Viking hoard was found, that's all.'

'I see,' he replied, although he didn't appear to understand why she'd be interested.

For some reason, she felt the need to justify her actions. 'You know the new library that's been built in Hereford?'

'Yes. What of it?'

'There's a special section set aside for the hoard now that funding has been raised to keep it in the town. I'm one of the people working on the exhibition, together with the archaeologist in charge.' She shrugged. 'I don't know why, but I somehow thought it would help me visualise the kind of person who had hidden such treasure if I went to look at the cairn myself. I'm sorry. I should have asked you first, but I was driving past and stopped on impulse.'

'No, that's fine. I thought . . . Well, I've been hassled by journalists a lot since it all happened, and I'm a bit fed up with them, to be honest.' He shook his head and suddenly held out his hand for her to shake. 'Can we start again? I'm Noah. Pleased to meet you, er . . . Alex?'

She hesitated, some residual anger still swirling inside her at his churlish behaviour last time they'd met. Evidently he'd had good reason for it, but she wasn't about to forgive him that easily. Her grandfather was watching the exchange, however, so she decided politeness was required at least. She put her hand in his and shook it lightly. 'It's Alix with an I. A bit of a weird name, isn't it, Grandpa?'

Morgan chuckled. 'That it is. I've no idea what your mother was thinking, but it's pretty. I like it and it suits you.'

'Mum read too many baby-name books when she was pregnant, and wanted something a little bit different.'

Noah merely nodded. 'Right. Got it. Al-ix.'

Alix realised she was still holding on to his hand and withdrew hers hastily, her cheeks heating up. Sitting this close to him, there was no denying the man was attractive. Light brown hair with golden highlights, no doubt from working outdoors in all weathers. Clear green eyes under straight brows. A nose with a bit of a tilt to it, and a beautiful mouth surrounded by darker brown stubble. His skin was already tanned from the spring sun, making his eyes stand out. They were the pale green of old moss, a most unusual shade.

She turned away and tried to steer her thoughts in other directions. Luckily, Morgan saved her.

'So what brings you here, young man? Having problems with my tenants?'

Noah gave himself a mental kick and concentrated on the old man, rather than his lovely granddaughter. Alix with an I. Of all the places to meet her again, he never would have thought of this one. And he'd acted like an oaf for no reason at their previous meeting – she wasn't a journalist at all, but a librarian. Yes, he could see it now. A very sexy one at that, despite the conservative way she was dressed, but he didn't want to think about that now.

He cleared his throat. 'Actually, I did come to talk about your tenants, but not because they've been causing problems. I was wondering how long their tenancy is going to last.'

'They've already left,' Morgan told him. 'Last week, in fact.'

'What? They didn't say anything to me.' Irritation flashed through him. Although the tenants hadn't been from around here, surely basic manners weren't too much to expect? He didn't say that out loud, but Morgan appeared to be of the same opinion.

'Rude lot, if you ask me. I'm glad to be rid of them, if I'm honest.' The old man fixed intelligent eyes on Noah. 'Are you interested in renting those fields? You never said anything before I left. I assumed you'd have told me if you wanted them then.'

'Yes, I would have, but I didn't think I could afford it at the time and I was still new to everything. I had a lot to learn after Uncle Ifan passed away, but now I would love to rent them if we can come to some sort of agreement.'

Morgan smiled and nodded at Alix. 'You'll have to talk it over with her. She's the new owner. As of today, actually.'

'What?' Noah turned to stare at the pretty librarian. 'Are you taking up farming instead of books?'

She scoffed and shook her head. 'Hardly. I'm not in any way qualified to do that. But I'm going to be moving into Grandpa's house eventually. If I can get it sorted out, that is. I haven't even been to look at it yet, so I don't know how much work it needs. I'm assuming quite a bit.'

'I see. And you've no need of the fields?' Noah let out a breath he hadn't realised he was holding. Morgan had surprised him when he said Alix was the new owner, and he'd been afraid his dream of expanding his operations was going down the drain. Now things were looking up.

'No.' She sent him an appraising glance. 'Not sure I want to rent them to my rude neighbour, though.'

'Ouch!' He clutched his heart as if she'd wounded him, then hung his head. 'I guess I deserve that, but please, can you forgive me? I really would like you to forget that and start again.'

'I'll think about it. I've only just taken over, as Grandpa said, so I should really explore all my options before committing to something like that.'

Disappointment washed through him, but he hoped she would change her mind.

'Fair enough,' he said, striving for a light tone. 'Perhaps we could discuss it over dinner one night? Or a drink at least?' He gave her his most charming smile, the one that had won over quite a few girls during his bad-boy teen phase.

Alix merely raised her eyebrows, suspicion lurking in her gaze. 'I don't think that will be necessary. If you give me your mobile number, I'll text you when I've made my decision.'

Again, he didn't allow her dismissive tone to get to him. Instead, the challenge in her gaze sent an arrow of awareness through him. She really was incredibly attractive. Her beautiful grey eyes were luminous in the afternoon sunlight. And today her lovely hair was loose, the long dark curls caught up with a small clip on top of her head and cascading down her shoulders. He had a sudden urge to run his fingers through it to see if they'd get caught. Somehow he knew they would, and he'd love the feel of the thick tresses against his skin . . . He shook off these thoughts and tried to act businesslike.

'Right. Give me your phone and I'll put in my number.'

That done, he had no reason to prolong the visit and reluctantly stood up to take his leave.

Morgan said he was tired so Alix might as well head off too. 'If you do decide to rent to Noah, just call the solicitor again and sort out an official agreement,' he told her. 'Always best to have things in writing.'

'Yes, of course.' She sent Noah a dubious glance. 'But I'm not rushing into anything. This is all so new. I can't believe I'm the owner of Howell's End. Thank you so much again, you're the best! Have a good rest now and I'll be back in a couple of days. Call me if you need anything.' She gave her grandfather a kiss on the cheek and headed for the door, which Noah was holding open for her.

'Goodbye, Morgan.' Noah sent the old man a final wave and followed Alix along the corridor to the main entrance of the manor. He took in their surroundings. 'Nice place, this.'

'Yes. I'm glad Grandpa isn't in some soulless home somewhere. Here he has his own domain, but lots of help if he needs it.'

'Sounds perfect.'

Outside, they fell into step with each other on the way to the car park. The silence between them was somewhat uncomfortable, and she must have felt it too, as she started to talk at the same time as him.

'I'll let you know . . .'

'Are you sure I can't . . .'

They both smiled awkwardly and he gestured with one hand. 'You first.'

Trying to capture a piece of her wayward hair that was blowing across her face, she cleared her throat. 'I was just going to say that I'll text you when I've had a chance to think things over. It might be a while, though, as we're very busy at the library right now, what with moving all the books and cataloguing them, as well as sorting out the exhibition about your hoard.'

'Fair enough, but actually it's not my hoard. It has caused no end of trouble for me, if I'm honest.'

'Oh. How so?'

'It wasn't me who found it. That was my sister, Niamh, and her boyfriend. Let's just say they "forgot" to inform the authorities.'

He rolled his eyes, still exasperated beyond measure by his sibling's idiotic actions. Not to mention that bastard Reece . . .

'Right. Of course. I . . . I read about that.' Noah could see the moment Alix put two and two together and came to the conclusion that his sister was a potential criminal. She tilted her head as if she was trying to recall something. 'I think maybe Autumn and I hung out with Niamh a few times when we stayed here, although she was a couple of years younger than us. Autumn definitely did.'

'Who's Autumn?'

'My sister. We're what's called Irish twins, born less than a year apart, so people often think we're real twins. Although these days we're nothing alike.' An expression of annoyance flashed across her features but was swiftly gone. 'She and Niamh went to pubs together, I think, before they were old enough. Got into trouble with Grandma. I, being a goody two-shoes, stayed at home.'

Noah smiled. 'That sounds about right. Niamh was forever getting into scrapes while I did my best to help Uncle Ifan. No time for pub crawls.' He sent her a teasing glance. 'Are you still a goody two-shoes, or are you more fun these days?'

A blush spread across her cheeks, blending with the smattering of freckles, and she raised her chin. 'None of your business.'

'Maybe I'll make it my business to find out,' he shot back. 'See you!'

Without giving her the chance to reply, he headed for his car and took off. He would definitely enjoy finding out if she was more willing to walk on the wild side these days. He had a feeling there was a passionate nature lurking under that prim exterior.

Challenge accepted.

Chapter Eight

West Mercia, May/Gaukmánuðr AD 874

Eirik really thought he'd died and gone to the afterlife when the young woman had crawled inside the cairn where he'd taken refuge. Fleeing from the locals, he'd soon realised that he wasn't far from where he and his uncle had hidden their loot. The stone structure was remote from habitation and offered a roof over his head, and as he was wounded and needed to rest, he couldn't be choosy. So he'd staggered towards this mysterious place and flopped down under the most massive slab of rock he'd ever seen.

He only hoped it wouldn't collapse on top of him.

Now, as he chewed the coarse bread with a bit of cheese, he felt better than he had for the last two days. Or was it three? He'd lost track of time. At one point he'd ventured out after dark, trying to find a brook in which to wash his wound and have a drink. After that, he hadn't had the strength to move that far, and the fever had had him in its grip. He was still hot and shivery, but the cool water and food helped, and with the gash in his groin properly bandaged, he was more comfortable. The spiderweb would staunch the blood. He should have thought of that himself, but he'd been too far gone. He sent up a swift thank you to the gods for bringing him this healer. It was probably more than he deserved.

He studied her while they ate in companionable silence. It was clear that she was kind and compassionate. She'd wanted him to have all the food, but he couldn't accept it. She had already been more benevolent than was warranted and he didn't want her going hungry because of him. His stomach had gone without for so long now, a little bit was more than enough.

As for her looks, he liked what he saw. Very much so. Curly dark brown hair, neatly braided in a long plait that hung over one shoulder but escaping in unruly wisps around her forehead and neck. Delicate dusky brows swooping over deep-set pale grey eyes, surrounded by dense sooty lashes. A small nose covered in freckles that spilled over onto her cheeks. A rosebud mouth that begged to be kissed, and a pleasingly shaped figure, judging by what he could make out in the semi-darkness of the cairn.

'You're staring,' she said. 'Do I have cheese on my face?'

'What? No.' He smiled. 'I was just wondering why a pretty young woman such as yourself is wandering the countryside on her own. Are you not anxious about more of my kind catching you unawares?'

He was teasing, but at the same time he caught himself worrying about her safety. Hastein wouldn't hesitate to capture any lone woman he came across. If he found her to his liking, he'd use her first before selling her on, and there wouldn't be a thing she could do about it. Personally, he liked his women willing, so he had never joined in that kind of activity. He didn't see the attraction.

'I have Sceadu. He'll kill anyone who threatens me. I'm on my guard as well and I know this area like the back of my hand,' she replied, putting the cloth she'd brought the food in back in her basket. 'Besides, you don't usually come in broad daylight.'

She was right. 'Well, be careful nonetheless. My uncle can be impulsive, so you never know.'

'Your uncle? Is he coming back for you?' She glanced out through the stones, a worried frown between her brows.

'I doubt it. He'll believe me dead by now. He left without making sure the other day, but he knows that anyone who didn't escape would have been killed. It was pure luck that I got away.'

He couldn't quite keep the bitterness out of his voice. Fourteen years with the man, viewing him as a father substitute, and Hastein hadn't even called out to ask if he was alive. He'd saved his own skin, no thought for anyone else.

When he'd arrived at the cairn, Eirik had been in excruciating pain, but most of all he had been angry. Furious at being left behind. When the tables had turned on the raiders, Hastein and the others had made a run for it. Any stragglers had been left to fend for themselves, which equalled certain death. It wasn't how they normally did things – they looked out for their brothers-in-arms – so he didn't know why it had happened this time.

Well, he wasn't going back to them, no matter what.

Why should he stay loyal to a man who cared so little for him? Hastein had always been selfish, but previously they had stuck together and Eirik had supported his uncle in every way. Family honour was paramount, and he'd thought they had a special bond. More fool him. Hastein should have rushed to defend him. He hadn't. There was no worse disgrace than being a coward, and Eirik felt that was what his uncle had been during that skirmish. The older the man got, the more self-centred he became. No doubt he had only been thinking of saving his own skin, the *argr*. He must have judged his nephew to be a lost cause and simply left him behind. If he could do that, why should Eirik feel the need to keep raiding? The loyalty should go both ways.

Right now, however, he was more intent on simply surviving. Decisions about his future could come later.

'Doesn't sound like a very nice man,' Merewen commented.

Eirik snorted. If only she knew. Some of the things Hastein had done would turn her hair grey. 'No, that he's not. Hopefully he's far away from here. Good riddance.'

She looked as though she wanted to ask more, but decided against it. 'I must go,' she said instead. 'I'm supposed to be looking for herbs.' She gathered up the soiled piece of linen and stuffed it into the basket. 'I'll come back as soon as I can with a poultice and a willow bark concoction for your fever. Will you . . . will you still be here?'

A sunbeam shone into the cavity under the stones, and Eirik noticed that her grey eyes were like drops of rain in the light, clear and lustrous. He wanted to drown in them. But that might be the fever affecting his brain. With an effort, he blinked and nodded. 'Aye, I should think so.' He reached out to take her soft hand in his callused one. 'Thank you again. I owe you a huge debt.'

She regarded their joined hands with a startled expression, as if she'd never had a man touch her that way. That made him want to hold on for longer, but at the same time he didn't wish to offend her. She had promised to come back with a poultice, and he needed her healing skills if he was to recover. He'd be in her debt, but he would compensate her, of course. Recalling that torn shift, he let go of her and opened one of the pouches hanging off his discarded belt.

'Wait. Let me pay you for your ruined garment.' He held out a couple of silver coins. They had the head of a Mercian king on one side, so he knew she'd be able to use them here.

'No, no, that's not necessary,' she protested, but he took her hand again, placed the coins in her palm and closed her fingers around them.

'Please. I insist. And I shall look forward to your return.'

That made her blush, the rosy colour almost obscuring her freckles. The sight made Eirik smile, but he was suddenly very sleepy. With his hunger and thirst sated at last, tired from the effort of talking, and the fever taking its toll too, he closed his eyes and shuffled back down onto his makeshift bed. 'Farewell and stay safe,' he muttered, before sleep claimed him.

Luck was with Merewen that evening. She had been wondering how she could possibly manage to sneak away again to tend to her patient. Since most of the family, including her, slept on benches in the hall, the main building of the settlement, she would have had to wait until everyone was asleep. She had envisaged an extended visit to the privy or some such, but she was spared having to lie when some guests arrived. They were relatives of her father, and she had forgotten they were due today. Burghild told her to go and bed down in the hut she used for concocting her healing potions, in order to make space for them.

'Father's cousin is elderly and needs to be near the main hearth,' her sister added. 'You'll survive a few nights without heat. Take a spare blanket. Oh, and you have that smelly hound to keep you warm too, do you not?'

Merewen glared at her – Sceadu was a constant cause of contention between them, as Burghild abhorred canines of any kind – but she didn't protest. 'Very well. I will sort out my bedding, then come and help with the chores.'

'Good. As you know, when they leave, they're taking our sisters with them for an extended stay, so there will be two pairs of hands fewer around here in the coming weeks. I will need your assistance even more.'

Their younger sisters, Aelfwynn and Eadgifu, were almost of marriageable age, and Merewen had heard her father mention that he hoped they might find husbands while staying with his kin. Perhaps there was more chance of that where they lived. It annoyed her that he hadn't extended the same offer to her instead of arbitrarily deciding to send her to a monastery She couldn't understand his reasoning, other than the vague ambition that she'd rise to the rank of abbess one day. Still, she knew there was no point arguing. Once he'd made up his mind, there was no changing it.

Before returning to her sister's side, she went through the meagre supplies she had left after winter and started repacking her basket. Willow bark was thankfully plentiful year-round, and she steeped some in hot water to bring to Eirik. She also crushed a bundle of yarrow leaves to make a poultice that she could smear on the wound. It should stop the bleeding, draw out any infection and help speed up the healing process. She packed a small oil lamp and some kindling too. Finally she added clean linen strips for bandaging, and a spare skin filled with cool spring water. If possible, she'd pilfer some food for him later.

Her preparations made, it was merely a question of waiting for everyone else to bed down for the night. The evening seemed interminable, but at last she was able to bid them all goodnight and slip outside. She sat on the bench in the little hut until all was quiet, Sceadu beside her. The dog could tell something was happening, but he was patient and made no sound. When she judged that no one was likely to be about, she put on her cloak, picked up her basket and the extra blanket and tiptoed out, closely followed by the hound.

Merewen climbed over a fence at the back of the settlement, while Sceadu easily jumped it. The guard, who was supposed to be alert to the slightest sound, was clearly inept, as no one challenged her. That ought to have been a worry, but tonight she was thankful. There was a full moon, and it helped to guide her along the tracks towards the stone monument. With Sceadu by her side, she wasn't afraid, but her insides still swirled with anxiety.

What if Eirik wasn't there any longer? What if he'd fooled her into thinking he was more hurt than he was, and he attacked her? Or, God forbid, what if he had already passed away, the fever and wound too severe?

'Please, no,' she muttered. 'Heavenly Father, please watch over him and help him to recover, even if he doesn't believe in you. Let my faith be enough for the both of us.'

Eirik was definitely not Christian. The amulet he wore was heathen; the hammer a symbol of the Norse god of thunder, Thor. Merewen had heard the occasional tale of the Norse gods from some of the itinerant bards that visited from time to time. They were a fascinating glimpse into other people's beliefs, even if the bards downplayed the religious aspect. Thor, by all accounts not the brightest of their gods, had many adventures, and those were amusing to listen to.

Slightly out of breath, she reached the cairn at last and halted outside. 'Eirik?' she whispered. The uncle he'd mentioned might have returned, and she stayed alert in case she needed to flee, knife at the ready.

'I'm here,' came the muffled reply.

Sceadu gave a muted bark and rushed inside, while Merewen followed more slowly.

'Oh, it's you again, is it? Yes, yes, it's good to see you too. Sceadu, was it? Thank you, I needed to be cleaned, clearly.'

Eirik's voice sounded amused as Merewen vaguely made out his and the dog's shapes in the darkness. It seemed the hound was pleased to see him, which was odd. He didn't normally take to strangers, but he was making a great fuss now, his tail wagging furiously.

'Sceadu, enough,' she murmured. 'Is it safe to strike a light, do you think?' she asked Eirik.

'Should be. I haven't heard a soul since you left. Unless they came by while I slept.'

Finding the oil lamp, fire iron, flint and tinder took a little while, but she managed it eventually and they had light. When she looked up, Eirik was sitting upright, leaning against the stone as before, with his cloak wrapped around him. It was kept firmly shut with the help of a bronze pin that glittered dully in the flickering light.

'I didn't think you would come this late, angel,' he commented with a smile. 'How did you manage that?'

She shook her head. 'I'm not telling you. You could use the knowledge to creep into our settlement unnoticed and steal everything we own.'

'Very wise.' He didn't appear to be offended that she was branding him a potential thief. 'But I make it a point never to bite the hand that feeds me.' He ruffled Sceadu's head. 'I'm sure you agree, eh, boy?'

'Well, good. And I'm not an angel.'

'You are to me.'

Merewen turned away before she became too intoxicated by the smile that accompanied his heartfelt words. 'I will need to see your wound again. I've brought a yarrow poultice. Oh, and please swallow some of this.' She handed him the willow bark concoction. 'It should help to reduce your fever. Have a quarter now, then another quarter morning, noon and night tomorrow.'

'Thank you.' He drank it without complaint and watched as she rummaged for the other items she needed.

In silence, he helped her uncover the wound again. It still looked sore, and Merewen prayed she wasn't too late with her herbs. First, she cleansed it once more with the spring water, noticing how Eirik's stomach muscles jumped when the chilly liquid was poured into the gash. She did her best not to stare at the fascinating expanse of taut skin and ridges. She squeezed the wound a little to make sure no pus was left inside, then dried it before applying the poultice she'd brought. While adding the slimy mess, she chanted a healing prayer under her breath as old Mother Mildred, her mentor, had taught her.

'*Flumina flumen aridum veruens flumen pallidum parens . . .*'

The words were in the foreign language used by the priests and monks, but Merewen knew them by heart and also understood their meaning. The sound was soothing and rhythmic, making her feel as though God would definitely listen and help the healing process. Yet she found it hard to concentrate with Eirik's hot skin under her fingers and his distracting physique so close. She could feel him watching her intently, but he didn't comment. It was a relief when she had bandaged him up again so that he could put his clothes back on.

'My thanks,' he murmured, his voice low and slightly hoarse. 'It is most kind of you to come to my aid.'

She shrugged. 'It's what healers do. I'll be spending the rest of my life on nothing but such tasks, no doubt.'

'How so? Do you not have a family? A . . . husband?'

'No. I was betrothed, but Oslac, my erstwhile husband-to-be, is now married to my older sister, Burghild. There's no one left for me.' A stab of pain pierced her, but she quickly suppressed it. Oslac's betrayal still rankled. Not to mention his recent attempts to possess her despite being wedded to Burghild. What on earth had he been thinking? It was wrong on so many levels, not to mention it would be a grievous sin.

'What? Why?' Eirik frowned as if he wasn't following.

She sighed. 'Burghild was betrothed to someone else, a man who went off to help King Burghred fight the *micel hæðen here*, but he fell in battle.'

When Ceolnoth had told them he was going to volunteer to fight the Great Heathen Army that was threatening the kingdom of Mercia, everyone had tried to dissuade him. Most men had to be actively conscripted to fight, as everyone was tired of warfare, but he'd seemed to think it would be an adventure. He'd been a farmer all his life, and although like most men he was trained in weapons skills to some extent, the Norsemen were said to be formidable warriors. Ceolnoth was no match for those who had practised fighting techniques from birth. At the time, Merewen hadn't thought his death would affect her, but she'd been wrong. Thanks to Ceolnoth, she would never have a family of her own. It was hard not to resent him for that, although he'd merely been the unwitting catalyst for what happened later.

'My father decided that it was more important for his eldest daughter to have a husband, so he dissolved my betrothal and gave my intended to Burghild instead,' she continued. 'Father has no sons, you see, so my sister stands to inherit his domains. He liked the idea of combining the two properties, as they are adjacent. It will make a sizeable estate. Oslac apparently agreed.'

'I'm sorry to hear that. What a *rass*.'

Merewen agreed, having understood the Norse word only too well. Oslac was most certainly an arse, although she wouldn't use such an uncouth expression herself. And Eirik sounded sincere, but for all she knew, he could have been the one who killed Ceolnoth. That was a chilling thought, but she suppressed it.

'Can your father not find you another match?' he asked.

'No, probably not. At least not here. Most of the other young men of marriageable age have left too, so there aren't enough to go round.' She sighed. 'I can only suppose that God didn't wish me to be a wife and mother, else he wouldn't have taken Ceolnoth and set this chain of events in motion. Father has decided not to try and seek another husband for me; instead I will go and live in a monastery. He has some strange notion that I can increase our family's standing by eventually becoming an abbess.' When Eirik raised his eyebrows in a silent question, she explained, 'The abbess is the woman in charge of such an establishment. She wields quite a lot of power and influence, by all accounts. I've been trained in the arts of healing since I was young, and the monks and nuns are always happy to have help from those of us with such knowledge. Many sick people seek their aid, so Father believes I'll be welcome to join them.'

'Monastery? You mean one of those places where they all wear the same clothes made of plain wool and pray to the god of the White Christ a lot?'

Merewen couldn't help but laugh at this description. 'Um, I believe there is more to it than that.'

He was frowning, and although his eyes were still glazed with fever, she could almost see his mind working as if he was trying to solve a conundrum.

'I've, er . . . come across a few of those places, and it doesn't look a very appealing way of spending your life. I mean, you're young and comely and would make someone an excellent wife. You shouldn't be shut away like that. What a waste of a good woman! Actually, I saw some of those people last autumn in Hreopandune, before Halfdan Hvitserk kicked them out. They looked rather pinched and unhappy, if you ask me.'

Merewen knew she was blushing, so she turned away and busied herself with repacking her basket. She didn't consider her looks remarkable and wasn't vain, although she'd been told she was the prettiest of the four sisters in her family. As for Eirik, he was merely being kind, but it warmed her that he thought she deserved to be married.

She sighed. 'Well, it's not as if I have a choice. If Father refuses to let me stay here, and I don't have a husband, I will have to go.

Although in a way I suppose I should thank you. I was meant to go to that very place – Hreopandune – to join the nuns there, but your attack last year put paid to that plan. Father has to find somewhere else for me now.'

'I can't say I'm sorry about that,' Eirik muttered, giving her a cheeky grin.

'Be that as it may, I should really return home now. Will you be all right?'

She reached out and touched the back of her hand to his forehead. It was still unnaturally hot and a bit clammy, and his face was pale. Studying him objectively, she could see he was sick and feverish, the ague making him shiver uncontrollably from time to time. The willow bark hadn't had time to work as yet. However, his eyes did appear slightly less glazed than before when she peered into them. For a moment, she lost herself in the depths of his gaze, and he seemed equally enthralled. They both stilled and stared at each other without blinking until Merewen became aware of the fact that she was still touching his forehead. She pulled her hand away as if scalded.

'I'm sorry. I just wanted to . . . You should lie down and rest.'

'Yes. Thank you. And I'll be fine, although I'll miss Sceadu's warmth. He's like a little brazier, aren't you, boy?' The dog was lying next to Eirik, snuggled up close to him. He thumped his tail at the Norseman's appreciation.

Merewen smiled at the sight of her big hound giving Eirik comfort and warmth. Although the man was supposedly her enemy, in this moment that seemed irrelevant. Here he was simply a wounded and feverish person who needed her.

'Just stay wrapped up and you should be warm enough,' she commented, tucking the blanket securely around him. 'Try to sweat out the fever.' She backed away from him. 'Sceadu, let's go.'

Eirik nodded. 'My thanks again for all you are doing, Merewen. My gratitude knows no bounds.'

'My pleasure.' And she meant that literally, although she'd never tell him so. She placed the waterskin and a cloth with some food next to him. 'This should tide you over until I can come again. I'm not sure when that will be, but please keep drinking the willow bark draught.'

'I will. And I will repay you somehow, I promise.'

'Not necessary. Goodnight.'

As she made her way home, her mind was full of images of Eirik. She was playing with fire, and yet she felt entirely safe in his company. At least, she didn't fear for her life. He was more dangerous to her equilibrium and her heart. She would have to be on her guard. With God's will, he would heal soon, then he'd be on his way and she would never see him again. That was probably for the best.

That thought was so depressing, she sighed loudly enough for Sceadu to send her an anxious glance.

'Oh, don't mind me. I'm being a fool.' She stroked the dog's soft head. 'At least I'll still have you when Eirik is gone, eh? It will have to be enough.'

Although if she went off to a monastery, she'd have to leave the hound behind as well. Best not to think about that now.

Chapter Nine

Hereford, May, present day

Alix had a busy week, she hadn't lied about that. She barely had time to eat, let alone think about whether to rent out her land to her hot neighbour. He did seem to pop into her mind quite frequently, however, much to her dismay. She didn't really want to think about him, as his parting shot had unsettled her. Why would he want to find out if she was fun? And what would he do when he realised she wasn't? No one had ever called her that. It was Autumn's domain being the life and soul of the party, the sister everyone wanted to hang out with. Alix was lucky to even be noticed.

'Argh! Stop thinking about that. It's irrelevant,' she admonished herself.

She had moved to Hereford to escape from her sister's shadow. Here she could be anyone she wanted, and although she might not be much fun, at least Autumn wasn't around for people to compare her with. Who knew, maybe miracles happened and Noah might like her the way she was? Although he'd seemed the type of man who enjoyed confident women, not nerdy shy librarians.

She sighed. She had to stop thinking about him. Yes, he was a very attractive man, and being in his proximity made butterflies dance in her stomach. But he wasn't for her. As soon as he discovered how boring she was, he'd run for the hills, like most of her ex-boyfriends. No, what she needed was a man with similar interests to her own. Someone steady who didn't mind if she wasn't a party queen. There had to be a guy like that somewhere, surely? But after her recent experiences, she wasn't in a hurry to find him.

When Saturday came around, she finally had time to pay a visit to her new property. Howell's End was situated south of Hereford, deep in the countryside, so she set off in her little Fiat and left the town behind. After a while, she turned right off the main road and continued on much smaller back roads. These quickly became narrow and lined with thick hedges either side. Summer had almost arrived, and recent rain showers had made the vegetation explode. Hedgerows that had consisted of dull bare branches all winter were now bright green and in full leaf, making the roads even narrower. The daffodils that edged every road hereabouts during spring had died off and been replaced with primroses, cowslips and hawthorn. The latter scented the air when she opened her window a crack. The sheer exuberance of nature made her happy to be alive.

Eventually she reached the turning for Howell's End and bumped down the potholed track leading to the farmhouse. She wondered if it might be prudent to exchange the tiny car for something like a small SUV if she was going to live here. Her current mode of transport was more suited for a city like London, where parking spaces were at a premium. It wasn't built for roads that turned muddy or slippery during the winter.

'Here we are,' she muttered to herself as she stopped on the gravelled area in front of the house. It was covered in weeds and had been sadly neglected, as had the garden by the looks of it, but that was easily remedied. The house itself might be another matter.

She climbed out of the car and stood for a moment taking in the sight of the old building. Parts of it dated from Elizabethan times, but it had been added to over the years, and the overall impression was of a haphazard construction. The various sections didn't really gel, but at the same time the very unevenness of it all added to its charm. Most of the outside walls were covered in a tangle of Virginia creeper, climbing roses, wisteria and honeysuckle, and this made the whole more harmonious. Although they could definitely do with a severe trim.

Alix had spent many happy summers here, but the house didn't feel as welcoming today as it had in the past. Perhaps because Grandma and Grandpa were no longer here. It was as though the soul had left the building. But that was silly. Fanciful. And temporary, even if it was true. Once she moved in, she'd make it a home again. She was determined to be happy here. It was a peaceful place and it would be her sanctuary.

She was just about to approach the front door when she heard the sound of a vehicle behind her. Turning around, she saw a Land Rover coming up the drive. It stopped next to her car and Noah jumped out, raising a hand in greeting. He was followed by a black and white sheepdog, who stayed close to him but regarded Alix curiously.

'Good morning,' he said, giving her that smile that made the butterflies inside her take flight again.

'Er, hello,' she said as he came over to stand in front of her. 'What are you doing here? And who's this?' She stretched out a hand for the dog to sniff and was given a small tail-wag in response, which made her dare to stroke his soft skull and ears.

'This is Shadow. We were in one of my fields and I saw you

passing. Thought I'd come and say hi. Isn't that the neighbourly thing to do?'

His tone was teasing, those moss-green eyes twinkling, and she felt her cheeks heat up. She had never known how to react to such banter. It only made her more awkward. 'Right. Yeah. Of course.' She gestured towards the house. 'I was going to take a look around, see what needs doing.'

'Mind if I tag along? I haven't set foot in this place for years.'

'Um, sure.' When he turned to Shadow and told him to stay, she shook her head. 'He can come. I'm sure the floors all need a good clean anyway.'

'OK, thanks. All right, boy, come on then.' The dog gave a short bark, as if to say he was pleased about not being left behind, and the plumed tail wagged once more.

Alix headed for the front door, very aware of Noah at her left shoulder. For some unknown reason she felt jittery and anxious, but his presence acted as an almost visceral buffer against anything unpleasant. A sensation of safety washed through her. With him there, nothing bad would happen. Not that there ought to be anything dangerous here in any case. Her imagination was just working overtime.

The old key fitted into the lock and the door opened with an audible creak.

'Guess the tenants had never heard of WD-40, eh?' Noah muttered sarcastically, making her smile.

'That's one thing I can handle myself.'

She stepped into the front hall. As she'd predicted, the dirty old flagstones were in dire need of mopping. An oak staircase rose up on the right-hand side, its banisters dull and lacking the polished shine her grandmother had always insisted on giving them. The plastered walls had several cracks, and paint flaked off both walls and ceiling. There were lighter patches where paintings had hung, but Alix didn't blame the tenants for that. Morgan had taken his favourites with him when he left, and they now decorated his flat at Pentwyn Place.

A sudden wave of dizziness overcame her, and the flagstones appeared to undulate in front of her. Her breath caught in her throat as they changed into something resembling hard-packed earth. Closing her eyes, she was flooded with images.

She was inside a huge barn-like building with wooden benches lining the sides. Upright posts supported massive ceiling beams, and one end wall had a pretty stained-glass window high up adding some light to the room. In the centre a stone-built hearth contained a smouldering fire. An iron tripod held a simmering cauldron suspended over the heat, and the smell of cooking permeated the air. The walls were rendered in between a timber framework and painted in an ochre colour, and on the benches lay folded blankets, sheepskin rugs and cushions. There were only a few people about – all dressed in some sort of tunics – but they were chattering and laughing . . .

'Alix? Are you OK?'

Noah's concerned voice brought her back to the present. 'Huh? Oh, yes. Sorry. Just felt a little dizzy there for a second. It's nothing. Let's go and explore.'

Trying to forget the strange experience, she concentrated on the here and now. They continued into the other rooms on the ground floor – a sitting room that Grandma had called 'the parlour', which contained a large inglenook fireplace; a den where the ancient TV had resided and whose walls were covered in empty bookshelves; a dining room; a small office where Grandpa had done the farm's accounts; and a large kitchen at the back of the house, with a laundry room and scullery attached. Everything was dusty and dingy, not to mention dark.

'I guess cleaning the windows will be a priority,' Alix said. 'Jeez, had those people never heard of Windolene either?'

Noah had followed her in silence, but now he gave her a lopsided smile. 'What's that?' he teased. 'Something I should know about?'

She smacked him playfully on the arm. 'Shut up. Don't tell me your windows are this bad. I won't believe you.' And she couldn't believe she'd hit him like that either. It was most unlike her.

'Hmm, you'd be surprised, but thanks for the heads-up. I'll be sure to polish every window before I invite you over to Vaughan Court.'

The thought of going to Noah's house made her cheeks warm again, but she turned away so that he wouldn't notice her reaction. It was silly anyway. They weren't even friends. Neighbours, yes, and possibly to be connected by a tenancy agreement. Nothing else. She'd have no reason to visit him.

'So far it looks like you mostly need to get a cleaning company in here,' Noah commented. 'Then some decorators. There's nothing major that needs doing, unless you're planning to knock down any walls?'

'Well, I was wondering whether it would be a good idea to open up an arch between the sitting room and dining room. The house is rather dark, with its low ceilings and beams, and the window in the dining room is much bigger. It would let more light into the sitting room.' Both rooms were on one side of the hallway, while the rest were on the other.

'Good idea. You'd have to ask a structural engineer if it's feasible. Wouldn't want the upper floors to collapse on you. Shall we look upstairs now?'

Shadow rushed ahead of them as soon as he saw the direction they were heading. He seemed to be enjoying exploring a new place and was happily sniffing every corner. His muzzle was soon covered in spiderwebs, and his claws clicked on the stairs and bare floors as he went. Noah had to tell him to slow down.

'Don't want you sliding and breaking a leg,' he said. 'He's invaluable in helping me with the sheep when they need moving,' he explained to Alix.

He was ushering her up the oak treads before him, and they creaked in protest at his weight. 'Sounds like I've been eating too much lately,' he joked. 'This house wasn't built for big men.'

Alix pretended to check his size, although she was already fully aware of it. 'I'm sure it can handle your weight. The staircase has been here for over four hundred years after all, so it must be pretty strong. The whole place was probably designed for slightly smaller men, though. From what I've gathered, the average male height in Elizabethan times was only about five foot six.' She eyed Noah's six-foot-plus frame. 'Make sure you duck through all the doors, especially upstairs.'

'Will do.'

There were three bedrooms and two bathrooms on the upper floor, all of them empty and forlorn-looking. In one, the ceiling had partially collapsed, leaving a pile of plaster and dust on the floor, but the others were merely dirty.

'You'd better have someone come in and check all the ceilings up here.' Noah poked one with a finger. It gave a little, making him frown. 'And shouldn't the former tenants at least have done some cleaning? I thought that was basic courtesy when you vacated a place.'

Alix sighed. 'Yes, but I gather they left in something of a hurry. A sick or dying relative who needed them. To be honest, I don't care, as it meant Grandpa giving me the house sooner. He would have had to wait another six months if they hadn't decided to end the contract early.' She took out her mobile and typed some notes, then brought out a tape measure. 'Would you mind helping me to take some measurements, please? I need to know what to get in the way of furniture, and I don't want to buy anything too big.'

'Sure.'

They spent half an hour measuring every room, then Alix declared that she'd seen enough.

'Thank you for helping me, Noah. You've been very patient.' She had to admit, him appearing like that had turned out to be a good thing. Measuring on her own would have taken a lot longer and been a pain. 'As have you,' she added to Shadow, patting his soft head. The dog had finished his explorations and had been waiting patiently for the last ten minutes. She received a lick on her hand in return and smiled at the beautiful canine.

'No problem. That's what neighbours are for, right?' Noah shoved his hands in the pockets of his jeans and grinned. 'And there's a possibility I'm trying to butter you up so you'll rent your fields to me. Is it working?'

'Hmm. I don't know. Very devious.' She didn't want to confess that it was definitely helping his cause. Besides, it wasn't as if she'd be inundated with offers. Who would want the fields other than someone who lived close by?

'Guess I'll have to try even harder.' His grin widened. 'Want to come back to my place for lunch before you drive home?'

'Are you sure you have time for that? Don't you have, like, farm stuff to do?'

He laughed. 'Of course, but I need to eat in any case, and it would be nice with company. The farm stuff can wait.'

'Then thank you, I'd like that.'

Alix wasn't sure she ought to be spending more time with him today, but the hopeful look in his eyes won her over. Also the thought that she should make him work for her goodwill after how rude he'd been the first time they met. That was only fair. Weirdly enough, something in his voice had made her think he might be lonely, which was probably crazy. She didn't know anything about his social life, but maybe working hard all day didn't allow him to go out much. Still, he was bound to have loads of friends.

And girlfriends, although she didn't want to think about those.

Stop it, Alix! Maybe it was time she tried to socialise a bit with her new workmates. One of them might be able to introduce her to some suitable guy. A man who wore suits rather than dirty jeans slung low on narrow hips, and flannel shirts over tight T-shirts, with the sleeves rolled up to show off tanned muscular forearms, and . . .

Good grief. She had to get a grip. 'I'll follow you,' she told Noah after locking the front door. 'I can't quite remember the way.'

Vaughan Court was only a five-minute drive along the winding lanes, and Alix was impatient to see it. She'd never been there, although she assumed Autumn had, back when she'd hung out with Noah's sister. That reminded her . . .

'Is your sister at home?' she asked as they got out of their respective vehicles.

'Maybe. She comes and goes as she pleases.' Noah's tone indicated that this was a sore subject, so Alix didn't want to pry. Relenting slightly, however, he added, 'She lives with me but is studying sociology long-distance. I don't see her much as she doesn't help with the farm. That's my domain.'

'I see.' She detected some resentment there, but it wasn't any of her business, so she didn't comment.

'I have two teenage boys helping out, Aidan and Pete,' Noah added. 'They're from London and are the relatives of some people I know from my time living there. I have them here sort of as apprentices so they can learn about farm work. I'm hoping they'll like it enough to want to go to agricultural college eventually. Beats hanging out with gangs in their old haunts.' He shrugged. 'It worked for me.'

That sounded admirable, and Alix was impressed.

'Do you have to feed them too?'

'No, I pay them a small allowance, plus a bit more for food, and they get free lodging in one of the outbuildings. They have their own kitchen and cook for themselves.'

The cluster of buildings that made up Vaughan Court was situated at the end of a long driveway that was less potholed than the one at Howell's End. It seemed Noah kept it in good repair. She stared up at the main house and couldn't help an awed 'Wow!' from escaping. It was a large, sprawling Victorian building, two storeys high, with a little turret or tower at one end, topped by a weathervane. Built partly of red brick and partly of the local reddish-grey sandstone, it had large sash windows, and the front walls were covered with the same sort of climbing plants as her grandfather's house. Here they'd been properly trimmed back, and the wisteria was starting to flower, the large purple and white clusters swaying in the breeze.

'This is beautiful, Noah!' she exclaimed. 'And now I understand why it's called Vaughan Court. It's a lot fancier than I expected.'

He smiled. 'Yes, I think some of my ancestors had delusions of grandeur. It used to be plain old Vaughan Farm before they extended the house. It's a pain in the neck to heat, let me tell you. The rooms are huge, with high ceilings and big single-glazed windows. In winter we practically live in only four of them – living room, kitchen and our bedrooms. On the positive side, it's a lovely cool refuge on a hot summer's day.'

They had parked in an old-fashioned stable yard surrounded by horse boxes. There were no equine heads looking out of them, however, and most of the double doors were closed.

'No horses here these days,' Noah confirmed. 'The family used to run a stud, but gave it up years ago.'

A huge barn and other outbuildings were next to the stables, and others could be glimpsed behind them. The familiar smell of a farmyard lingered in the air. Alix didn't mind it; the odour of manure had never bothered her. She associated it with her happy summers at Grandma and Grandpa's.

'How many rooms are there?' She peered up at the house as they walked towards the back door.

'Well, there are the usual rooms downstairs, and ten bedrooms and eight bathrooms upstairs if you include what used to be the servants' quarters on the attic floor. Back in the nineteenth century, the Vaughan family owned a lot of land around here, but my great-great-grandfather had so many children that a huge chunk of it was sold off to pay for dowries and such. Then all the male heirs except one were killed during the First World War. The only survivor had two grandsons – my uncle Ifan and my dad. Ifan was eventually left with the house and outbuildings, but not enough land and no extra cash. He'd bought out my dad, who had no interest in staying here, so he was already low on funds.'

'And now it's your burden?' Alix studied his face to see how much of a strain this was putting on him, but he didn't seem bothered.

'No. I see it as an unexpected gift, and I'm hoping to make it prosperous again. Maybe buy back some of the land eventually. If I ever have any extra energy, I might even run the house as a B&B one day. There's certainly enough space!'

'Great idea.'

Alix followed him into a kitchen that was cavernous to say the least. A long workbench of white marble with two Belfast sinks set into it ran along one wall, underneath massive windows. Another wall held the most enormous pine dresser she'd ever seen, which was covered in an assortment of old tins and blue-and-white glazed china. A large black AGA heated the room and was surrounded by a selection of polished copper pans. Meat hooks in the ceiling also had copper pots suspended from them. She was glad, as she wouldn't have liked to see slabs of meat or dead pheasants hanging there.

'Again, wow!' she said, twirling around to take it all in. 'This is what you call a proper kitchen.'

Noah laughed. 'Yes. A shame I don't have the time to cook much. Or the ability.' He walked over to the fridge and extracted an armful of items. 'Bread with cold stuff OK? I'm afraid I haven't gone food shopping yet today.'

'That's absolutely fine, thank you. Here, let me help you.' She grabbed some of the packets of cheese and a tub of tomatoes that were threatening to topple out of his grip. They spread everything on the old kitchen table and Noah brought over a farmhouse loaf.

'At least the bread is fresh,' he said. 'I had some in the freezer and I left it out on top of the AGA to defrost this morning.'

He put out plates and cutlery, and Alix admired the old-fashioned blue-and-white porcelain, its pattern a vivid floating indigo hue. 'Are you sure we should be eating on this? It's beautiful, but it looks too fancy for everyday use.'

'Nah, there's tons of the stuff here. I think it must have been a dinner service for at least twenty people originally. Maybe more. So no worries if we break a few.'

The tomatoes and cucumber turned out to be home-grown – the first of the season – and tasted much better than shop-bought ones. Noah had also put out hard-boiled eggs, which he told her came from his own hens.

'Oh, I'd love to meet them sometime. Maybe I should have hens too?' Alix had always loved feeding her grandmother's.

'Why not? As long as you have a safe place to lock them up at night so the foxes don't get them. I can give you a couple to start you off.'

'Thank you, but you don't have to do that. I'm sure I could easily get some ex-battery hens.'

'Whatever you prefer.'

Conversation flowed easily throughout the meal, although Alix was barely aware of what they talked about. It was mostly superficial stuff, but she felt unexpectedly relaxed in Noah's company. It helped that Shadow seemed to have taken a liking to her and spent most of the meal sitting next to her with his head on her lap, gazing up with soulful eyes.

'Don't fall for it,' Noah advised. 'He's trying to make you think he's starving, and he's not. He knows very well he's not allowed to cadge for food.'

Alix slipped the dog a couple of pieces of cheese anyway. Noah just shook his head and smiled.

When they were more or less done eating, they were interrupted by a snarky voice from the doorway.

'Well, this is cosy.'

They both looked up, and Alix saw a young woman leaning against the door jamb with her arms crossed. She had ash-blonde hair shot through with artificial highlights, caught up on top of her head in a messy bun. Unlike her brother's, her eyes were brown, and she was much smaller in stature as well. Alix couldn't see any sibling resemblance other than perhaps the straight nose with a slight tilt at the tip. There was a strange expression on the woman's face – half annoyed, half intrigued, and something a tiny bit malicious when she looked at Noah.

'Niamh. I didn't think you were at home.' He scowled in his sister's direction. 'Your car wasn't outside.'

She walked towards them. 'I lent it to a friend.' She plonked herself down on a chair next to Noah. 'Left anything for me, or did you eat it all?'

'Don't be ridiculous. There's always plenty, as you well know.'

He sent her an irritated glance, then appeared to remember his manners. 'This is Alix Howell, our new neighbour.' He nodded in her direction. 'And this is my sister Niamh, as you've probably gathered.'

Niamh's eyebrows rose and she smirked. 'You don't look like an Alex.'

'It's Alix, actually, with an I.' She was used to having to explain her name, as most people got it wrong at first, but she had the feeling Niamh had done it on purpose. How rude. And what on earth did an Alex look like? Was there a type? She decided to ignore the comment, as it didn't make sense. 'I think you used to know my sister, Autumn.'

'Oh. Yes, we hung out a few times. She was fun.' Niamh helped herself to a slice of cheese without bothering to put it on a plate or a piece of bread, then studied Alix with her head tilted to one side. 'In fact, I chat to her on Instagram sometimes. You don't look much like her. I thought she said you were twins.'

The words were uttered in an even tone, but the underlying taunt was unmistakable. Niamh was implying that Autumn was much better-looking. Again, not the first time Alix had been told this. She clenched her fists under the table, but decided not to rise to the bait. Instead she gave Niamh a bland smile.

'We're not, but people sometimes think we are because we were born less than a year apart. Anyway, why would we want to look the same, even if we *were* twins? I, for one, would much rather be my own person than a copy of my sister. We are individuals after all.'

Noah, who must have seen his sister opening her mouth to spew some more snark, intervened. 'Alix, if you're finished, why don't we head outside? You can take a look at the chickens before you drive back.'

'That would be great, thanks. And thank you for lunch, it was delicious.'

'You're doing tours of the place now? Didn't you say you had a thousand things to do around here?' Niamh taunted, reaching for the loaf of bread.

Noah put a hand on the small of Alix's back and guided her out of the kitchen, closely followed by Shadow, who hadn't greeted Niamh in any way. 'Ignore her,' he murmured. 'She's a spoiled brat.'

That certainly seemed to be the case, and Alix wondered why he put up with her. It was none of her business, though, and from what she'd gathered, Niamh was the only close family he had, so perhaps he didn't have a choice.

They had a quick look at the chickens, then Alix headed towards her car. She didn't want to take up any more of Noah's time, and Niamh's comments rankled, despite her trying not to think about them.

As they came to a halt next to the Fiat, Noah turned to her with a worried look in his eyes. 'I'm really sorry about my sister. I hope she hasn't put you off your neighbours.'

'Still worried about me not renting you the fields?' she dared to tease with a small smile.

'Yes, very. I desperately need them.' He smiled back. 'How about if I take you out for a drink or a meal? Would that help my cause?'

She stared at him, feeling suddenly flustered. 'A drink? Oh. Er, yes, that might be . . . nice?'

He chuckled. 'No need to sound so enthusiastic. I'm a big boy. I can take no for an answer without having a tantrum. Although it makes the task of buttering you up more difficult if I can't see you again any time soon.'

A fiery blush spread across her cheeks. 'Sorry. Automatic reaction. It's just that I've recently been through a bad break-up and another unpleasant experience involving men, so I'm a little cautious at the moment. But if all you want is an opportunity to try and persuade me to let you be my tenant, that's fine. It's not like my diary is full at the moment. I don't know many people here yet.'

At his raised eyebrows, she added, 'I only recently moved to Hereford. I've lived in London all my life, except for during the summers when I visited Grandpa and Grandma here.'

'OK, then how about a drink tomorrow night? If you text me your address, I'll pick you up.'

'Tomorrow?' She hadn't thought he meant so soon, but she couldn't think of a reason to refuse. 'All right. Seven p.m.?'

'See you then.'

Chapter Ten

West Mercia, May/Gaukmánuðr AD 874

For the next few days, Merewen came to the cairn at least once a day, although she didn't stay long. She brought food and water, and changed the dressing on Eirik's wound, adding a fresh poultice of yarrow each time. He battled the fever for another day, but the willow bark draught helped, and he finally started to feel halfway human again on the third day. So much so that he managed to hobble to the nearest brook to wash both himself and his shirt and tunic. It was indescribably wonderful to feel clean and refreshed. He didn't even mind the chilly water, but dunked his entire head and then tried to comb out his hair.

Merewen arrived just as he was fighting with the final tangles, and he heard her draw in a sharp breath. When he looked up, she was staring at his naked torso as if she couldn't take her eyes off it. While he ought to have been embarrassed – men should not go around without a shirt on at any time – her fascinated gaze made him heat up in other ways. It was clear that she liked what she saw, and he had to hide a smile. This woman was *not* suited for the monastery. She had needs and emotions that would never be fulfilled there.

He had to find a way to save her from that fate.

'What . . . what are you doing?' she stammered, when she had recovered her wits enough to turn away. 'Has the fever returned? Are you too hot again?'

Eirik liked that she sounded worried. Who would have thought an enemy woman would care whether he lived or died? But then again, here they were merely two humans, thrown together by fate. Neither was engaged in warfare, and truth be told, he didn't want to ever fight anyone again. He was heartily sick of that life.

'No, I think it's gone. Unfortunately, all my belongings are on the ship I arrived in, and I needed to wash my shirt. I apologise if the sight of me offends you.' He knew it didn't, but couldn't resist teasing her a little.

'Hmph. You could have worn your tunic while the shirt dries,' she grumbled.

'No. I washed that too,' he informed her, smiling widely when she deigned to glance at him. 'My trousers will be next.'

She narrowed her gaze. 'You did it on purpose, didn't you? If you're well enough for mischief, there's no need for me to keep coming.' Her chin went up a fraction, as if she was truly miffed, although he was sure she was only pretending.

He found it endearing and captured her chin with his fingers, turning her face towards him. 'Please don't stop coming. I still need you.'

Staring into the deep, clear pools of her eyes, he felt a frisson of awareness shimmer through him. She was lovely, and not merely because of the way she looked. To him, everything about her was pleasing. The determined chin he was holding, the pert nose, the delightful freckles and her tempting little mouth. Not to mention her willingness to help him, and her efforts to heal him and care for him. He owed her a massive debt, and he wasn't going to pounce on her or treat her in any way that was inappropriate. She deserved better than that.

It was possible that he could have survived on his own, but her care had certainly helped speed up the process. Maybe she had even saved his life. He was determined to pay her back somehow, and he was beginning to come up with a plan for that, but he also realised he'd have to go slowly. She didn't fully trust him yet and she hadn't seen him at full strength. He was a big man and could be intimidating, but he never wanted her to be afraid of him. He wouldn't ever hurt her.

All he had to do was convince her of that.

Merewen was flustered. Well, what else would she be, with a half-naked man within touching distance? And she did want to touch all that smooth skin, she had to admit. Desperately. Thankfully, he had no way of knowing that her thoughts were extremely inappropriate. Sinful. That was her secret shame. She couldn't shake the suspicion that he'd shed his clothing on purpose, but his explanation had sounded plausible. There was no denying he smelled a lot better now, and his hair was lovely and shiny, and free of tangles. She had heard tell that the Norsemen bathed a lot more often than her own countrymen, and that they changed their clothes frequently. If they all smelled as fresh as Eirik, she could see the appeal. Oslac hadn't bothered with such niceties for the most part. He always washed his hands before a meal, but she'd never noticed the rest of him being overly clean, and she hadn't expected it.

Perhaps she was in need of washing herself? Yes, she'd have to do something about that when she got home.

'Can you stay for a while? I'm very bored and restless today,' Eirik said, bringing her out of her strange thoughts. 'Would you care to play a game with me?'

'A game?' Even she could hear the distrustful tone in her voice, so it was no surprise when Eirik grinned at her.

'Not that kind,' he assured her. 'A board game.'

'Um, I'm not sure I'd be able to smuggle one out. Someone would be bound to notice.'

He shook his head. 'You don't need to do that. Look, I'll just draw a grid here on the ground, then we can use stones as gaming pieces. I collected some by the brook earlier.'

She watched as he drew in the dirt with a stick, his squares surprisingly neat and even. Then he produced a handful of little pebbles, and one larger stone, which he held up. 'This one is the king, that's why he's bigger.'

'King? What are we playing?'

'*Hnefatafl*. I'll teach you.' He gestured for her to sit on the opposite side of the makeshift board. 'Let me tell you the rules.'

Merewen had played board games before, of course, especially one called Merels, although the objective of that was different and it was played with fewer gaming pieces. She listened as Eirik explained about *hnefatafl* and went through a practice game with her. It was a fairly easy concept. One player had a smaller number of pieces plus the larger one, the king, which he called *hnefi*. The other had more pieces and was supposed to surround and capture the king, like an army in warfare. It required strategy and deep thought, not merely luck, just like Merels. You had to try and second-guess your opponent's next move in order to best him. Merewen found it intriguing, and once she'd grasped the rules, exciting and absorbing.

They played two rounds and she tried her utmost to concentrate on the pebbles rather than the charismatic man sitting opposite her. The entire experience was surreal. They were inside an ancient stone monument playing a board game as if it was nothing out of the ordinary. She shouldn't be alone with him, an enemy – nor any man for that matter – especially not in this remote place. And definitely not with him in a semi-nude state. Now that he was recovering, he was becoming more dangerous every day. She'd seen him standing up – he was a tall man, big and powerful. A wiser person than her would have left him to fend for himself, but she couldn't resist the pull he exerted on her. Couldn't make herself walk away.

'What are you thinking about?' His voice brought her out of her reverie and she realised it was her turn, but he was staring at her rather than the board.

'Er, nothing. I mean . . . I don't know what I'm doing here,' she blurted out. She was confused and befuddled. Completely out of her depth. All because of him.

'You're tending to a sick man,' he said, but his twinkling green eyes told her he knew what she'd really meant. 'And you're losing,' he added, nodding at the game.

'What? Oh.' He was right. His pebbles had her king surrounded. Again. 'Bother.'

He chuckled and gathered up the little stones, putting them to one side. 'We can practise more another day. Tell me about yourself,' he urged. 'I want to know more about you.'

'What? Why?' Merewen felt perturbed, not sure where he was going with this.

Eirik shrugged. 'I'm interested. You said you had sisters, and you mentioned your father. No mother?'

'She died five winters ago. My older sister, Burghild, runs the household now. As I mentioned, she's married to Oslac and the two of them will inherit the property one day. It's her dowry. In fact, she already acts as if she owns it,' Merewen added grumpily.

'I see. A tyrant, is she?' Eirik smiled. 'I've met a few of those in my time.'

'Indeed. I'm the second oldest, then there are my two younger sisters, Aelfwynn and Eadgifu, but they've gone off to stay with kin for a while. Burghild is with child, which makes her even more impossible to be around than usual. There are various other relatives living with us, and of course the *ceorls*, the free peasants who help to work the land. They have their own dwellings near the main hall.'

'So it's a large settlement then?' Eirik seemed merely interested in general, rather than in an avaricious way, so Merewen didn't see why she shouldn't tell him. He was but one man and couldn't attack on his own.

'Yes, very. Father is what we call a *thegn*. He owns several hides of land, a mixture of grazing and fields for growing crops.' A hide was an area large enough to support one family, so she knew her father was fortunate to own much more. 'And it will become even larger when combined with Oslac's.'

'That is what I aspire to.' Eirik gazed through the opening of the cairn and into the distance, as though visualising what he wished for. 'I want my own domains.'

'Then why are you raiding? I assume you've been part of the Heathen Army.' They hadn't spoken about this before, both of them instinctively holding back, but she felt it was time to face the truth.

'Yes, I was until recently. I've been with my uncle and his men since I was a young boy, and I swore fealty to him.' He sighed. 'For some time now I've been urging him to find a place for us to settle, but he always resists. I don't think the life of a landholder is for him. He's much too restless. And greedy.'

'Were you aiming to travel back to your own people and settle there?'

A fleeting shadow of grief passed over his features, but he masked it quickly. 'I have no one other than my uncle. My parents were living in Frisia when I was born, my father a mercenary like his brother. I'm not sure where they came from originally – Hastein won't talk about it – so I've nowhere to return to. No, I will seek a place of my own here. Well, not in Mercia, but Northumbria perhaps. I'm told there's land for the taking there. In fact I saw the perfect place last year and I'm hoping to return to it before anyone else claims it.'

'I see.'

'Tell me more about your life. How come you have no say in whether you enter a monastery? Shouldn't your father take your opinion into account? Surely you can earn your keep by being a healer in your own community?'

'No. It is a man's right to decide for the females of his household. Women have to obey their fathers and husbands, that's just the way it is. St Paul teaches that women should keep silent in church, and I think he meant for us to be meek in general as well. We are expected to tend to our homes and do our duty; not be too forward or assertive, nor sow discord, but act as a *frythwebba* – peace-weaver – whenever possible. Even queens have to abide by these rules.'

Eirik muttered something clearly extremely rude in his own language that made Merewen's eyes open wide. She understood the meaning but had never heard that word before. Then he shook his head. 'That is not how things work where I come from. Women are respected, their opinions sought on various matters, especially to do with a household. I've never lived in one place for very long, but I know for a fact that the wives of some of the jarls are running their estates back home while they are out campaigning. A married couple are equals, two parts of a whole, each with their own duties and domains. Women can be married off without their consent, but for the most part they are asked whether they agree.'

'That sounds . . . good?' Merewen had never thought to rebel against her father, and had been fully prepared to submit to a husband in every way. It was what she'd been taught from birth. The strange ideas Eirik was promoting appeared dangerous and forbidden, but also rather tempting.

'You don't really want to spend the rest of your life in a monastery, do you?' He was peering at her intently, those green eyes filled with genuine concern.

'What else can I do? At least I wouldn't have to stay here and watch my sisters with their future husbands and children, something I will never be granted. Truth to tell, it would be a relief to get away.'

Sadness welled up inside her. She had so looked forward to becoming a mother, as she adored children. Now that dream was gone.

Unexpectedly, Eirik reached out to stroke her cheek with his knuckles. 'You could come with me,' he said softly. 'I'll need a woman to run my household.'

'What?' Alarm bells rang in her mind, and she jerked away from his touch. He was still shirtless, temptation personified, and she shouldn't even be here, never mind go anywhere with him. 'No! I . . . I can't.' He was a heathen and she refused to be his woman, living in sin, no matter how wonderful that sounded.

He studied her for a moment, then turned away to put on his shirt, which must have been dry enough by now. 'At least give it some thought,' he said. 'The offer is there, and I promise to treat you well, always.'

Merewen didn't reply. Her traitorous body wanted her to throw herself into his arms and say she'd follow him wherever he wished, but common sense held her back. This interlude with Eirik was a time out of the ordinary, but sooner or later she had to return to reality.

The two of them were enemies. They had no future together.

*

Well, that didn't go very well. Eirik wanted to kick himself. He shouldn't have mentioned her coming with him so soon. They had only known each other a short while, after all, and she had no reason to trust him. But he'd meant well and he was serious. The life he could offer her had to be better than being immured in a monastery for the rest of her days, though perhaps she didn't see it like that.

It would have been a way to thank her for everything she'd done for him, though honesty made him admit to himself that he didn't want to part from her either. She made him feel things he never had before. Desire, certainly, but also affection and respect. Liking. Perhaps even more than that. Her courage and kindness were admirable qualities, but there was a vulnerability in her too that brought his protective instincts to the fore. There had always been willing women in his life, but no one he'd considered spending the rest of his days with. Merewen, however, was different.

She was clearly virtuous, for one thing, and he assumed no man had ever touched her. Judging by the way she'd recoiled from his light caress, the mere thought terrified her. He was a patient man, though, and he could show her how pleasurable it could be if only she'd give him the chance. Perhaps she was put off by his beliefs. Should he offer to be baptised in order for her to accept his suit? He knew of quite a few jarls who had allowed priests to pour water on their heads and intone their rites over them. It didn't necessarily mean anything and could be expedient when dealing with foreign rulers. In secret, those jarls had stuck to their own gods, merely adding the White Christ and his so-called Heavenly Father to that pantheon. Their Christian counterparts didn't need to know that.

But it would feel wrong to deceive Merewen that way.

She'd stood up and was preparing to flee. He could tell he'd spooked her and was afraid she wouldn't return. Not that he really needed her any longer – he was well enough to set some snares for rabbits and catch fish in the nearest river – but he wanted her to come back. Needed to spend more time with her. It was dangerous for both of them, but addictive. Irresistible. If they were found out, the consequences would be disastrous, but he didn't care. He would take that chance rather than lose her.

What could he do to show his sincerity?

'Wait,' he said as she shook out her skirts and started backing towards the opening between the stones. He turned to rummage in one of his leather pouches and found what he was looking for. 'Here. I want you to have this as a token of my appreciation for your care.'

He held out a gold ring with an engraved image of a lamb in between two letters. They were unlike the runes he was used to, but he'd made it a point to learn to read the native writing and knew they were an A and a D. Presumably they meant something, but he had no idea what.

'That's not necessary,' she replied, but she took the ring to study the engraving. '*Agnus Dei*, the Lamb of God,' she murmured.

'What?'

'It's a symbol of peace.' Merewen looked up at him. 'You didn't know?'

'No. I just thought the design seemed fitting for you, but this is good. I do want there to be peace between us. Always.'

She nodded. 'Then I thank you for this gift. I shall treasure it.'

Before he could ask whether she intended to come back, she'd fled with Sceadu following in her wake. He could only hope he hadn't scared her away for good.

Chapter Eleven

Hereford, May, present day

Alix was standing inside a tiny building of some sort, its wattle-and-daub walls drab and a bit dirty. There was a sweet scent of herbs in the air from various bunches hanging from a low beam, but in her immediate vicinity it was tainted by the rank smell of the heavyset man standing in front of her. Too close. And coming closer, his expression menacing. Her back was already pressed up against a workbench that contained all manner of pots and jars, as well as a pestle and mortar. Right now, though, she was oblivious to her surroundings, and her heart was beating fast enough to leave her chest.

He shouldn't be here. She hated him.

A low growl from a large hound standing next to her imbued her with courage, and she grabbed a knife from behind her and pointed it at the man. 'Leave,' she hissed, but he only smirked, and she knew she couldn't hurt him. She wasn't strong enough.

His eyes told her that nothing would stop him. He was going to take what he wanted and there was not a thing she could do about it. She watched in horror as he moved further towards her. He was coming and she was helpless. A scream formed in her throat, but no sound emerged. She tried again, desperate now to call for help. Her lips made the right shape but her vocal cords refused to function. Only a tiny mewling noise emerged, and no one would hear that. It was going to be too late ...

The sound she'd made in her sleep woke Alix from the nightmare and she lay still, staring at the ceiling, while her erratic heartbeat slowly began to calm down. The images were still clear in her mind, and she willed them away. It wasn't real. It was just a dream.

But it was eerily similar to what had so recently happened to her. And she never wanted to be that frightened ever again.

She couldn't believe she'd said yes to going out for a drink with Noah. She'd sworn off men after leaving London, and not just because of Sean's treachery.

The week leading up to that discovery had been one of the worst in her life. At the library where she had worked, she'd had a male colleague, Ed, who had cornered her in the staff room one evening after everyone else had gone home. The two of them were supposed to lock up and make sure everything was turned off for the night. Alix had gone to fetch her coat and handbag from her locker when a pair of arms suddenly enveloped her from behind.

'Finally, we have the place to ourselves,' Ed had murmured, attempting to nuzzle her neck. 'I've seen the way you've been looking at me recently. Now all your dreams are about to come true.'

Alix had frozen at first, unable to believe this was happening. As far as she could recall, she'd never regarded Ed with anything other than the friendliness due a co-worker. Panic shot through her, galvanising her into action. 'What on earth are you talking about? I have a fiancé! Let go of me!'

She struggled to free herself, but Ed was surprisingly strong.

Not a big man, but wiry and with corded muscles in his arms, perhaps from lifting heavy boxes of books every day.

He chuckled. 'The lady doth protest too much. No need to pretend any longer, sweetheart. Your eyes don't lie.'

His hands were wandering, one palm squeezing her left breast while the other wrapped around her stomach to pull her tighter to his body. She struggled to free herself, but his arms were a vice that wouldn't budge. She could feel the unmistakable evidence of his arousal, and nausea threatened to overwhelm her.

'Get off me!' she shouted, elbowing him in the sternum. 'Stop it!'

This time he laughed outright. 'Not a chance. You want me, I know you do. Just admit it.'

Terror was gripping her insides now, immobilising her. Eyes flickering around wildly, she tried to find something to hit him with, but there was nothing except her handbag. She tried swinging that round behind her to bash his head, but he merely ducked. It wouldn't have done much damage in any case. Alix was sobbing by this time, her lungs constricted with fear, but she forced herself to take a couple of deep breaths.

Think! She had to come up with some way of stopping him. What did the heroines do in the romantic suspense books she read?

Ed's hand had stopped fondling her breast and moved to her crotch instead. He was tugging the hem of her skirt up with impatient movements, and while he was focused on that, she suddenly went completely limp in his arms. This caused his grip to loosen slightly, allowing her to twist around. Without hesitation, she jabbed her fingers into his eyes, nails first, and he howled and stumbled backwards.

'You bitch!' he screamed.

She ignored him, grabbed her coat and fled before he could reach for her again. Once outside the staff room, she knew she was safe, as there were security cameras everywhere, but she still ran towards the front doors as if the hounds of hell were chasing her. Tears flowed down her cheeks, and great sobs erupted from her throat. Her legs were shaking so badly she wasn't sure she'd make it outside, but somehow she did. To her immense relief, an empty taxi was passing just as she barrelled through the doors, and she waved frantically at the driver. He stopped, and by the time Ed emerged behind her, she was speeding away.

'Fight with your boyfriend?' the cab driver asked, studying her tear-stained face with concern, but she didn't want to talk about it.

'Something like that.'

The following day, she'd reported Ed for sexual assault, but no one had believed her. When confronted by their manager, Ed had apparently told them Alix was trying to besmirch his reputation so that she would be given the promotion they'd both been competing for. Since there were no cameras in the staff room, there was no evidence of what had happened apart from her headlong dash towards the front doors, which proved nothing. It was her word against his, and the male manager chose to believe Ed.

Alix had resigned on the spot. There was no way she'd be able to work with Ed ever again. It simply wasn't safe. Before leaving, she had sent an email to all her female colleagues to be on their guard around him, but she didn't know if they'd replied, as her work address had been shut down soon after that. She'd done what she could.

The very next day was when she'd heard Sean and Autumn plotting together, and it was all too much. She never wanted to see another man for as long as she lived.

So why had she agreed to meet up with Noah? She must have gone mad.

*

Noah had arranged to meet Alix outside the Green Dragon Hotel in Broad Street, not far from Hereford Cathedral. He didn't know exactly where she lived but assumed it was somewhere near the centre of town. He respected her wish not to tell him and to meet nearby instead. Perhaps she didn't want him in her space, presumably because of the bad experiences she'd alluded to. It was a shame, but he would do his best not to spook her as he definitely wasn't a threat to her in any way.

He'd have to earn her trust.

He was leaning against his Land Rover, studying the passers-by, when she appeared on the other side of the street, rushing towards him. She came to a halt in front of him, looking adorably flushed. Noah felt something shift inside him at the sight of her and realised he'd been afraid she wouldn't show up. Now she was here and he was flooded with relief. He wanted to get to know her, spend time with her, and not just to persuade her to rent him her fields. It surprised him, as it had been a long time since he'd been truly interested in a woman.

'Sorry I'm late. I forgot the time as I was working on something,' she explained, sounding a little out of breath.

He smiled. 'No problem. I haven't been here long.' Gesturing to the Land Rover, he asked, 'Do you want to go to a pub out in the countryside, or would you prefer to stay in town? If so, I'll have to pay for more parking.'

She bit her lip, drawing his attention to the fact that she had a delectable mouth and she wasn't wearing lipstick. He approved. Lipstick was something he'd never understood. The few times he'd kissed a woman wearing some, he'd disliked the taste and feel of it. Natural lips were so much nicer. Softer. Although why he was thinking of kissing already, he had no idea. He forced himself to concentrate on Alix's eyes while he waited for her reply.

'Where did you have in mind? Outside of Hereford, I mean.' It was clear that she was reluctant to go anywhere with him that was just the two of them, and he felt bad for suggesting it.

'I was thinking the Carpenters Arms in Walterstone, but if you'd rather stay around here, there's a place down by the river that's pretty good.' Looking her straight in the eyes, he added, 'I swear you're safe with me, Alix. I don't molest women or mistreat them in any way. You can call your grandfather and tell him you're with me if you want, so that someone knows your whereabouts. Then check in with him after we get back.'

Her cheeks turned pink and she ducked her head. 'I'm sorry,' she whispered. 'I had an, um ... altercation with a male colleague, but there were no witnesses and no one believed me.'

'What? Why not?'

'My word against his.' She shook her head. 'I'd rather not talk about it right now. I want us to have a nice evening.' Taking a deep breath, she visibly squared her shoulders. 'I'm going to trust you because Grandpa knows your family, so you're not a complete stranger. And if you want to rent those fields, you have to behave, right?'

He could tell she was trying to joke about it in order to lighten the mood, so he played along. 'Absolutely. My sheep are very important to me. I'd never do anything to jeopardise that tenancy agreement. They'll stampede me to death if I don't give them enough grazing.'

She rewarded him with a small smile. 'Good. Let's go, then.'

He held open the passenger door for her and tried not to stare at her legs as she climbed in. She was wearing tight black jeans that moulded to shapely thighs, and little half-boots with a spiky heel. A far cry from the flat librarian shoes and prim skirt she'd been wearing the first time he had met her. A short black leather jacket over a V-neck top that showed a glimpse of cleavage completed her outfit. Around her neck she wore a gold chain with some kind of amulet, and her long hair was once again caught up only at the front, leaving the rest to tumble around her shoulders. Understated but elegant, and he liked what he saw. Very much so.

'Um, are you going to stand there and stare at my boots all night?'

There was amusement in her voice, and Noah blinked, realising he'd been ogling her legs for too long. 'Sorry, just remembered something. Not important.' He bustled around to the driver's side, and soon they were on their way.

'Have you been to Walterstone before?' he asked as they headed south out of the city.

'I think so, but it's been a while. Don't they do a lovely Sunday lunch?' Alix was fidgeting with the strap of her handbag and Noah realised she was still nervous.

'Oh yes! I'd go every week if I could, but I hardly ever have time.'

She half turned towards him as if studying his profile. 'You must be very busy with farm work. I remember Grandpa never really got a break. Why did you want to be a farmer? It's tough, right?'

He nodded. 'It's physically demanding, that's for sure, and the work never really ends. It was kind of my salvation, though.' He didn't normally share his life history with people he'd only just met, but he sensed that she needed confidences from him in order to feel safer and keep her anxiety at bay. 'I grew up in London, and not in the nicer parts. Single mum, father God knows where, and friends who were always up to no good. I did some things I'm not proud of and it could have ended very badly, but then my mum died. I was nineteen and suddenly responsible for a fourteen-year-old half-sister who was angry at the unfairness of life and grieving the loss of our mother. She was almost taken away by social services to be placed in a foster home, but then Uncle Ifan and Aunt Jane stepped in. They offered us a home on condition that I helped out around the farm. Ifan was getting older and couldn't cope on his own any longer but didn't have the money to hire much help. I realised this was my chance to straighten myself out, and I was grateful to them. By working hard, I was able to pay them back for their kindness.'

'And now you own Vaughan Court?' Alix seemed fascinated by his tale.

'Yes, my uncle left it to me in his will. Said it should stay in the family if at all possible. My dad had died by then and there were no other relatives. And as I said, Dad had sold Ifan his share a long time ago. He wouldn't have wanted the place anyway, from what I understand. I didn't see him very often and we never talked about that. I'm doing my best to take good care of it. Wouldn't want to disappoint the ancestors.'

Alix sighed. 'Grandpa has given me Howell's End for the same reason. My dad – his son – was never interested, but he knows I love it here. I can't carry on with the farm, though, and I feel bad about that. I'm sure he would have liked me to do what you're doing.'

Noah reached out and gave her arm a light squeeze. 'Hey, don't be so hard on yourself. The farming life is not for everyone, and I'll make good use of those fields if you'll let me. I'm sure Morgan is pleased you'll be living in his ancestral home at least.'

'Yes, that's true.' She flashed him a quick smile. 'Thanks. I'll contact the solicitor on Monday and ask him to draw up an agreement between us. I'm glad Grandpa's fields won't fall into ruin.'

'Trust me, my flock will be ecstatic to use them. Speaking of Howell's End, have you had a chance to think about the renovations you want?'

'Yes, I made a list when I got home, but it will depend on costs. Hopefully I have the funds for any necessary work, but I might have to do it a little bit at a time.' There was some uncertainty in her voice, which made Noah want to reassure her.

'You can probably do a lot of it yourself. Painting and such. I'm happy to help if you need me. I'm great at wallpapering.'

Alix blinked at him. 'Really? I mean, are you sure you have the time?'

'I'll make time. I get that it might be daunting to tackle it on your own. At least at first.'

'Thank you. That's very kind. But you don't have to, honestly. I'll be fine.' The fingers fiddling nervously with her handbag strap told a different tale and strengthened Noah's resolve.

'No worries. Just let me know.'

They had arrived at the pub and he pulled into the car park. 'Now, how about that drink I promised you?'

She gave him a wide smile. 'Sounds perfect.'

Chapter Twelve

West Mercia, early June/Gaukmánuðr AD 874

'Do you ever go anywhere without that mangy hound? I think it's time we got rid of him before he eats us out of house and home.'

Merewen startled, and turned to find Oslac standing much too close behind her while Sceadu growled and bared his teeth at the man. She'd been busy making up bundles of the herbs she'd picked, tying them with string and hanging them to dry on a beam above her workbench. She took a step to the side to avoid the unwelcome proximity.

'No. Father gave Sceadu to me and I'm sure he wouldn't take kindly to anyone harming him,' she replied. 'Besides, it wouldn't be wise to be without a guard dog in these uncertain times.' She carried on with her task, trying to ignore Oslac, but she was supremely aware of him. It made her skin crawl, because she sensed he wasn't here merely to talk.

Unlike Eirik, he smelled of man and sweat, and not in a good way. It overpowered the sweet scent of the herbs. And he was large; a hulking presence next to her that was intimidating and menacing. Although not as tall as the Norseman, he still exuded strength, being heavyset and robust. She had once considered him handsome, but not any longer. At least not on the inside. She wasn't under his spell the way she had once been, and since his marriage to Burghild she had seen a side of him she thoroughly disliked. He was selfish and domineering. A good match for her sister, come to think of it, as they were very alike in that respect.

Thank the Lord she hadn't ended up married to him. He would have made her miserable.

Unfortunately, though, he still hadn't given up his pursuit of her.

With Burghild growing larger with child each day – and grumpy and bloated with it – Merewen had found herself increasingly frequently cornered by Oslac. It would seem he was still determined to bed her without the sanctity of marriage. It was outrageous, and why he thought she'd go along with it, she couldn't fathom. At first he had tried to charm her with flattery and flirtation. When that didn't work, he'd resorted to more forceful tactics. He kept appearing when she was alone and no one else could overhear their conversations. Even in company, he would often brush against her deliberately, touching her under the guise of ushering her along or inadvertently bumping into her. He had squeezed her backside on numerous occasions, and even one of her breasts.

Yet her constant refusals to engage with him had only made him redouble his efforts. It made her want to scream.

Sceadu was her only defence and there was no way she'd allow him to be harmed. She glared at Oslac. 'If you hurt so much as a hair on his head, I'll tell Father,' she warned. 'And I'll make sure he knows why you wish to be rid of my dog, as well.'

He smirked. 'Do you really think he'd believe you? You're a mere woman and it would be your word against mine.' He moved closer, and out of sheer self-preservation, Merewen picked up the knife she'd been using to cut stems and pointed it at him.

'Then you'd best be on your guard, because I'll take my revenge when you least expect it,' she hissed. 'Now please, leave me alone and stop harassing me. You have a wife, and a child on the way. Be content with that.'

Oslac's mouth tightened as he stared down at the knife. 'You think you can hurt me with that?' he sneered.

She smiled back, grimly determined. 'I could if you were asleep. Perhaps I'll cut off that which you prize so highly.' A glance at his crotch made her meaning clear, and his expression darkened.

'Curse you, you insolent girl! I'll have you know I'm in charge here and you're to obey my every wish or else. One way or another, I'll have you before they ship you off to that monastery. I'm sure it won't matter to them if you're soiled goods, and no man would want you anyway.'

Then why do you? She wanted to shout the question at him, but she knew the answer. Burghild was a competent wife, but since becoming pregnant, she appeared washed out and constantly tired. It didn't help that her expression was habitually sour and dissatisfied. Merewen suspected that Oslac had already strayed with other women, and poor Burghild was bound to have heard the whispered rumours. She also couldn't have failed to notice her husband's interest in her sister, a fact that contributed to her waspishness whenever she interacted with Merewen. The latter would have loved to reassure Burghild that she'd never accept Oslac's advances, but it wouldn't make any difference. The fact that he wanted her and not his wife was enough to cause enmity.

'One of these days I'll catch you without the hound and then you'll see.' Oslac's words made a shiver of foreboding slither down her back, but she tried not to show it.

'I really hope for your sake you don't mean that, but thank you for the warning. I'll make sure to carry a larger knife with me from now on,' she retorted, jabbing the small one in her hand towards him. 'And one of these days *I'll* catch *you* asleep and defenceless.'

With a scowl, he left the hut and Merewen sank into a crouch, leaning her arms on her knees and her forehead on top. A warm lick on her cheek reminded her that she wasn't alone.

'Thank you,' she whispered to the hound. 'I suppose the sooner I leave here, the better. That man is dangerous and I won't be able to thwart him much longer.' She put her arms round Sceadu's neck and hugged him. 'He'd better not hurt you, though, or I'll cut his manhood off, see if I don't. Hateful swine!'

A little voice inside her whispered that she should take Eirik up on his offer instead of urging her father to find a monastery sooner rather than later. That would mean giving her virtue to another man. Living in sin. Could she really do that?

She didn't know. But she was sure of one thing – she'd much rather do it with Eirik than Oslac.

For the next few days, Merewen stayed away, and Eirik missed her company. Missed seeing her altogether – her lovely face, her smile, her intelligent remarks, everything about her. He came to the realisation that he loved her, and wanted to court her, but how could he do that when she wouldn't come anywhere near him? It wasn't as though he could enter her father's settlement and ask for her hand in marriage. Despite his ability to speak like the locals, he'd be identified as a Norseman straight away, he was certain. He had the riches to propose to any woman he wanted, but he was a stranger here, and their enemy. It was doubtful he'd even make it as far as holding a conversation with anyone, let alone telling them what he could provide in the way of a bride price.

They would kill him on sight.

Feeling glum and morose, he dedicated himself to regaining his strength. He mostly slept during the day and went outside the cairn to exercise at night. Weapons training, pulling himself up and down on a nearby tree branch, and pushing off the ground horizontally using only his arm muscles. The wound in his groin was still painful, but not unbearably so, and it was healing rapidly. He wasn't able to run yet, but he built up his stamina with long walks through the dark countryside and swimming in the river. It was freezing, but invigorating, and the water helped speed up the healing process.

It was during one such nightly outing that he became aware of dark figures moving stealthily through a field adjoining Merewen's father's settlement. He'd scouted out the place himself, noting the cluster of wooden buildings of various sizes, the fenced-in paddocks close to the dwellings, and the cultivated fields and grazing all around. There were plenty of lambs and calves, this year's newborns, as well as horses with foals, a small herd of goats and kids, and several sows with large litters of piglets. As it was still early in the year, they were kept in close proximity so that people could keep an eye on the little ones and make sure they thrived.

Eirik followed the flitting figures, wondering if Hastein and his men had returned to the area. Somehow this felt different, though, and he watched as the shadowy men made their way towards the paddocks rather than the dwellings. They weren't attacking openly but were obviously hoping to steal sheep or cattle without anyone noticing.

He had heard tell that Norsemen weren't the only threat in these parts. There were also raids from across the Welsh border from time to time. From what he could see now, the group making its way towards the paddocks wasn't huge, but it was large enough to take quite a few animals, ushering them out of their pens and driving them towards their own domains.

He came to a decision and circled round to the gate leading into the settlement. There was a man on guard there, but he was half asleep.

'Hey, you, wake up!' Eirik materialised beside the man, making him jump. Before he could grab a weapon, Eirik had disarmed him and held his wrists together, pushing them up behind his back. 'Listen to me,' he hissed. 'I mean you no harm. You need to know that there is a group of men currently stealing your master's herds from the paddocks. Go and raise the alarm this instant.'

'What? Who are you? Why would I—'

'There's no time to argue, and it matters not who I am. Run! Before it's too late.' He let go of the man and gave him a push.

Still looking befuddled, the guard did as he was told. He must have been used to following orders. Eirik limped after him, intent on helping to repel the cattle rustlers. As he passed a small hut, he heard a muted *woof* that sounded familiar.

'Sceadu?' he called softly. Another bark answered him, and soon afterwards, the door of the hut opened.

'Eirik? What are you doing here?' Merewen, sleepy and tousled, stared at him with a mixture of anxiety and pleasure, as if she wasn't sure how she felt about his presence. Sceadu had no such reservations and rushed out to greet him effusively. He reciprocated, but only for a moment.

'No time to explain. There are men trying to steal your father's animals,' he told her, nodding towards the paddocks. 'Can I borrow Sceadu?'

'Of course, but—'

He didn't allow her to finish the sentence. Instead, he ordered Sceadu to come with him, and the dog obeyed, causing Merewen to frown. Eirik took off at a half-run, the fastest he could manage, closely followed by Sceadu. The movement made his wound twinge, but he ignored it. The alarm had been raised by the guard, and there were men pouring out of the other buildings now, all rushing towards the back of the property.

When he arrived there, the startled raiders were either fleeing or preparing to fight. They must have thought they could carry out their nefarious business without anyone being the wiser. Sheep milled around baaing loudly, desperately calling out to their lambs. Some of them had been picked up by the rustlers, who carried one under each arm. It was pure chaos. Eirik hadn't brought his weapons, but he had a Saxon *scramasax*, a foot-long lethal knife that always hung off his belt, and he threw himself into the fray wielding that. He was helped by Sceadu, who stayed close to his side, dancing out of the way of any blades and inflicting damage with his large jaws. Eirik and the dog worked well together, making him wish he owned one himself. The skirmish didn't last very long as the would-be thieves were soon outnumbered. A few managed to escape with a couple of lambs, but the majority were killed or wounded.

'How dare you?' a middle-aged man bellowed at a captive. 'Thought you could steal from me, did you?'

Eirik assumed this was Merewen's father, Beorthric. A younger man had fought alongside him, and had been eyeing Eirik. As Eirik whistled softly to Sceadu and prepared to return him to his owner, the man stepped into his path, staring him up and down.

'Who are you?' he asked rudely. 'And who asked you to help here?'

'I was merely passing by and saw the raiders creeping up on your settlement,' Eirik explained. 'I thought it was my duty to raise the alarm. Did I do wrong?' He glanced at Beorthric, who had come to stand next to the other man.

'Easy, Oslac. We owe this man our thanks,' Beorthric said. 'I am grateful for the warning. We could have lost a great many animals tonight.' He cast a glare at the man who'd been on guard. 'It would seem I need to post more vigilant men. You, report to me in the morning for punishment.'

The guard hung his head in shame and slunk off, presumably to resume his post by the main gate.

'It was nothing,' Eirik said. 'I'd best be on my way.'

'Won't you come inside for a cup of ale? And perhaps you'd like to bed down on a bench for the night. It's late to be out and about.' Beorthric was studying him as if he wanted to know why he'd been abroad at night but wasn't sure how to ask without sounding rude to someone who had just done him a huge favour. Then he caught sight of Sceadu and frowned. 'Is that my daughter's hound?'

Eirik feigned ignorance. 'I've no idea. He appeared by my side and seemed to want to help. An obedient dog, I must say.'

For some reason, his words caused Oslac to send Sceadu a vicious glare, but Beorthric was a different matter.

'That he is. Come here. Good boy.' He patted the dog, who accepted the praise with a small wag of his tail.

'He's a menace,' Oslac grumbled, but Beorthric wasn't listening to him.

'Come inside, do. It's cold out here and a spell beside the hearth will be most welcome, am I right?'

Eirik had no choice but to accept, despite the hostility he felt coming off Oslac in waves. He trailed after his host, walking right past Merewen when she came up to them to retrieve her hound. It seemed prudent not to let on that he knew her, and she must have come to the same conclusion.

'Sceadu, what on earth has got into you!' she exclaimed. 'Where did you run off to?'

'Now, now, daughter, the hound was most useful. Don't scold

him. He must have heard the commotion and wanted to help,' her father told her. 'Come into the hall. Your sister will need assistance.' As if recalling the stranger in their midst, he added, 'This man raised the alarm about the rustlers. We owe him thanks.'

'I see.' She blinked at Eirik, but her gaze didn't dwell on him for long. 'Come, Sceadu, let's see if Burghild has need of us.'

'He should be left outside,' Oslac muttered, but when they entered the main building, there were other dogs inside, so there seemed no reason for Sceadu to be excluded.

Eirik sank down onto a bench when invited to do so and took the mug of ale he was offered. He looked around, studying his surroundings. He was in a large hall, the walls made of timber frames interspersed with wattle-and-daub, and painted a pale ochre. There were woven hangings depicting various Christian motifs on some of them, and one of the end walls had a window covered in painted glass, a rare luxury. The central hearth was a long rectangle, the embers having been stirred into a proper fire despite it being the middle of the night. All the surrounding benches were occupied, and he could feel the curious stares being aimed his way. He ignored them, feigning a calm he didn't feel.

'So, er, you were just passing, were you?' Beorthric sank down next to him and cradled his own cup of ale. Oslac stood nearby, as if ready to attack Eirik at the slightest provocation.

'I was out for a walk.' Eirik shrugged. 'I was camping near the river but couldn't sleep. I'm a travelling pedlar, although mostly I make combs. A week or so ago I was attacked and robbed of everything except this knife.' He indicated the *scramasax*. 'I was wounded and left for dead, and it ended up underneath me, which is probably why they didn't take it. Somehow I managed to survive, although I'm still limping slightly. Ever since, I've been following the river, hoping to join up with a merchant ship carrying some of my acquaintances. I'm sure they would let me join them until I can get back on my feet again, but I don't know how far along the river they've gone.'

'What's your name? I'm Beorthric, and this is my son-in-law, Oslac.'

'I'm Eirik.' He saw the look passing between the other men and hastened to fabricate an explanation. 'My father was a Norseman, hence the name, but my mother came from Northumbria. They're both dead now.'

'Hmm. You certainly don't sound Norse, and I suppose we cannot help who our sires are.' Beorthric did not appear to hold it against him, which was a relief. Nor had he mentioned the recent raid by Hastein and his cronies.

'Indeed. I have often wondered whether to change my name, but it seems wrong when that is how I was baptised.' Another outright lie, but Beorthric didn't need to know that.

'No, no. That might be a sin,' the older man agreed. 'A comb-maker, are you? Perhaps you'd care to stay here for a while and make some for us. I for one could certainly do with a new one. We would pay you for your work, of course, to help you regain some of what you lost. It's the least we can do after tonight.'

'Thank you, that is most kind. I'd be happy to take you up on your offer, but as I said, I lost everything. I have no tools or materials with which to work.' His tools were still in his kist on board the ship, if Hastein hadn't sold them.

'Not a problem. We can lend you tools, and we'll come to an arrangement regarding the materials. There are antlers in our stores waiting to be used for various things.'

'Then I'm very pleased to accept. My thanks.'

Throughout this conversation, Oslac had been throwing Eirik suspicious glances, but since Beorthric was the owner of the settlement, he couldn't protest. Eventually everyone settled down for the night, and Eirik was given a blanket and shown to a bench in a corner. He stayed vigilant until he saw Oslac disappear into a chamber at the other end of the hall with his wife; only then did he allow himself to relax.

As for Merewen, he'd noticed her slipping outside earlier with Sceadu, but thought it best not to look her way. He would have to find an opportunity to speak with her on the morrow.

Chapter Thirteen

Hereford, early June, present day

'So how are things with you? Had any fun lately, or is it all work and no play?'

Alix saw the glint of mischief in her grandfather's eyes but pretended she hadn't noticed.

'I went to look at the house and I've made an appointment with a structural surveyor.'

'Oh? What are you wanting to do?' Morgan seemed curious rather than worried, so Alix told him about her plans. 'Sounds perfect,' he said with a smile. 'I always thought that room was a bit poky, but your gran wouldn't let me change it.'

'Well, phew!' Alix smiled back. 'I was worried you'd be offended that I'm not keeping it exactly as it was.'

'Don't be silly. It's yours now and you should do what you like. I can't wait to see how it turns out.'

'I'll take you over there as soon as it's ready, but that'll be a while yet.' She didn't mind, though. It was more important to get it right, and for now she was fine living in the small flat she rented in Church Street.

'What about the outbuildings? I don't suppose you'll have much use for them, and I don't know what state they're in anyway.'

'I haven't had a chance to look at those, but I'm thinking of keeping chickens and I'll have to find a suitable place to lock them up at night.' Alix had loved seeing Noah's hens and noisy rooster, and he'd promised to teach her the basics if she decided to go ahead.

'Good plan. They're easy enough to start with.' Morgan seemed pleased that at least part of the outbuildings would be used. 'And did you make up your mind about the fields?' His words were innocent enough, but Alix could tell he was dying to ask if she'd had any more interactions with her neighbour.

She hid a smile as her mind flashed back to that evening. Despite her initial fears, she had enjoyed her time with Noah immensely. He was easy company and could be very charming when he set his mind to it. And he'd behaved like a perfect gentleman, giving her no cause for alarm. In the end, she'd felt comfortable and relaxed with him, not something she'd expected.

'Yes. The solicitor was most helpful,' she told Morgan now. 'Noah and I have signed the contract already. Noah says he's going to fix the fences before using the fields for his flock. He's kindly agreed to do the work for free as long as I pay for half the materials.'

'Very neighbourly of him.' Morgan chuckled. 'Don't suppose it has anything to do with you being young and pretty?'

'I doubt it,' she replied somewhat tartly, but because she knew he wasn't teasing her in order to be mean, she relented and added, 'He did come over when I was looking at the house, though. And invited me to lunch at Vaughan Court afterwards.' She decided not to mention the pub visit the following day.

Morgan's expression brightened. 'Did he now? What did you think of it?'

'It's a bit overwhelming, isn't it. A great big barracks of a place. He said he has trouble heating it in winter.' She had the inappropriate thought that she could help him keep warm, but quashed it. They were only just getting to know each other. One date – if it even was a date – didn't constitute a relationship of any kind.

'Mm-hmm. And what do you think of *him*?'

'Who, Noah?' Alix busied herself with straightening the sofa cushions so that her grandfather wouldn't see her cheeks heating up. 'Now that he's stopped being rude to me, he's OK.'

Morgan laughed. 'Damned with faint praise! Poor boy.'

She turned to frown at him. 'He's not a boy, and I'm not damning him with anything.' Seeing his gleeful expression, she pretended to threaten to throw a cushion at him. 'Stop it! If you're trying to matchmake, it's early days. I barely know the man.'

'Fine, fine. I'll leave you be for now.' But his eyes danced. She was sure he could read her clearly and knew that she was very attracted to Noah. It surprised her how much, actually, following their initial rather disastrous introduction. There was just something about him that drew her in and made her want to spend time with him. As if they had a connection on a deeper level. Very strange.

After they'd had their tea, Morgan pointed to an antique chest of drawers. 'Could you look in the top drawer for me, please? There should be an old wooden box in there. Fetch it out, would you?'

Alix did as he'd asked and placed the box in his lap. 'Here you go.'

It wasn't huge, about half the size of a shoebox, and looked to be ancient. The dark wood had a patina that could only be achieved by age and repeated handling. The clasp must have once had a padlock to keep the contents secure, but that was no longer there. Morgan opened it and lifted the lid, revealing that the inside was lined with faded blue velvet.

'This was your grandmother's. She kept it locked away in the farm safe, so you probably never saw it.' There were a few small silk parcels, folded into squares, and he rummaged among them. 'These were her jewels, and I'd like you to have first pick.'

'Grandpa—' She began to protest, but he held up a hand.

'I know, I know. I'm being partial and I shouldn't favour one grandchild over the other, but your parents have always put Autumn first, so I want to redress the balance a little. And I promise she will get her fair share.' He extracted one particular package and held it out to her. 'This one, however, I want you to have. As for the rest, you can fight it out between you.'

Alix accepted the parcel and carefully unwrapped the silk. She couldn't stop a gasp from escaping when she saw what was inside. 'Whoa! Grandpa!'

On a long silver chain dangled a piece of polished rock crystal encased in silver filigree, as though set inside a cage. The crystal was an almost perfect sphere, without blemishes, and the silver that surrounded it was reflected in its depths. It would have been a beautiful object worthy of any number of gasps whatever the circumstances, but Alix felt a frisson of awareness slither down her spine.

She was sure she'd seen this pendant before.

Not only that, but it was uncannily similar to the one that was part of the library's Viking hoard.

'Where on earth did Grandma get this?' she asked, holding it up so that the light from the windows was refracted through it, bouncing off the walls.

'It was an heirloom, passed down the generations in her family from mother to daughter. She was originally from Northumberland, did you know that? I always assumed that style was common there. She never showed it to you or Autumn because she wasn't sure which of you to give it to. She didn't want to hurt anyone's feelings, so she was torn. Now I've made the decision for her. I consider you worthy of it, and you are the firstborn in any case. I believe it's your right to have it.'

Alix continued to study the pendant. 'But it's probably ancient. I saw one just like it not long ago and was told it was from the fifth or sixth century. Anglo-Saxon, Grandpa! It should be in a museum.'

He shook his head. 'No. Your grandmother was adamant it should stay in the family. I suppose you could loan it to a museum if you want – it is yours to do with as you wish – but I know she would have wanted you to wear it on special occasions. She wore it for our wedding. Besides, it might not be that old. It could be a replica.'

'I . . . I'm speechless. I'm going to have to buy a safe. Not sure I'll ever dare to wear it, to be honest.'

Morgan patted her hand. 'Put it on and hide it under your shirt. No one'll know it's there. And once you move into Howell's End, you can use the farm safe. It's still there, isn't it? I'll tell you how to change the combination for the lock to something only you know.'

'I'd forgotten about that. Good idea.'

She hesitated, then slipped the chain over her head, unable to resist. It was as if it was calling to her, reeling her in and making her want to wear it. The chain itself seemed sturdy enough to hold the heavy pendant, and once it was in place, the crystal ball settled between her breasts. It was cool at first touch, but soon sent a wave of heat shooting through her sternum.

She closed her eyes for an instant and her mind was immediately flooded with images. *A man's hand holding the pendant on his palm. The deep murmur of his voice as he told her he wanted her to have it. The feel of it as it settled against her skin when he slipped the leather cord holding it over her head. The soft touch of his lips as he kissed her neck, her cheek, her lips, and she tilted her head to accommodate him . . .*

Morgan's voice pulled her back to the here and now.

'There, all hidden.' He nodded in satisfaction. 'And I'm glad to have fulfilled your grandmother's last wish. She told me to give it to one of you before I go so that you'd know how important it is. Will you promise to pass it on to your own daughter if you have one?'

'I promise.' Alix's eyes stung with threatening tears, but they were tears of joy and gratitude. And she would keep it a secret from Autumn. Her sister would have coveted the pendant simply for its material value, whereas to Alix its history was worth a lot more. 'Thank you so much. I hope Grandma knows how much I'll treasure this. I'll keep it safe, I swear.'

'She knows, dear. She knows.'

It was late afternoon the following Friday, and Noah was in one of the Howell's End fields, working on the fence, when he saw Alix's electric-blue Fiat flash past. She probably hadn't noticed him, as he was crouching to fix something at the bottom, and he hurried to finish the job. He hadn't seen her for nearly a week, and although she'd sent him a text message, it had only been to say thank you for taking her to the pub. No mention of meeting up again. He couldn't help but feel disappointed, but had forced himself to be patient. It had seemed as though they had a real connection, and he'd thoroughly enjoyed the evening they'd spent together. He had hoped she would want to see him again, but perhaps he needed to give her a nudge.

He put his tools and left-over materials away in the trailer he'd hooked up to the Land Rover, and whistled for Shadow to jump into the back seat, then drove in the direction of Howell's End. A little voice was telling him he might be acting too pushy, but another egged him on. Where was the harm in being neighbourly? He could update Alix on the progress of the fencing work, and enquire how she was getting on with the renovation plans. Just a friendly exchange, then he'd leave her alone.

He pulled up outside the old house, and as he climbed out of the car, Alix opened the front door. Noah was pleased to see that her eyes lit up at the sight of him. A good sign, hopefully.

'Hey! I hope you don't mind me stopping by, but I saw your car speeding past.' He indicated the fields with his thumb. 'I was over there working on the fences and thought I'd come and tell you I'm nearly done.'

'Already? That was quick! But I guess the sooner it's done, the faster you can put your sheep in those fields to graze.'

'Exactly.'

She opened the door wide and bent to greet Shadow, who seemed pleased with the attention. 'Come in. I've brought over a kettle, some tea, milk and mugs. I figured I'd be coming here a lot from now on, and those are absolute necessities. Want a cup? The kettle's just boiled.'

'Yes, please.' Noah followed her into the kitchen at the back of the house, Shadow at his heels.

'I've cleaned the fridge and turned it on. I called the electricity company too and made sure I'm up to date with payments. Wouldn't want sour milk.' She smiled at him and busied herself making two mugs of tea. 'Milk? Sugar?' She looked apologetic when she added, 'Sorry, I only have sweetener, not proper sugar.'

'Just milk is fine, thanks.' He accepted a mug and looked around for something to sit on. There was nothing except an old bench against one wall. He walked over to inspect it. 'Is this going to be strong enough to hold my weight?'

'Yes, it looks pretty sturdy. If it collapses, so be it. I won't blame you.'

They sat side by side, drinking their tea in companionable silence for a while. Shadow lay down, his front paws crossed, and closed his eyes. Alix glanced at Noah and cleared her throat. 'How have you been? I was going to text you this evening to see how much I owed you for the fencing stuff.'

'Not because you wanted to see me again?' he teased. 'I'm gutted.' Although the truth was that he was extremely relieved she had been intending to contact him at all.

'Cut it out!' She smiled and elbowed him, nearly making him spill his drink. 'Oops, sorry! I haven't had time to see anyone this week. I've honestly been extremely busy. One of my colleagues went down with flu, so the rest of us have had to cover her shifts. And in my spare time, I've been trying to get quotes out of builders. I don't know what's wrong with them, but I've had to chase several times before anyone gets back to me.'

'OK, I'll let you off this time.' He grinned and flinched as if he thought she was going to elbow him again. 'As for the workmen, sounds about normal. You'd think we were doing them a favour offering work. I usually do most things myself to save time.' He took a sip of his tea. 'What about the structural surveyor?'

'He came the other day, thank goodness, and said it's fine, I can knock down that entire wall if I want. It's not a load-bearing one, so I can have my archway. He's going to write an official report for insurance purposes, but it's OK to go ahead, according to him.'

'That's great news.'

She made a face. 'Yes, if I can actually get someone to do the work.'

Having finished her own tea, she bent forward to place her mug on the floor. As she did so, a necklace on a long chain slipped out of her shirt, which had the top three buttons undone. Noah blinked as he was dazzled by a glint of silver and a ray of sunlight reflected through a glass marble of some sort. 'Whoa! New jewellery?'

To his surprise, her cheeks flushed. 'Um, sort of. Grandpa gave it to me. I'm not supposed to show it to anyone as it's some kind of heirloom. I wear it every day because I don't have anywhere to store it yet. There is a safe here, but as I'm not around much, I don't really want to leave anything in it yet.'

'Can I see?' Noah wasn't normally interested in jewellery, but for some reason he felt compelled to touch this piece. It was almost as if it was calling to him.

She had quickly pushed the pendant back inside her shirt, where it glittered enticingly in her cleavage. He tried not to stare, but both the jewel and her smooth skin mesmerised him.

'Do you promise not to tell anyone about it?' She peered at him, clearly torn. 'I don't want people to know I have it. Although I suppose you've already seen it now, so it's too late to hide it.'

He held up a hand like a president swearing an oath. 'I swear on my mother's grave not to tell a soul.' Giving her a quick grin, he added, 'And I promise not to steal it either. Don't think it would suit me.'

'Idiot,' she muttered, but she was smiling, so he took it as a win. 'It's not like it's a diamond or anything, merely rock crystal. Here.' She fished it out of her cleavage once more, making him swallow hard, and pulled the chain over her head before handing it to him.

The moment it landed in his palm, Noah had the feeling that it was familiar. That he'd held it before. But that was crazy. It looked extremely old and probably very valuable. He could understand Alix not wanting anyone to know about it. He would have wished to keep it safe too. As he held it up to the light to look through the crystal, he thought he could see a scene inside it featuring two people, a young couple. It was kind of like a snow globe or a fortune-teller's crystal ball. In the next instant, his brain was invaded by strange images and sensations.

A woman's bent neck, caressed by dark curls. The urge to kiss her, just there under her ear where he knew she was extra sensitive. The pale skin of beautiful breasts with the pendant resting in between them. Velvet softness as he nuzzled her in that enticing valley. The smell of lavender and herbs that clung to the clothing he pushed aside. Her sweet moans as he allowed his fingers to roam . . .

'Noah?' Alix's voice brought him back to the present, but when he stared into her eyes, he saw confusion and questions. 'What . . . what just happened?'

'You felt it too? Saw it?' His heart was beating frantically, the sound of blood being pumped through his veins blocking his hearing.

'Yes. I mean, I saw something. And I felt . . .' A fiery blush spread across her cheeks and she ducked her head to stare at the floor.

'Turned on,' he whispered. She didn't reply, but that was answer enough. Noah scowled at the pendant. 'What the hell?' he muttered. 'Is it bewitched or something?'

'It can't be. There's no such thing as magic,' Alix protested, but when they exchanged another puzzled glance, they both knew she might be wrong. 'Actually, I had some sort of vision the first time I held it too. Nothing since, though. Until now.'

They were sitting close together, shoulder to shoulder, and when she shivered, the tremor passed through her body and into his. He pretended like he hadn't noticed, then cleared his throat and held the necklace out to her.

'You'd better put it back on. Maybe it's some sort of protective amulet with a spell on it?' It sounded far-fetched, but what else was he to think? There was definitely something strange about it. 'Did you say Morgan gave it to you? Then perhaps you can ask him.'

A slightly hysterical giggle bubbled out of her as she slipped the chain over her head again. 'And what if he knows nothing about it and thinks I've lost my mind?'

'Then we both have.'

Chapter Fourteen

West Mercia, early June/Eggtið AD 874

It wasn't until two days later that Eirik managed to speak to Merewen in private. He'd kept his distance, only giving her a polite greeting when Beorthric introduced her along with the rest of the family. There was no way he could let on that they knew each other. That would obviously be extremely dangerous for both of them.

Finally, his chance came when he was walking towards the little workshop he'd been told he could share with a carpenter, and saw her enter a small hut nearby. He checked his surroundings to make sure no one was looking and dived inside, startling her. To his surprise, she was holding a knife in her hand as she turned, pointing it right at him.

'*Hei!* It's only me. No need for violence,' he said, holding up his hands with what he hoped was a disarming smile.

Sceadu, who had been lying on an old blanket on the floor, rushed to greet him, and Eirik bent to make a fuss of him. 'Yes, I'm happy to see you too. Thank you for your assistance the other night. It was most welcome.'

He looked up at Merewen, who appeared to be frozen. Slowly she relaxed and put the knife down. 'I'm sorry,' she mumbled. 'I thought you were someone else.'

Eirik frowned. 'Who?' He gathered it wasn't someone she wanted to see. In fact, she was visibly trembling, so it must be a person she was afraid of.

'Oslac,' she admitted, closing her eyes and taking a deep breath. 'He's been . . . harassing me.'

'Your brother-in-law? That's disgusting!'

She let out a wry laugh. 'Try telling him that.' Her cheeks turned pink. 'He thinks I need to experience what it's like to be with a man before I leave for the monastery. And he believes he should be the one to show me. Swine.'

So not only had the man married Merewen's sister out of sheer greed, now he was also under the impression that he was entitled to have Merewen as well. Much ruder epithets than *swine* hovered on Eirik's tongue, but he kept them to himself. Instead he put a hand on her arm and squeezed gently to show his support. He moved slowly, so as not to spook her, and she leaned forward of her own accord, her forehead touching his chest. When she stayed that way, he allowed his arms to encircle her, drawing her closer but not too close, while he stroked her back in a soothing motion. She was shaking, and no wonder. Oslac must have given her a fright, and now Eirik himself had inadvertently done the same. 'He won't succeed as long as I'm here,' he vowed. 'I'll keep an eye out.'

Her trembling lessened and her breathing evened out. She let him hold her for a moment longer, then leaned back to look up at him. 'But you won't always be here. And why *are* you here? I couldn't believe it when you turned up the other night. It's not safe for you.'

Her concern warmed him, but he would have risked a lot more

to be near her. He reached up and pushed a wayward curl behind her ear. 'You hadn't been to see me for a while, angel, so I had to come to you.'

She smacked him on the arm and took a step away from him. 'Be serious, Eirik. I refuse to believe you're that foolhardy.'

He hadn't wanted her to leave his embrace, but knew it was best for now or he'd never let her go. 'Very well. The truth is, I was out for a walk and saw the rustlers. I know I've been guilty of raiding myself in the past, but I couldn't stand by and see your father robbed without having the chance to defend himself. That seemed wrong, especially as it would have affected you as well. So I decided to sound the alarm and help out. I'd intended to leave immediately afterwards, but he insisted I should stay.' He shrugged. 'Since he believed my story about being a travelling pedlar of half-Norse origins, I think it's safe for now.'

'I don't know. Oslac isn't as trusting as my father. He could harm you. Perhaps it would be better if you went back to the cairn.'

'I will if I feel threatened, I promise. For now, I'm going to make some combs and keep an eye on you. Surreptitiously, of course.'

'Do you even know how? To make combs, I mean. If not, they'll soon find out that you lied.' She bit her lip and he wished he could do the same. Or at least kiss the spot where her teeth had been.

He cleared his throat, pushing down the almost irresistible urge, and chuckled. 'Of course I do. I'm not stupid enough to claim skills I don't have. You'll see. I will make you the prettiest comb you've ever owned.' He bent to give her a quick kiss on the cheek. It was tempting to do more, but he couldn't risk staying in here with her for any length of time.

'Eirik . . .' Her protest was half-hearted, and he suspected she craved more as well, but he had no wish to be like Oslac, pushing too far. He wanted her trust and her love, and she had to come to him willingly. She wasn't quite there yet.

'Shh. All will be well. Now I'd better go. Check if there is anyone about, will you, please?'

He patted Sceadu goodbye and slipped out the door when she said the coast was clear. From now on, he vowed to guard her at all times. That *rass* Oslac wouldn't have his way, he was determined about that.

The following day was Sunnandaeg, and all the inhabitants of the settlement gathered in the small wooden chapel situated near the main hall. Each family usually prayed together in their own home morning and evening, but sometimes, like today, a priest came to perform a proper service. He'd be holding Mass and giving a sermon, and although Merewen was used to this, she couldn't help but think that she would soon be forced to spend a lot more time in religious observance than she really wanted to.

As she entered the dimly lit building behind her father, Burghild and Oslac, with the rest of their relatives following, she threw a furtive glance around the congregation. She spotted Eirik at the back and wondered if he knew what he was doing. He definitely wasn't a Christian, but could he pretend to be one convincingly? She certainly hoped so, or he'd be in danger.

Incense smoke hung in the air, heavy and cloying, making it difficult to breathe at first. She stood with the others and listened as the priest recited the Latin phrases of the Mass. Then he elaborated in her own language on a specific text from the Gospels, one she knew by heart. As he prayed loudly for the Lord's help to repel the Norse marauders who had recently attacked nearby, Merewen had to force herself not to turn around and look at Eirik. If anyone should find out that one of those raiders was currently in their midst, there would be instant bloodshed. The thought of him being killed made her shiver with dread.

She didn't want him to be hurt. She cared about him. More than cared. How on earth had she allowed this to happen?

It was wrong, but she couldn't help it. Eirik was a decent man. Better than some, she thought, sending her brother-in-law a sideways glare. The Norseman hadn't hurt anyone here. Instead, he'd helped prevent them from being robbed. She prayed silently for him to be kept safe. Not to be discovered for who he really was.

Please, dear Lord, don't let anyone harm him.

Everyone kneeled on the cold flagstone floor to take Communion, and she heard Eirik mumble the right responses. Either he'd learned them before, or he was quick to copy those around him. When it came to the Lord's Prayer, she added her voice to everyone else's. A quick look over her shoulder showed that he was mouthing the words as well, and she wondered how he knew them. But he was an intelligent man. He might have thought it prudent to memorise them just in case.

Either way, her relief that he had survived the service without giving away his identity was almost overwhelming. She went back to her herbs on shaky legs and had to sit down next to Sceadu for a long while to recover. She wanted Eirik gone, for his own safety, but at the same time she couldn't bear the thought of him leaving.

She was in serious trouble.

'What are you doing?'

Burghild's querulous voice interrupted Merewen's thoughts. She'd been daydreaming about a certain handsome Norseman yet again, and not really paying attention to her surroundings. That wouldn't do. Oslac could sneak up on her at any time and she needed to stay vigilant. Being hounded by her sister was only marginally better.

'Hmm? Oh, I'm heating some water to wash with,' she replied, checking whether the water had begun to boil yet.

'For whom?' Burghild put her hands on her hips and frowned.

'Myself,' Merewen admitted.

'Why? Didn't you wash the other day before the church service?' Suspicion lurked in her sister's sharp gaze.

'Yes, but I got very dirty helping with cheese-making this morning.' It was a feeble excuse and Merewen knew it, but it was the best she could come up with on the spur of the moment.

The truth was that she'd been trying to keep herself extra clean for Eirik's sake. She'd seen him go off down to the river several times, coming back with his hair wet and wearing a clean shirt. Now that he was making combs, he'd apparently had the wherewithal to buy himself an extra one, and he appeared to change them often. She assumed he washed the one he wasn't wearing himself, as he hadn't asked anyone else to launder it for him.

Whenever she happened to be near him, she noticed there was a fresh smell of the outdoors on him. His hair was always clean and neatly combed, and his beard trimmed short. She didn't want him to think her slovenly or smelly, although it shouldn't really make a difference to her.

'Hmph.' Burghild didn't look like she believed her for an instant. 'There are plenty of other things you could be getting on with. I need you to come and help me with the weaving now. We've not been making as much progress with that as I'd hoped. You can wash some other time.'

Merewen stood her ground. 'Please start without me. I'll be along as soon as I'm done. You wouldn't want me to make the fabric dirty, would you?'

She lifted the cauldron off the tripod with a cloth to protect her hands from getting burned on the handle and poured the water into a bucket. 'I'll be as quick as I can, I promise.'

Burghild opened her mouth as if to protest, but Merewen turned her back on her and walked towards the door carrying her bucket. She needed the privacy of her hut because she was going to wash herself all over. And if her sister didn't like it, that was too bad.

Safely inside the hut, Merewen hurried to undress and made short work of washing with a cloth and some lye soap. She'd left a linen drying sheet and a clean set of garments in there earlier, so it didn't take her long to finish her ablutions. Once dressed, she pushed the bucket under the workbench and folded her old clothes into a bundle to be laundered later. Just as she was about to comb out her wet hair, there was a soft knock on the door. She opened it a crack and was surprised to find Eirik outside. Without thinking about it, she widened the gap and ushered him inside before sticking her head out to check that no one had seen him enter.

'Eirik? What are you doing here?' She closed the door and turned to him, feeling self-conscious about the wet tresses dripping onto her shoulders and back.

'Forgive me. I didn't mean to startle you, but your father and brother-in-law have gone to see a neighbour about a bull, so I thought I'd take the opportunity to speak to you.' He noticed her hair and the old comb in her hand. 'Do you need help with that?'

Merewen's cheeks turned scalding hot. 'No. No, thank you. I can manage.'

He held out his hand for the comb. 'Please, let me do it,' he insisted. 'It will be faster.'

'If you say so.' She shouldn't let him. It was too intimate, too much. But it would seem she had no willpower whatsoever when it came to this man.

'Sit down,' Eirik murmured. 'Then I can reach more easily.'

She sank onto the bench and he began to separate the wet

strands of hair with his fingers. 'This isn't seemly,' she muttered, her cheeks on fire yet again. This man always had her discombobulated, one way or another. Letting him do such a thing for her seemed wrong, but she craved his touch, even if it was only on her hair.

He leaned forward and kissed her cheek. 'I won't tell anyone if you don't,' he whispered.

Picking up one long tress at a time, he began to methodically comb his way from top to bottom. The sensation of having someone else perform this task for her was sheer bliss. Merewen closed her eyes and allowed herself to simply enjoy it. At no time did Eirik pull too hard or scrape her scalp. He undid any knots with patience, and then continued with sure strokes. When he had finished, he ran one hand down the length of it from the top of her head to her backside. A shiver raced down her spine.

'Beautiful,' he murmured. She squirmed, delighted with the praise but fully aware that she shouldn't allow him to touch her like that. 'Keep still and I'll plait it for you.'

'I can do it myself,' she protested, turning around to look up at him.

'I know, but I want to.' He bent down to place another soft kiss on her other cheek, then firmly swivelled her shoulders. It didn't take him long to make a very presentable plait, and he held the end while she tied on the cord.

'Thank you.' She gazed into his mesmerising green eyes. They were twinkling, but in their depths lurked something else. She didn't dare think about what that might be.

'It was entirely my pleasure,' he said. 'But I'd better go. I'm sure you have things to do.'

Things to do? Her brain woke from its stupor. 'Oh! Burghild is waiting for me. She's probably going to scold me for taking so long.'

Eirik caressed her cheek. 'Then let her. She won't be in charge of you for much longer. And remember what I said – I'd be happy to take you away from here any time. Goodbye for now.'

After he left, Merewen stood for a moment in the stillness of the hut, trying to calm herself. His words had stirred a longing inside her, fierce and insistent. She wanted to take him up on his offer, even if that meant living in sin, but did she really dare?

She needed more time to consider such a huge step.

Chapter Fifteen

Hereford, early June, present day

'So what are you up to this evening – a night on the town?' Noah had enjoyed spending time with Alix and didn't want to leave her quite yet, but he didn't want to make assumptions. If she was busy, he'd let her be. He had already foisted his company on her uninvited this afternoon.

She laughed. 'Hardly. As I said, I don't really know anyone here yet. Most of my work colleagues are a little older than me and have families, and those who aren't don't seem to have realised I might want to tag along.' She stared at the floor. 'I'm not very good at making friends, to be honest. I don't like to push in where I'm not wanted.'

'I'm sure they wouldn't mind, but you have me. We're friends now, right?' He was starting to hope they might become more than that, but with the recent bad experiences she'd alluded to, he knew he'd have to take things slowly.

'I guess.' At his raised eyebrows and pretended wounded expression, she smiled. 'OK, yes, we're friends. But I'm sure you're going out with your mates as it's Friday. Or perhaps you have a hot date? I wouldn't like to be in the way. And I don't mind being on my own, honest.'

'No date. I'm not going anywhere. Too knackered.' Not to mention jaded, but she didn't need to know that. He didn't have any really good mates here, just acquaintances. There wasn't anyone his age to hang out with in the neighbouring area, and he never had much time to socialise with fellow farmers either. As for dating, he'd long since tired of the local scene and hadn't felt like participating in quite a while. Right now, the only person he wanted to spend time with was Alix. 'How about we buy some fish and chips for dinner from the nearest village? There's an award-winning chip shop. You've got to try it.'

'Only if you're sure . . .'

'Absolutely. You'll have to excuse me eating in my work clothes, though,' he added. 'I'm too hungry to wait, but I promise I'll go and shower afterwards if you want to hang out and watch a movie or something.'

'No problem. That sounds good.'

They picked up the food on the way and she followed him to Vaughan Court in her own car. When she parked it next to his in the stable yard, it looked ridiculously small beside the Land Rover.

Noah laughed when she said as much. 'It is rather dinky, isn't it, but it suits you.'

'Are you saying I'm short?' She pretended to be offended and straightened up to her full height, which wasn't very tall. Maybe five foot five on a good day.

He slung an arm around her shoulders and gave her a one-armed hug as they headed for the back door. 'No, I'm saying you're both cute. Small, yes, but perfect.'

Alix blushed and ducked her head. 'Um, thank you.'

He tried to catch her gaze. 'What, you don't think you're cute?'

'Definitely not perfect,' she mumbled.

'Then you need to buy yourself a new mirror.' He could see that she was uncomfortable with the compliment and changed the subject so she didn't need to reply. 'Come on, let's eat quickly before the food goes cold. Want a beer with your meal? Or a soft drink?'

'Soft drink, please.'

They were soon enjoying the succulent fish and perfectly cooked chips, and Alix gave a sigh of pleasure. 'Mm, this is so good! I haven't had decent fish and chips in ages. Thank you for suggesting it.'

'Well, it's not exactly fine dining, but then I'm just a farmer so that's not really my scene.'

'You're not "just" anything. Farmers are important. Where would the rest of us be without you?' She felt strongly about this, as her own father had always seemed to look down on Morgan, which was incredibly unfair. Just because he himself didn't want to work the land, that didn't mean it wasn't a great profession.

'OK.' Noah smiled, then regarded her quizzically. 'But as a former London girl, aren't you into Michelin-starred restaurants? Posh meals?'

She shook her head. 'No, that's more my sister's thing. Anything that's supposedly luxurious, she'll enjoy. Brand names, expensive handbags, blingy jewellery . . . you name it. Shame she's got a boyfriend who can't afford to spoil her.'

'How come? She couldn't find someone richer?' Noah took a sip of his beer, drinking it straight from the bottle. For some reason, Alix found this sexy. She averted her gaze and concentrated on answering his question.

'I'm sure she could, but she's always wanted what I have, and he was mine so she took him.' The familiar feelings of resentment rose up inside her, but she realised that it no longer hurt to think about Sean's betrayal. She was well and truly over him. The only thing that was painful was the way her sister had acted. That stung, as always.

'What? She stole your boyfriend?'

'Not just boyfriend – fiancé. We were in the process of buying a flat together and had discussed wedding dates and venues.' She sighed. 'But yes, she stole him. In fact, I don't think I've ever had a boyfriend she didn't seduce. She's never happier than when she's managed to wrest something away from me.' Alix shrugged. 'I don't know what's wrong with her, but I'm done letting her ruin things. I've moved to get away from her and I hope she doesn't follow me here.'

'Wow!' Noah looked stunned. 'That's . . . messed up.'

'You could say that.' She smiled at him, but it was a bit half-hearted.

'Can't your parents talk to her?' He was frowning, his meal forgotten for the moment.

'Nope. She's the golden child who can do no wrong. It's as if they forgot I existed the minute she was born. I'm told she was a beautiful baby, and apparently I was very demanding, while she was an angel. Could have something to do with the fact that I wasn't even a year old yet at that point, and presumably wanted some of their attention, but there you go. Water under the bridge.' It wasn't really, but what could she do about it? Nothing. 'Let's not talk about Autumn. I hope you never have to meet her.'

'If I do, I'll give her a piece of my mind.'

Alix doubted that very much. Most men who met her sister fell under her spell and forgot that any other woman existed. The thought of Noah being enthralled by Autumn made something twist inside her. She acknowledged that she wanted him for herself, but she would always be afraid of having him snatched away like all the others. It would be better not to date anyone, but at the same time, that would mean allowing Autumn to win.

If she really wanted someone, she would have to fight for him. And Noah might just be worth fighting for.

Noah went to have a quick shower, wanting to wash the smell of the farmyard off completely before sitting next to Alix on the couch. It had been a while since he'd had to worry about such things. He hadn't brought a woman back to the farm in years. Whenever he'd hooked up with someone, they had gone to her place. And naturally he had showered and made himself presentable before going out on the town.

Now he pulled out all the stops, even adding a dash of aftershave, although he didn't actually have time to run a razor across his cheeks. He doubted he'd get close enough to Alix for his five o'clock shadow to bother her, but at least he could smell good.

When he came out of his en suite bathroom, he paused at the sound of voices downstairs. Female ones. 'Dammit!' he muttered.

His sister must have returned. Why was she at home on a Friday evening? That was unheard of. And what was she saying to Alix? Niamh's sarcastic laughter rang out and a sense of foreboding gripped him. He quickly ran a towel over his hair, then stepped into a pair of boxer briefs and sweatpants before walking down the stairs. Niamh was still talking, and when he heard his name mentioned, he stopped outside the door to the sitting room to listen.

This could not be good.

'Wow, you've managed to get yourself invited twice in one week?'

Alix looked up from the *Country Life* magazine she'd been leafing through while she waited for Noah. His sister was loitering just inside the doorway, her arms crossed and a distinct sneer on her face. Alix frowned at her.

'What is your problem? Are you this rude to everyone who visits?'

'Nah. Just you.' Niamh laughed, but it wasn't a nice sound. 'I really don't know why you're hanging around. You're not Noah's type, so if I were you, I'd give up. Would be a shame to get your heart broken, eh?'

Alix lowered the magazine with exaggerated care. She was very tempted to roll it up and bash the stupid woman's head with it, but she'd been brought up with better manners than that. This conversation was surreal, but she figured Niamh must feel threatened by her somehow, otherwise why would she be so hostile? Did she not want to share the house with another woman? Was she afraid of being kicked out if Noah had a girlfriend? Surely she didn't expect her brother to live like a monk or to never have relationships? That would be unreasonable in the extreme.

She didn't feel she owed Niamh an explanation, so she decided to ignore her and returned to leafing through the magazine in silence.

But Niamh wasn't done. 'You have desperation written all over you,' she sneered. 'You're what, twenty-eight, twenty-nine? So staring thirty in the face without a husband or kids to show for it. I bet that kills you. You look like the settling-down kind who needs a man to feel worthwhile. If you've set your sights on Noah, you'll be in for a major disappointment. He's a player. Never hooks up with anyone more than once.'

'Jesus!' Alix was genuinely shocked at the vitriol coming out of Niamh's mouth. 'I'm guessing that with you around he doesn't get the chance.'

'What the hell, Niamh? What is wrong with you?'

Noah burst into the room wearing only a pair of sweatpants, and with a towel slung round his neck. There were still droplets of water making their way from his hair down his well-muscled chest, and Alix was momentarily sidetracked by this mesmerising sight. The guy was ripped. Not in a bodybuilding kind of way, but in the working-outdoors fashion. She tore her gaze away and watched as he grabbed his sister's arm and propelled her towards the door.

'If you can't act like a civilised human being, you have no business talking to my guests. Get out!'

Niamh shook him off. 'I live here. And I'm an adult. You can't tell me what to do.'

'I can in my own house. If you want this to be your home too, I suggest you learn some manners or you'll be looking for another place to live sooner than you think. Apologise to Alix. Now!' He was glaring at her and practically growling. Gone was the easy-going man Alix had become used to. This one was no pushover, though his sister wasn't backing down.

'No way! What for? I was telling her nothing but the truth,' she countered. 'Saving her from heartbreak. You don't do girlfriends. You haven't had one since we lived in London.'

'That's none of your business. At least I don't hang out with criminals.'

'Arsehole,' she muttered, before heading towards the stairs. She hadn't taken more than a couple of steps, though, before Noah caught hold of her shoulders and turned her around, steering her towards the front door instead.

'Out!' he ordered. 'I'm not having you in the house this evening. And don't come back until you're ready to apologise.'

For a moment it looked as though Niamh was going to argue, but then she wrenched the door open and stomped out, slamming it behind her so hard the walls shook.

'Bloody hell,' Noah muttered, pushing his fingers through the wet strands of his hair. When he turned back to Alix, his cheeks were red and he shook his head. 'I'm so sorry about that. I honestly don't know why I put up with her. Or why she said all that. Please don't be offended. It was complete bullshit.'

Alix gave him a tentative smile. 'No worries. For the record, I'm only twenty-six, so not quite at the desperation stage yet.'

That made him relax a little, and his mouth quirked up in an answering smile. 'Oh good. You have at least four years to try to lure me into marriage then,' he joked. 'Looks like I don't need to run away screaming for a while.'

'Nope. I promise not to try my wiles on you for a good few years. You're safe.'

Something flashed in the depths of his eyes, but it was gone almost as quickly. He looked down at himself and seemed to finally take in his half-naked state. 'Um, I should probably go and get a T-shirt or something. Sorry. Be right back.'

When he returned, bringing snacks and drinks, he sank down onto the sofa next to her. He smelled gorgeous, but she tried her best not to notice. Niamh might have been malicious on purpose, but there was probably some truth in what she'd said. Alix could well believe that Noah was a player, and she wasn't going to fall for that. Not again.

No matter how tempting he was, she'd keep him at arm's length. And let's be real, she thought to herself, why would he want her when he could clearly pull any woman who took his fancy?

Noah was very aware of Alix sitting next to him, but he didn't want to let on as that might make her uncomfortable. He could tell she was tense at first, but as they chatted and sipped their drinks, she relaxed a fraction. At least until Niamh returned unexpectedly and stuck her head back in through the door, shouting, 'I won't be back until tomorrow, or maybe even next week, so you can have wild monkey sex in the kitchen if you want. Just make sure you disinfect the counters afterwards.'

'Give me strength!' Noah tugged at his hair and looked at the ceiling, praying for patience. What on earth had got into his sister? She was unbearable. 'Please don't run out screaming,' he begged Alix, feeling mortified. 'She's never acted like this before, I swear.' Then again, as he hadn't brought anyone else home, she hadn't had the chance.

To his relief, Alix burst out laughing. 'Sorry, but your expression . . .' She giggled some more. 'I guess Niamh knows how to push your buttons.'

'You could say that.' He took a deep breath. 'I think me bringing you here twice in one week has her rattled. Although she comes across as brash, she's actually very insecure, and not particularly mature. When Mum died, Niamh went through a rebellious phase, then had some sort of meltdown, spiralling into depression. It wasn't until she met her douchebag boyfriend that she started to get back on an even keel. Now that he's in prison, I think she's feeling scared and lost, but she won't admit it or accept that she needs help. And it still doesn't excuse her behaviour towards you. Anyway, let's forget she exists for now, please. What film do you want to watch?'

'How about *The Northman*? I haven't seen that yet.'

Noah blinked. 'Are you sure? I think it's pretty violent, and I've heard it has a sad ending.'

That made her smile. 'I'm not a delicate flower, you know, and since I've been working on that exhibition I told you about, I've developed an interest in the Vikings. They were very interesting people.'

'Right. *The Northman* it is.'

He settled back with another beer and hid a smile when Alix proved not to be quite as brave as she'd thought. 'Oh my God,' she muttered at one point, as the violence in the film became rather graphic. Without thinking, she turned to hide her face against his shoulder, and he took the opportunity to put an arm around her.

'Hey, we can watch something else if you want,' he said, but she shook her head.

'No, I need to see this. I don't know why.'

Noah too felt a strange compulsion to watch. He didn't find the plot very realistic, but the parts about Viking life and beliefs resonated with him. Why, he had no idea. At one point, images flooded his brain, just like earlier that day, but nothing as peaceful.

There was fighting all around him and he could feel the heft of a heavy sword in his hand. It took all his strength to wield it, but he knew he was used to it, and the movement came as naturally as if he'd done it hundreds of times before. The smell of blood and fear hung in the air surrounding him, and there were shouts and grunts. Someone's scream behind him came to a gurgling end, but he didn't turn to see what had happened. He was sure it would be a gruesome sight, but one he'd seen often. There were three men attacking him at once and he just had to concentrate on them or all would be lost ...

He blinked until the TV screen came back into focus, then took a deep breath and tried to calm his racing heartbeat. Although he'd been in fights when he was a stupid teenager, he hadn't hit anyone since. He wasn't violent by nature, so where did those horrible images come from?

It was probably just his brain working overtime, influenced by what they were watching. Best to forget it and focus on the here and now. He had a gorgeous woman next to him and life was good. It got even better when he pulled her closer and she instinctively snuggled up to him.

Hopefully she'd stay there.

Chapter Sixteen

West Mercia, early June/Eggtið AD 874

'That mangy hound seems uncommonly fond of you.'

The comment was made in a sarcastic tone of voice with an undertone of suspicion. Eirik looked up from his carving and found Oslac standing in front of him regarding Sceadu with something akin to hatred. The dog, in turn, growled low in his throat and bared his teeth.

'Easy, boy,' Eirik muttered and reached out to stroke the soft fuzzy head. He maintained his composure when replying. 'I seem to have a knack with animals. Always have done.' He shrugged and added with a smile, 'Although it could have something to do with the treats I've been sharing with him.'

To prove his point, he dug his hand into the leather pouch hanging off his belt and retrieved a piece of hard cheese. He threw it to the hound, who caught it with a snap of his jaws, then licked his muzzle as if savouring every last crumb. Although it wasn't the main reason Sceadu enjoyed Eirik's company, he was sure it didn't hurt. The dog had been seeking him out whenever his mistress was in her workshop. Since Eirik was sitting outside the building diagonally opposite, the two of them kept an eye on Merewen together. And he couldn't deny that it was pleasant to have company while he worked. The other inhabitants of Beorthric's settlement were still wary of him and mostly gave him a wide berth.

'Hmph.' Oslac didn't seem convinced. He crossed his arms and widened his stance, deliberately trying to look intimidating.

Eirik pretended not to notice. He went back to carving an intricate pattern into the piece of antler he was working on.

'Well, if he likes you so much, you should take him with you when you go,' Oslac continued. 'He's nothing but a menace, and it's not as if Merewen can bring him with her when she leaves.'

'Merewen is leaving?' Eirik pretended that this was news to him. He had exchanged a few words with her in public, but nothing beyond a polite 'good morning' or thanks for serving him ale or food. He couldn't let on that he was already aware of her father's plans for her.

'Aye. As soon as Beorthric finds a suitable place, she's off to a monastery, and I doubt they want smelly mongrels in their hallowed precincts.' Oslac sent the dog yet another glare.

Eirik had to hide a smile when Sceadu retaliated again with a menacing growl. There was clearly no love lost between man and dog. 'I see. I'd have to ask her permission, as I'm fairly certain she wouldn't be best pleased otherwise. But in principle, I wouldn't mind taking the hound with me. I could do with a travelling companion.'

And he was hoping to have more than one.

'Do that and good riddance.'

He had the impression Oslac's words were meant to encompass both him and Sceadu, but didn't comment on the man's rudeness. Instead, he deemed it wise to change the subject. 'Are you wanting me to make you a comb?' he asked. 'I've a bit of a backlog at the moment, but I might be able to accommodate your request in a week or two.'

'A week or two?' Oslac's arms fell to his sides, where he clenched his fists. 'I thought you'd be leaving soon.'

Eirik raised his eyebrows. 'Oh? Beorthric told me to stay for as long as I wished. He said there's a market day coming up and that I could go with you to sell any spare combs I make. Did he not tell you?'

'No. And if he had, I would have advised him against letting you remain. We don't need your sort here.'

'My sort? You mean itinerant comb-makers?' Eirik made a show of concentrating hard on a particularly intricate swirl in the pattern.

'I mean half-breeds,' Oslac hissed. 'With a Norse father, how do we know where your allegiances lie?'

'I guess you don't.' Eirik feigned unconcern. 'But by all means take it up with Beorthric. If he wants me gone, I'll go.' He knew the older man wasn't likely to order his immediate departure, as he felt beholden to his guest for saving him from losing a large number of animals.

'I will.' Oslac sent him a look of acute dislike and stomped off, but he didn't go far. He stopped to chat to a man who was on his way in the other direction, the two of them throwing glances at Eirik every now and then. He again pretended to be oblivious.

'I'm guessing he doesn't like either of us much, boy. And he'd rather we didn't sit here guarding Merewen.' Sceadu put his head on his paws and stared up at Eirik with soulful eyes. His twitching ears showed that he was listening. 'Too bad.'

Eirik kept an eye on the two men while continuing with his task. Beorthric had let him have his pick from a pile of red-deer antlers, and he'd selected the most suitable ones. Out of those, he had cut pieces to the exact length he needed to form long plates for the back and front of the top of the comb, and smaller pieces for the tines. The top plates were decorated with a pattern, and this was where he excelled. He'd discovered early on that he had a knack for creating beautiful motifs – either symmetrical lines and swirls, or sometimes things like a sinuous animal shape with a dragon's or snake's head. If a comb was commissioned for a particular person, he might add the owner's name in runes or other letters as well, and he had done that on the comb he'd made for Merewen. Once the carving was done, the prongs had to be cut. This was a painstaking job, as they needed to be fairly close together and evenly spaced. Finally the pieces were assembled by drilling holes in the various plates and securing them with small iron pins. Fortunately the settlement's blacksmith had been able to make some of those for him at a reasonable cost.

He finished his carving and glanced across to where Oslac was continuing his conversation. 'How about we give him some rope to hang himself with, eh, Sceadu? Let's go inside for a moment.'

He stood up and gestured for the dog to follow him into the workshop, but he didn't go far. Lurking by the doorway, he made sure he was hidden from sight by the shadowy interior, Sceadu peeking out next to him. It wasn't long before Oslac wound up his discussion with the other man and sent him on his way. As soon as the man was gone, he glanced around as if checking to see if he was truly alone, then approached Merewen's hut with swift strides. He slipped inside without knocking, and Eirik swore under his breath.

'The utter *bakrauf*,' he muttered, but stopped himself from storming over there immediately. He had to give the man long enough to incriminate himself, but not so long that he had the opportunity to hurt Merewen.

After counting to fifty, he signalled to the dog again. 'Come on, Sceadu. We can't allow him too much time with your mistress.'

Picking up the beautiful comb he'd completed earlier that day, he headed for Merewen's hut and knocked on the door.

Oslac wouldn't be best pleased to see him, but that was too bad.

Merewen had been busy all morning with a basket full of newly gathered herbs. Some needed to be trimmed, tied together in bundles and hung up to dry. Others she mixed into goose grease to make salves and unguents, while the rest were boiled or turned into liquid remedies. She'd lost track of time and hadn't noticed that Sceadu had left. It wasn't until the door opened abruptly and Oslac slipped inside that she realised the dog was absent. By then it was too late.

'At last I find you alone, without your stinky companion.' Oslac's expression was gloating and triumphant. In the next instant it turned into a leer. 'I hope you've given my suggestion some thought. I promise it will be worth your while to cooperate with me.'

Merewen had spun around to face him, feeling as if all the air had suddenly been sucked out of the hut. Her brother-in-law took up so much space, and he was advancing on her, backing her up against the workbench yet again.

'Your suggestion?' she snorted, while fumbling behind her for the knife she'd been using. She stared him in the eyes, refusing to show any weakness. 'It sounded more like a proposition to me. A sinful, disgusting one at that.'

'Now, now, let's not quibble. I want you, Merewen, and I mean to have you. There's nothing you can do about it, so you may as well resign yourself to your fate. What good is your virtue going to do you in a monastery? I'll give you something to dream about during those long, cold nights in your little cell. It'll make the time pass much more pleasantly, I assure you.' He was smirking now, certain he had her cornered.

'It's more likely to give me nightmares,' she retorted, and pulled the knife out from behind her back, pointing it at his groin.

'Take one more step towards me and you won't be able to create any more children with my sister.'

He halted, looking down at the knife in disbelief. 'Why, you little bitch . . .'

Unfortunately, he was faster and stronger than her, and in a flash he had her wrist in a hard grip, twisting until she had no option but to let go of her weapon, which dropped to the floor with a muted thud. Just as swiftly he pulled her arms behind her back, pinning her wrists in place with one meaty hand. Her front was now pushed up tightly against his, and he chuckled as her heaving breaths made her breasts brush his chest. Panic assailed her, making her heart rate speed up to the point where it was the only thing she could hear. Her legs trembled and her knees went weak as she cast around frantically for a way out of this nightmare.

There was no way she would submit to this oaf without a fight. She had to escape him somehow.

'Get away from me!' she hissed, doing her best to kick him in the shins while simultaneously wriggling out of his grasp. Neither move was successful, and she let out a little scream of frustration and fear.

'Shush now, or I'll have to gag you. This won't take long, so you'd best give in gracefully.'

'Never!'

She continued to fight him, but his free hand was roaming and there was no way of stopping it from squeezing various parts of her anatomy. As a last resort, she sank her teeth into his upper arm, but it only stopped him for a short while and served to make him even more hell-bent on claiming her quickly.

'Do that again and I'll clout you so hard you'll see stars,' he threatened.

Merewen wasn't listening. She was lost in a haze of fear, her brain going round in circles, unable to come up with a solution to this predicament. Just when she had almost given up hope, there was a knock on the door. Oslac froze and scowled at it.

'What the devil?' he snarled.

'Merewen? Are you in there?'

It was Eirik's voice, accompanied by a sharp bark from Sceadu. She almost sagged in relief and called out to them instantly. 'Yes, come in!'

Thankfully Oslac hadn't thought to bar the door, and it flew open. Eirik stood in the opening, taking in the scene before him with narrowed eyes, his mouth a grim line of disapproval.

'Oslac. I thought you left a while back,' he commented, staring pointedly at where the man's hand was still gripping Merewen's hip, and undoubtedly taking in the fact that she was plastered to Oslac's front with her arms behind her back. 'Is something amiss?'

Reluctantly Oslac let go of her and took a step back. 'No. I was just helping her with her tasks,' he murmured, his eyes shooting daggers at Eirik. 'Why are you here?'

Eirik directed his answer to Merewen. 'I've brought the comb you ordered.' He held out the item in question and made a show of bowing as he offered it to her. 'I hope it's to your liking.'

'Thank you.' Her voice came out sounding shaky, so she cleared her throat and added, 'How much do I owe you?' even though she hadn't actually ordered a comb from him. She had forgotten his promise to make her one when they'd discussed his skills a while back.

'Seeing as your father is allowing me to stay here a while, I'll give you a special price. Three pennies. Does that sound reasonable to you?'

Merewen took a deep breath and prepared to join in his game of pretend. For whatever reason, he had appeared just when she needed him, and she was grateful. The least she could do was follow his lead. She tilted her head and frowned at the beautifully carved comb. There was a lovely pattern swirling all over one side, and when she turned it over, she found her name in runes surrounded by even more intricate whorls. It was finer than any comb she'd owned before, but she couldn't say that or Oslac would become suspicious.

'Is that your best price? I'm sure the local comb-makers don't charge half as much.'

'Really? You surprise me.' Eirik spread his hands. 'But have you ever seen such fine craftsmanship? Not to boast, but my combs are usually sought after. You'll not find a better one this side of the country.'

'Hmm, if you say so.' She turned the object this way and that, studying it in more detail. 'It is well made, I'll give you that, but three pennies?'

He sighed. 'Very well. I'll let you have it for two. Is that acceptable?'

'Thank you, yes, that will do.'

Oslac had been regarding them both with impatience and a deep scowl throughout this exchange. 'Are you done haggling?' he enquired now, sounding royally peeved. 'If so, you may leave so that I can conclude my business with Merewen.'

'Oh, but I'll have to go back to the main house to fetch the coins,' she said, heading for the door. 'I don't have any to hand and I like to discharge my debts immediately.'

'Excellent. A customer after my own heart,' Eirik declared. He held out a hand to indicate that she should precede him, while simultaneously placing himself between her and Oslac. 'After you.'

Leaving a fuming Oslac behind, they hurried through the door and headed towards the main building, followed by Sceadu. Merewen led the way, walking a few steps ahead of Eirik with her head held high, as if she was above him in status. She was for now, although she had a feeling he would never be inferior to anyone.

As soon as they were out of earshot, she whispered, 'Thank you so much! You saved me from a fate worse than death. I'm in your debt.' Her legs were still shaking and her breathing was erratic.

'No, I'm the one who owes you, remember? And it was my pleasure. Literally.' He chuckled. 'Did you see the expression on his face when you said you were leaving? Priceless.'

She couldn't help but laugh, and it eased the knot of anxiety inside her. 'Yes, indeed.' Throwing a stern glance at her dog, she added, 'But Sceadu, you can't go off and leave me on my own ever again. It's too dangerous and he hasn't given up. He'll be back.'

'Do not fret. He was with me and we were both keeping an eye on your hut. I wanted to teach Oslac a lesson today, so I gave him the opportunity to get you alone. It was only ever going to be for a moment, as I wanted to show him that he can't get away with it. I'll be watching over you, I promise. I apologise for giving you a fright, but if you'd known about my plans beforehand, you would have given the game away.'

A warm feeling spread through her veins, and she smiled at him. 'That's very kind of you. If only you could stay until I have to leave.'

'Oh, but I will. I'm not leaving you to his mercy. He'll have you over my dead body.'

Merewen could see that he meant every word, and it was reassuring. Let Oslac do his worst. She had two protectors now.

The cairn stood sentinel on top of the small hill as usual as Merewen approached. It was early morning, and she'd pretended she was going on another of her foraging trips, but that wasn't the true reason for her outing. The day before, Eirik had managed to catch her alone for a moment and had whispered, 'Meet me at the cairn tomorrow morning. Please?'

She had given him a small nod to show she agreed, then hurried away. Now here she was.

'Eirik?' she whispered, and to her relief he peeked out from under the giant stones.

'I'm here. Come in, *unnasta*.'

She ducked inside, wondering what he meant by the endearment. It had probably just slipped out and she shouldn't attach any importance to it. She was closely followed by Sceadu, who greeted Eirik with extreme enthusiasm. Merewen laughed.

'You seem to have usurped me in his affections. Faithless hound!'

'Never.' Eirik grinned. 'He just knows I'll give him more treats than you do.' But he seemed equally happy to see the dog.

'Hmm, sneaky.'

He indicated that she should sit on his cloak, which he had spread out on the ground. She sank down on it and arranged her skirts so that they covered her legs as modesty dictated. Not that there was anything modest or prudent about meeting a man in secret on her own. If anyone found out, she'd be in deep trouble. She swallowed hard. Hopefully no one would ever know, but she wouldn't think about that now.

'You wanted to see me?' she said, turning her gaze on Eirik, who was regarding her with those amazing green eyes.

'Yes. I don't know if you've heard, but your father is taking me with him to some sort of small marketplace tomorrow. It will give me a chance to sell a few of the combs I've made, and also to see if there is any news of my uncle and his men.'

A cold knot formed in Merewen's stomach. 'You think he's still around?'

'It wouldn't surprise me. He's likely been going up and down the river, raiding wherever he finds some suitable target. There's no saying where he'll go next. He doesn't plan ahead but only lives in the moment.'

'I see.' She hesitated, then blurted out the question that hovered on her tongue. 'And will you go and join him if you find out where he is?'

'Absolutely not!'

Eirik's reply was uttered forcefully and with conviction, which made Merewen draw a sigh of relief. It shouldn't matter to her what he did after he left her father's settlement. She wouldn't be around for much longer to care, as Beorthric had apparently found another monastery that was willing to take her in. But for some reason she didn't want to think of Eirik raiding and fighting in bloody skirmishes. She wished for him to stay alive and live in peace.

He took both her hands in his and looked her in the eyes. 'That's not the kind of life I want any longer. I told you, I dream of owning my own settlement, and I'm ready to put down roots. My wound is almost completely healed now, and as soon as I am back to full strength, I will leave. I don't wish to go without you, though. Please will you come with me?'

Merewen was torn. She had come to care for this man during the short space of time they'd known each other. More than care, if she was honest, but she didn't know how he felt. He needed a woman to run his household, and she was fully capable of doing that. But as what? His lover?

'I . . . I don't know if I can be your, um, woman.' She closed her eyes and sighed. 'I too dreamed of running my own settlement, but as a properly wedded wife with the status that entails. I—'

'Merewen,' he interrupted her. '*Ást mín*. Of course you'd be my wife. That is what I meant.' He gave her a rueful smile. 'We may be barbarians, but us Norsemen do have marriage, you know. And if our rituals aren't enough for you, I'm willing to wed you the Christian way. You have my word. I'll even let them pour water on my head if that's what it takes.'

'Really? You want to marry me?'

'Of course I do, you goose. Why, what did you think? That I merely wanted a bed partner?'

Her cheeks flamed, since that was exactly what she'd thought. 'I'm sorry,' she murmured. 'I didn't know. I mean, I wasn't sure.'

'*Unnasta*, trust me, I want you to be my wife any way you'll have me. But I doubt your father will agree, so you're going to have to run away with me. Can you do that? I realise I'm asking a lot. You'd have to leave behind everyone you know and love. And it probably won't be easy for the first few years, even though I have enough riches to last us a while. You won't go hungry, I promise, but there will be much hard work ahead of us. Are you willing to take a chance on me? I swear I will treat you like a queen, and I'll be faithful to you until the day I die.'

Merewen could see that he was sincere. He meant every word. He hadn't said he loved her, but most marriages weren't founded on such sentimental and foolish emotions. If he cared for her and stayed true to her, that ought to be enough for any woman. Running away with him was a gamble, but really, what did she have to lose? The prospect of years in a monastery, always serving others and never living for herself. That wasn't what she wanted out of life. Eirik was offering her the very thing that had been snatched away from her by Burghild and her father – a household of her own. Now she had the chance to reclaim the future she'd lost. She would be a wife and, hopefully, a mother. And she'd have Eirik . . .

'Yes,' she said, squeezing his hands, which were still holding hers. 'I'd like to be your wife. And yes, I'm willing to leave everything behind, but they must never know.'

'Good.' He beamed at her. 'Then that's settled. We'll aim to leave two weeks hence. I'll find us a horse for the journey. I suggest you choose the things you can't live without and slowly start to bring them here to the cairn, then we can pick them up on the way. If you remove one thing at a time, no one will notice.'

'That sounds like a good plan.'

'Now I'll be gone all of tomorrow, but I understand Oslac is coming with us as well, so you should be safe. Keep Sceadu with you at all times, though, just in case. I wouldn't want anyone to harm you while I'm gone.'

'I will, I promise.'

'Good. Then there's only one thing left to do – seal our pact.'

Merewen didn't know what he meant, but she soon found out. He leaned forward and kissed her, his mouth meeting hers in a series of caresses so soft she wasn't sure if she was imagining it at first. Startled, but curious, she didn't stop him, and he grew bolder. Soon his lips were pressing against hers in the most delicious way, the bristles of his short beard adding a teasing sensation that she loved. He surprised her by gently biting her bottom lip, sending shivers down her spine. She opened her mouth to draw in some much-needed air, and he took advantage of this to touch his tongue to hers, stroking gently. It felt strange at first, but tantalising, thrilling. She dared to join in and copied his movements. He murmured encouragement and deepened the kiss. It went on for what seemed like for ever, and she would have been happy if it had never ended.

Eventually they broke apart, and he put his arms around her to pull her close, both of them breathing heavily. 'That will have to hold us until I return,' he whispered. 'I'll be dreaming of that kiss while I'm away.'

Merewen was certain she would as well. It was the most magical thing that had ever happened to her.

Chapter Seventeen

Hereford, early June, present day

Alix woke to the smell of bacon wafting through the air and making her stomach grumble. At first she had no idea where she was, but as she took in her surroundings, realisation hit her – she was still at Vaughan Court. *Shit!* She hadn't meant for that to happen.

Not that anything had occurred. Noah had been a perfect gentleman. After that first movie, he had suggested watching something slightly less violent in order to prevent them from having nightmares, and she'd agreed. They had settled on some innocuous romcom, but the large meal and a long week at work must have caught up with her, and she'd fallen asleep halfway through. Instead of waking her and sending her on her way, she guessed Noah had covered her with the soft blanket she was currently clutching. And he'd placed a proper pillow under her head – one from his own bed if she wasn't mistaken, as it smelled vaguely like him. Very thoughtful.

But embarrassing.

What must he think of her? After the hateful words his sister had flung at her, Alix had been supremely aware of her every move and hadn't wished to overstep in any way. The last thing she wanted was for him to think she was hitting on him. Despite this, she'd buried her face in his shoulder during a scene of graphic violence, and he had kept his arm around her after that. It had made her second-guess herself and wonder if he thought she'd done it on purpose.

Aargh! She should just go home and stop overthinking things. He hadn't so much as tried to kiss her, even though he hadn't removed his arm for the rest of the evening. She should have pulled away, but it had felt so good to snuggle up to someone, and he'd been so warm and smelled wonderful . . .

'Ah, you're awake.' Noah's voice from the doorway interrupted her thoughts. 'I was just coming to tell you that breakfast is ready.'

Despite the early hour – an old grandfather clock in the corner told her it was only 8 a.m. – he looked fresh and energetic. And good. The man would probably be handsome no matter what he wore, and the jeans, T-shirt and plaid overshirt combo really worked on him. It enhanced his quiet strength, and the green in the faded shirt brought out the colour of his eyes, which were regarding her quizzically.

'You OK?'

'Oh, um, yeah. I'm sorry. I didn't mean to fall asleep. You should have woken me up and told me to go home.'

He smiled. 'And miss the sight of you snoring softly on my couch? No way.'

Alix sat up and started to fold the blanket. 'I don't snore,' she muttered, but of course she had no way of knowing that.

Noah laughed. 'No, I was just kidding, but you're cute when you sleep. You wrinkle your nose – did you know that?'

'What? No.' And there was that word again – cute. Did he really think so, or was he just being kind? And was 'cute' a good thing, or more like something sweet you smiled at and passed by? She stood up. 'I'm just going to use the bathroom. I need to wash my face and hands. And really, you don't need to feed me. I should get going.'

'Please don't. I've cooked enough to feed an army, so you have to help me out.' He gestured towards the cloakroom behind the stairs. 'Take your time. I'll put the food in the warming oven for now.'

Noah could tell Alix was uncomfortable with the fact that she'd stayed the night. He didn't want her to be, and although he wished she'd slept in his bed rather than on the sofa, at least he got to spend some more time with her this morning. She was a fetching sight, despite being dishevelled and sleepy, with panda eyes from yesterday's mascara. When she came into the kitchen after her visit to the cloakroom, her face was scrubbed clean of make-up. Her cheeks were slightly rosy and her silver eyes more alert. As they were surrounded by dense sooty lashes, she had no need of make-up. Noah found her beautiful just the way she was.

He put a big plate of food in front of her as she sat down. 'Here. If there's anything you don't like, just pass it over to me. I'm an omnivore.'

That made her smile, and she gave him a once-over. 'I'm guessing you use up a lot of calories every day. Farming is hard work, right?'

'Yep, but rewarding. I love it, actually. I get to be out in the fresh air, not tied to a desk somewhere with a boss hovering over me. Here I decide what to do each day, and if it doesn't get done, there's always tomorrow. Dig in, please.'

He waited until she'd taken her first mouthful of bacon and scrambled eggs before starting to eat himself. His stomach growled, as he was ravenous. He'd been up since six and had already been outside to do his morning chores. Normally he wouldn't have bothered making a cooked breakfast, but he'd wanted to impress his guest. Make her stay. He didn't want to let her go.

'Mm, this is delicious,' she told him, closing her eyes as she savoured the bacon. 'Home-grown?'

He sent her a teasing smile. 'Well, we don't grow pigs, but yes, that one was reared here.'

Alix pretended she was going to throw a piece of toast at him. 'All right, smartass. Whatever. It tastes divine anyway.'

'Thank you. I'm glad you like it.'

Her expression turned pensive. 'Doesn't it bother you to eat an animal you've known and loved, though?'

'Um, I wouldn't say I fall in love with my pigs. I prefer women, to be honest.' This time she really did throw the toast at him, but he caught it in mid-air and stuffed it into his mouth. When he'd finished chewing, he replied properly. 'But yes, I know what you mean. I try not to get attached, but there are days when I can definitely see why people become vegetarian. It helps that I don't give the animals names.'

Alix nodded. 'Yes, I suppose you have to block such thoughts or you wouldn't be able to do your job. If it was me, I'd want to keep every adorable lamb, piglet or calf and never let them go.'

'Well, fortunately they grow up quickly and the cuteness factor declines. It's easier when there's a whole herd of them. I find it hardest when I have to hand-rear a lamb. Then it becomes personal, but usually in cases like that I keep them.'

'I see. That makes sense.'

They ate in silence for a while and Noah enjoyed the sight of Alix savouring the food he'd cooked for her. Such a caveman reaction, providing for the woman of his choice, trying to impress her. Inwardly he shook his head at himself. He'd never acted like this before, but Alix was special. He'd felt it the moment he met her, even if he had been cross that day.

'Would you like to come with me to check on the lambs before you go home?' he blurted out. 'I'm going to do my rounds after breakfast.'

Alix looked up, her crystal eyes shining with sudden enthusiasm. 'Oh, yes, please! I'd love that. But only if I'm not in your way. I wouldn't want to stop you from your work.'

'No worries. I just drive around on the quad bike to check that no one is hurt, lost or stuck in a fence somewhere. You can sit behind me and enjoy the sights.'

'Thank you. That sounds fab!'

They had both finished their meal, and Alix stood up and reached for his plate, carrying it over to the sink. 'Let me help with the dishes. It will be quicker.'

'No, you're a guest. I'll do it.' He put his hands on her waist and moved her to the side, turning on the tap.

To his surprise, she bumped him out of the way with her hip. 'No way. You cooked, I clean up. That's how it's always worked in my family. The chef gets a pass.'

He held up his hands. 'OK, fine, I won't fight you for it. I'm just going to brush my teeth and I'll be right back. Want to borrow a toothbrush?'

A fiery blush spread across her cheeks, and she turned away from him, muttering, 'Yes, please.'

It was clear that she felt awkward, as if this was the morning after a one-night stand. If only. Although that wasn't what he wanted from her at all. Hopefully, she'd spend many more nights here in the future. For now, he was content to take her out into the fields with him.

*

Riding pillion on a quad bike was a novel experience. Alix held on tight, her arms around Noah's waist, as they bumped over ruts and clumps of grass. It wasn't a smooth ride by any means, but she was loving every minute.

'You OK back there?' He glanced at her over his shoulder. His green eyes were bright and radiated happiness. Alix had the feeling he was enjoying this almost as much as she was.

'Yes, fine. Not sure my kidneys will agree later, but who cares? This is fun!'

He smiled, and she noticed he hadn't shaved this morning. His stubble was a darker brown than his hair, but shot through with hints of gold that shimmered in the sunlight. She had an urge to put her hand against his cheek to see how those bristles felt, but she resisted. It wasn't like she was his girlfriend. She had no right to touch him like that.

'Almost there,' he said, bringing her thoughts back to the here and now. He stopped the bike and got off to open a gate, then closed it behind them after he'd driven through. 'I'm going to go round the perimeter of this field,' he explained, 'just to make sure no one has escaped and there aren't any holes in the fence.'

Alix relaxed in the morning sunshine and kept an eye out herself in case she spotted anything out of order. No doubt Noah's eagle eye would catch any problems, but she liked to feel she was helping, if only a tiny bit. Finally he stopped and jumped off the bike, then helped her down.

'You want to pet a lamb?' he asked, and grinned when she nodded enthusiastically. 'Let me see if I can catch one.'

He was calm and unhurried, and managed it on the third try, much to the accompanying ewe's displeasure. He handed the little critter to Alix.

'Make sure you're supporting him properly, like this,' he said, and placed her hands firmly underneath the small, warm body so that she was cradling it with both of them.

The lamb was soft and didn't appear to be frightened, and Alix beamed at Noah. 'He's so precious!' she whispered. 'But I'd better not keep him from his mum.'

Gently she placed him on the grass and watched as he scurried back to the ewe. The whole flock was watching them warily, but not running away as long as she and Noah stood still.

'Wow, you have so many,' Alix commented. There were hundreds of sheep, more than she could count.

'Yes, and thanks to the additional fields I'm renting from you, I can have an even larger flock now. I'll be buying some more next week.'

'I'm glad.' Alix took in the neighbouring fields, some of which had crops in them and some that were filled with yet more sheep. 'Will you have time to look after them all?'

Noah shrugged. 'I have no choice. If I want to make money, I've got to increase the numbers. Farming is tough economically these days. I've tried lots of things, but so far rearing sheep is the most profitable.'

'I hadn't thought about it that way.' Alix realised she knew very little about farming, despite all the summers she'd spent with her grandparents. They hadn't bothered to talk to her or Autumn about the financial side of things either, and she'd been too young to wonder about it. 'Well, I hope you do really well then.'

'Thank you.' He looked as though he was about to say something else, but changed his mind. 'How about we go to the cairn? You said you wanted to take a closer look, didn't you? I owe you, after how I behaved that day.'

'If you're sure you don't mind?'

'Not at all. Let's go.'

*

The Neolithic stone monument rose up before them and Noah stopped a few yards away, killing the engine.

'It's pretty impressive, isn't it?'

'Yes. I can't imagine the effort it must have taken to build it,' Alix replied. 'Do you think it's safe to go inside? I remember crawling in there with Autumn once or twice, but we were terrified the whole time.' She smiled at the memory. 'I'd like to try it as an adult.'

'I actually asked the archaeologists who were here recently, looking for the find site of that hoard. They said it was extremely sturdy and not likely to fall down for another thousand years at least.' Noah took her hand and started walking towards the cairn. 'Let's do it. I haven't been in there for ages either.'

Alix blinked at their hands but didn't pull hers away. It felt safe and reassuring, as if they were meant to be joined like that. *Had held hands before.* What a strange thought. She wondered where it had come from.

'OK. You first.'

'Chicken,' he teased, but he hunkered down and shuffled inside. He didn't let go of her, though, and tugged her in after him. 'Come on. I'm taller than you, so if the stones fall on our heads, they'll crush me first. You'll be fine.'

'How reassuring,' she muttered sarcastically, but she was smiling so he'd know she wasn't serious.

Once inside, the light was dimmer, but they could see everything perfectly.

'Awesome,' Noah breathed, as they took in the large upright stones and the enormous granite slab over their heads.

'Yes, it's amazing,' Alix agreed. It really was the most incredible construction, and to think it had been there for thousands of years was mind-boggling.

Being underneath the stones was cosy and snug. It reminded

Alix of the dens she and her sister had built out of sofa cushions and blankets as children. The floor consisted of packed earth, with tufts of grass growing round the edges and near the openings at either end. Sunlight filtered in, but it was muted, and Alix felt as though she was in another world. A magical one, where she was safe and protected. A strange tingling sensation came over her, and her vision blurred. She glanced at Noah, and he was frowning as if the same thing was happening to him.

'Noah?'

He tilted his head slightly to the side and sank down onto his knees right in front of her, reaching out to cup her cheek with his palm. 'Alix,' he whispered. His gaze was intense, boring into hers. Then he lowered his head, murmuring something that sounded like '*Ást mín.*' She watched, mesmerised, as his mouth came closer to hers. He was going to kiss her, and she couldn't have moved if her life depended on it.

She wanted this. Craved his kiss more than she'd ever wished for anything in her life. 'Yes,' she whispered, and in the next second his lips claimed hers and she closed her eyes.

He was tentative at first, dropping butterfly kisses on her mouth that were so fleeting it was as if they were barely there. Then he grew bolder, the touch of his firm lips more assured. He nibbled playfully at her lower lip until she opened for him and he could plunge his tongue inside. Alix lost all reason and threw her arms around his neck, pulling him close. Her tongue tangled with his, stroking, playing, revelling in the sensation. She allowed herself to touch his stubbled cheek, as she'd wanted to do earlier. The bristles against her palm made her shiver in delight. She moaned, and an answering growl came from deep inside his chest. This was heaven and she never wanted him to stop.

She was only vaguely aware of their surroundings, but as she stroked her hands down Noah's back, something niggled at her. It didn't feel right. The material of his worn plaid shirt should have been as soft as thistledown, but her palms were connecting with something much coarser. Woven wool, scratchy and sandpapery. Moving her hands up, her fingers encountered soft strands of hair. Long ones. And as Noah's kiss came to an end and he moved to trail his mouth along her chin, he murmured, 'Merewen, *unnasta*.'

Alix recoiled and put her hands on his chest, giving him a shove. 'Stop!' she said, her voice quivering, breathing erratic.

For an instant, the man before her wasn't Noah, but a stranger with long golden-brown hair. When she blinked, he disappeared and was replaced by Noah's familiar features and shorter strands. She stared at him, her heart hammering in her chest.

'What the hell just happened?' she asked.

He shook his head, as if he was trying to clear his vision. 'I have no idea. I . . . You weren't you.'

'You neither.' Alix scanned their surroundings and shuddered. 'There's something weird going on in here. I feel safe, but also . . . not.'

Noah nodded and stared pointedly at her crystal pendant, which must have escaped the confines of her shirt when she crawled inside the cairn, as it was now hanging on the outside. 'Yeah. More magic?' He speared his fingers through the hair on top of his head. 'Shit. What is going on with us? I'm sorry. I didn't mean to maul you like that.'

Alix felt her cheeks heat up. 'It's fine. We obviously weren't ourselves.' Which was terrifying, as that would mean they had both been possessed by someone else. A spirit? A soul? Was that even possible? She didn't dare speculate and would prefer to forget all about it. Not to mention that it was depressing because she'd wanted Noah to kiss her when she was her normal self. Not some strange woman who had somehow invaded her psyche and appeared to be influencing her actions.

'Alix, I—'

She held up a hand. 'Let's forget about it. We've seen this place now. It's time to go back.'

His shoulders slumped. 'OK. If that's what you want.'

He crawled out from under the stones and headed for the quad bike. Alix didn't know how to reply, so she didn't say anything. It was probably better that way.

Chapter Eighteen

West Mercia, early June/Eggtið AD 874

It felt odd to be travelling along the river legitimately. Eirik studied his surroundings and noted the beauty of the banks they passed. Before, he'd always been alert and on the lookout for either danger or opportunities. He'd never had the option of merely enjoying the sights. Now he took in the trees and dense vegetation overhanging the water on either side of the river, interspersed with fields and meadows. The river itself was calm, apart from where dangerous undercurrents could be seen to swirl beneath the surface in places. Fish splashed occasionally. Ducks, moorhens, swans and other birds floated leisurely along the edges, and insects hummed among the reeds.

It was peaceful and idyllic. Beautiful. Deceptively so, because Eirik knew that at any given moment men like his uncle could disrupt the tranquillity. For so long, he had been part of that menace lurking around every bend. It was a strange sensation to be on the other side.

He was manning one of the oars of the small boat they were travelling in. Oslac sat on his right, rowing in tandem with him while casting him suspicious glances from time to time. Eirik ignored him. The man had a right to be cautious. He would have been the same in his shoes. But at present, Eirik wasn't a threat to these people and he didn't intend to cause them any harm.

'We'll be there shortly,' Beorthric informed them. There were two other men in their party and the boat was stuffed with produce they were hoping to sell.

The market turned out to be fairly small, a dozen stalls at most, but it was well attended and commerce was lively. It was clear that people had come from quite far afield to seek out bargains and goods they needed after the long winter months. Eirik soon sold all the combs he'd brought, and made a tidy profit, half of which he gave to Beorthric as payment for room and board, not to mention the materials he'd used.

'That's not necessary,' the older man protested, but he was persuaded to accept it in the end. Eirik didn't want to be beholden to the Mercian, especially since he was planning to run away with his daughter.

He helped out at Beorthric's stall for a while, then someone else took over and he wandered round the rest of the market. A woman was selling ale nearby, and he bought himself a mug. She had quite a few customers, who were chatting and gossiping, their tongues lubricated by her excellent brew. Eirik started conversations with a few of them and listened when they told tales of marauders on the river. He knew it was likely his uncle, and asked questions to try and figure out if they were in the vicinity.

'They raided a settlement about half a day's journey south of here a few days ago,' someone told him. 'Why, have you come across them before?'

'No. I was robbed recently, but that was by a small group of men,' he replied, trotting out the lie he'd told Beorthric. 'And they were definitely not Norse.'

It sounded as though Hastein and his men weren't far away, and Eirik's stomach muscles clenched. He wished they would go elsewhere for the next few weeks, until he had left safely with Merewen.

'Well, best to keep an eye out,' his drinking companion said. 'I post guards at all times. Not that I have much worth stealing.'

Eirik could have told him that didn't matter to Hastein. If his uncle was hungry or fancied a barrel of ale, he'd raid whatever settlement he came upon first.

He took his leave of the man and continued to wander, casting his eye over the goods for sale. Most of it was produce, but there were a few stalls offering things like leather items and jewellery. He considered buying Merewen a gift, but the wares on display were paltry, and he had better things hidden in his stash near the cairn. Come to think of it, he knew the very thing he wanted to give her – a beautiful crystal pendant he hadn't had the heart to have melted down. That would suit her perfectly, as it would match her ice-grey eyes.

Smiling to himself, he headed back towards Beorthric and the others. He caught a glimpse of a figure in the crowd who looked familiar, but the man disappeared in the next instant. He frowned. It hadn't been Hastein or one of the men who had come with him from Hreopandune. Could it have been one of the crewmen they'd joined forces with, perhaps? Eirik hadn't had time to get to know them before that fateful raid that went wrong, and hoped the man hadn't recognised him if it was one of them.

He tried to follow him, but it was as if the earth had swallowed the man up. There was nothing for it but to be on his guard.

'I hear you've been sneaking around with my husband, making eyes at him in order to seduce him. Did you think I wouldn't find out?'

'I beg your pardon?' Merewen looked up from the tedious task of setting up a warp on one of the looms that were kept in the hall, and found Burghild standing next to her. She had her hands resting on her stomach, the bump very noticeable now, and a more than usually severe scowl on her face. In fact, her eyes were shooting daggers and there was a distinctly malicious glint in their depths.

'Someone saw him entering your hut. Several times, in fact. And I've noticed you keep glancing at him whenever we're gathered in the hall at mealtimes. I won't have it, do you hear?'

Without warning, she slapped Merewen hard across the cheek, making her stumble backwards. She dropped the ball of yarn she'd been holding, and blinked at her sister in disbelief.

'What are you talking about? I wouldn't go anywhere near Oslac, not for all the silver in the world. I loathe the man.' Her cheek stung and she raised a hand to the hot skin, which was no doubt bright red. 'How dare you accuse me of something so foul?'

'Hah! You think I believe that? You were forever mooning after him when the two of you were betrothed, and I know it galled you to lose him to me. I'm telling you, I have a witness. Now that Father isn't here to protect you, I'm going to see to it you receive your just punishment.'

'Burghild, for the last time, I want nothing to do with your husband! He's an uncouth boor and I'm glad he married you instead of me.' Merewen glared back, infuriated that her sister could be so obtuse. And so wilfully blind. It wasn't just Merewen that Oslac importuned. She'd seen him groping several of the serving wenches too, and none too subtly. He'd been growing increasingly bold of late.

Another slap landed on her cheek. 'You're not only a fallen woman, you're disrespectful as well!' Burghild's voice was rising, her cheeks mottled with fury. 'I hate you, and I can't wait for you to be carted off to a monastery. You're always so high and mighty, think you're better than the rest of us. Well, you're not. *I'm* in charge here, and I won't stand for your arrogance.'

Merewen wanted to laugh. Arrogance? If that wasn't the height of hypocrisy. 'And I'll be very pleased to leave this place. Having you lording it over everyone is unbearable. You have no right to slap me for something I haven't done. If you weren't with child, I'd hit you back.'

'Well, that's where you're wrong. I have every right and I'm going to make you see the error of your ways. Edgar, Cuthbert, come here,' Burghild shouted.

Two of Beorthric's men came running. 'What is it, mistress?'

She pointed at Merewen. 'I want you to take her to the old hut and lock her in. She needs to repent of her sins, and she's not to come out until she's ready to apologise and show remorse.'

The two men looked at each other in consternation. 'But she's a lady of this settlement. We can't . . . . I mean, your father wouldn't like it.'

'He's not here and I'm in charge!' Burghild shrieked. 'Take her away. Now! Or I'll have you flogged.'

Merewen decided that her sister was clearly unhinged and any moment now the situation would spiral even further out of control. She clenched her fists, threw Burghild a look of disgust, and marched over to the two guards. 'Let's go. I don't want you harmed on my account.'

Bewildered, but obviously wanting to escape Burghild's presence, they followed her out of the building and marched either side of her towards the old hut. It was an empty one that Beorthric used for temporary confinement if someone had transgressed or needed to cool their heels for a while. Merewen hadn't been in there in ages, and when she entered, she gagged. The stench of stale urine and sweat hit her square in the face, and the only bench inside was covered in a filthy sheepskin. The floor was none too clean either, and there were gaps in the walls' planking that had let in rain and wind, making the place damp as well.

'Take that away, please,' she ordered, pointing at the pelt. 'And then you'd best lock me in for a while until she calms down.'

'Yes, Mistress Merewen. We're right sorry,' one of the men told her, his eyes holding sincere regret. 'We'll try to free you as soon as we can, I promise.'

'Very well.' She noticed Sceadu skulking behind the pair, as usual not letting her out of his sight, but she shook her head at him. 'Stay outside, Sceadu. I've no idea how long I'll be in here, so you're better off guarding me.'

The hound appeared to understand and lay down outside the hut. The last thing she saw before the door closed was him lowering his muzzle to rest on his front paws. She would have liked to have him inside with her for comfort, but at least now he would hopefully be fed, even if she wasn't.

Eirik was bone tired from rowing upstream, as well as wet and cold from a sudden rain shower that had begun almost as soon as they'd left the marketplace. When they finally reached Beorthric's settlement that evening, it was almost fully dark. Or as dark as it got this time of year. They could still see where they were going, thankfully. He couldn't wait to change into dry clothing, have a meal, and lie down on his allotted bench. His leg ached, but he didn't want to let on that he was hurting. It wouldn't do to show weakness, or the likes of Oslac would take advantage.

He also couldn't wait to catch a glimpse of Merewen before he drifted off to sleep.

Beorthric was in a good mood, having sold all the produce he'd brought to the market. And Oslac had spent a considerable amount of time at the ale stall, so he was pleasantly mellow. He'd even sung a few songs as they rowed, one of the other men joining in. Eirik pretended that he didn't have a good voice, but in reality he didn't know the words or tunes.

As they trooped inside the hall, the delicious smells of stew and bread wafted towards them, and his stomach rumbled. He glanced around to see if he could spot Merewen, but she was nowhere in sight. Perhaps she'd gone to fetch something. Anticipation fizzed in his veins. Although he couldn't greet her openly, he hadn't forgotten their kiss, and he knew that if he could catch her eye, he'd remind her of it silently. They had an agreement. She was to be his wife and she was willing to run away with him. He was content to wait, because it wouldn't be long now until he could make her his in every way.

Oslac made a beeline for Burghild, whose face flushed with pleasure as he greeted her with a smacking kiss. Eirik hid a smirk. Oslac wasn't normally that affectionate with the prickly woman, but ale had a tendency to blur a man's vision. At the moment, she would be perceived as his quickest route to a swift tumble in the sheets. Poor thing probably had no idea that her husband normally lusted more after her sister.

'Come, sit by me,' Beorthric invited, after Eirik had exchanged his wet shirt for a dry one and wrapped himself in his cloak to get warm. 'You've worked hard today.'

The older man hadn't done any rowing. Instead he had manned the steering oar and occasionally urged them to pick up the pace.

Eirik sank down onto a stool next to Beorthric's chieftain's chair and accepted a bowl of stew from a serving woman. There was still no sign of Merewen, and a niggle of worry wormed its way into his brain. Where was she? What was taking her so long?

He chatted to Beorthric, but he was grateful the older man did most of the talking, because he was having trouble concentrating. Merewen continued to be absent, and the niggle turned into full-blown anxiety. Why wasn't she here? Was she ill? Just as he'd finished his last morsel of food, he noticed Sceadu slinking in and stopping to scan the room. When he caught sight of Eirik, he came trotting over purposefully, but instead of greeting him in his usual way, with effusive tail-wagging and licks, he grabbed hold of his sleeve and tugged at it, growling softly.

'What on earth's got into you?' Eirik tried scratching the dog behind his ears, as he normally would, but Sceadu shook him off and redoubled his efforts.

'What's the matter with the hound?' Beorthric peered around Eirik with a frown. 'Isn't that my daughter's dog?'

'Yes, and I believe he's trying to tell me something. Do you think anything has happened to her? Perhaps she's taken a tumble somewhere and twisted her ankle.' Eirik couldn't think of any other reason why Sceadu would be behaving so strangely. Coupled with the fact that Merewen was nowhere to be seen, he had a horrible feeling that something bad had occurred.

Odin's ravens! Please don't let my uncle have found her . . .

Beorthric's eyebrows came down in a fierce frown. 'We'd best find out. Let's see if he leads us somewhere.'

They stood up and followed the dog, who had let go of Eirik's garment as soon as he saw that they understood his silent message. The two men headed for the door.

'Where are you going, Father?' Burghild called out. She was sitting next to her now even drunker husband, but cast an anxious glance their way.

'To find Merewen. You wouldn't happen to know where she is, would you?'

She lowered her gaze. 'I'm sure I couldn't say. She is a law unto herself.'

Beorthric didn't waste any more time, but strode out of the door with Eirik in his wake. 'Where to, dog?' he said to Sceadu.

The hound took off through the darkness, and they followed him to the outskirts of the settlement. The night had turned even more rainy and cold, unseasonably so, and Eirik shivered despite the cloak he was wearing. 'Where on earth is he taking us?' he wondered.

'Merewen? Are you there?' Beorthric bellowed. '*Merewen!*'

After they had passed all the other buildings, they came upon a dilapidated hut whose timbers had sizeable gaps in between them. Not large enough for a person to crawl through, but they must let in the cold air and rain from outside. Sceadu barked and sat down outside the door, scratching at it with one paw.

'Merewen?' Beorthric called again, and this time there was a muffled reply.

'In here.'

'In the name of all the saints, what is she doing in there?' Beorthric muttered. Eirik helped him lift the sturdy bar, then they threw the door open. 'Daughter?'

'H-here, Father.' Merewen stumbled out, shivering and bleary. She wasn't wearing a cloak and looked to be frozen stiff.

Fury coursed through Eirik and he clenched his fists. He had to make a huge effort to stop himself from rushing forward to envelop her in his arms and check her all over to make sure she wasn't injured. Who had done this to her? Whoever it was, he vowed to make them pay.

'What happened?' her father demanded, equally angry judging by his scowling countenance. 'Why were you locked in there?' He reached out to steady her, but she flinched away from him, making his scowl deepen. Eirik gathered the man wasn't normally so concerned about his daughter, and she in turn wasn't happy with her father.

'You'd h-have to ask B-Burghild,' she stuttered, her teeth chattering badly. 'She h-had some foolish notion, s-said I needed to repent of my sins.'

Beorthric muttered a curse, while Eirik swung his cloak off his shoulders and draped it around her. 'She needs to get warm,' he said. 'We can find out the details later.' He turned to her. 'Can you walk, or would you like me to carry you?' He hoped he wasn't overstepping by offering, but right now, he didn't care.

'I can walk.' She pulled the cloak tightly around her body, still trembling. Sceadu whined softly and plastered himself to his mistress's legs, as if he wanted to give her warmth too. She stroked his ears, then started to head in the direction of the main hall.

Along the way, Beorthric managed to get the full story out of her. How Burghild had accused her of seducing her husband. The fact that Merewen didn't want him and hadn't so much as looked at the man. How Burghild had slapped her – twice – and forced two of the guards to lock her up. Then apparently forgotten about her for the rest of the day. She'd been in the hut since morning without food, water or any way of keeping warm once evening came.

By the time they reached the hall, Beorthric was seething. He immediately confronted Burghild, who denied any wrongdoing.

'She was insolent and disrespectful, Father. I had no choice but to punish her,' she said, although it was clear from her darting eyes that she knew she'd overstepped her remit.

'Rubbish!' Beorthric declared. 'If you weren't with child, I'd lock *you* up in that hut for the rest of the night. And you lied to me when I asked if you knew where your sister was. How dare you? Honestly, carrying a babe has muddled your brain. I don't want to see your face again until the morrow. In fact, from now on, Merewen will be in charge of the household until she leaves. You should stay in bed and rest, then perhaps you can start to think clearly once more.'

'What? No! You can't do that, Father.' Burghild looked aghast.

'I can, and it's settled. Hand over the keys.' Beorthric's expression brooked no further argument. His eldest daughter reluctantly gave him the set of household keys she always carried, while simultaneously sending Merewen a death glare. 'Oslac!' he barked. 'Take your wife away, please.'

'With pleasure. Come, wife. Let's go to bed.' Oslac got to his feet, none too steadily, but managed to hold on tight when Burghild tried to tug her arm out of his grip.

'Father, I was in charge here while you were gone. I had every right to act as I saw fit,' she protested in a last-ditch attempt to justify her actions.

'Merewen is the gentlest of creatures, as obedient a daughter as I could wish for,' Beorthric said firmly, clearly overlooking the fact that she hadn't seemed very respectful when they freed her from the hut. 'Didn't she step aside for you when I asked her to? Make barely any fuss about the fact that this settlement will be yours one day? What more do you want? Really, it makes me wonder if I didn't make a mistake. I should have sent *you* to the nuns instead.'

Burghild blanched and shook her head, eyes bulging in horror. Without another word, she followed her husband to their private sleeping chamber.

Beorthric turned his attention back to Merewen. 'Come and sit by the fire,' he urged, steering her towards the hearth. 'Someone bring a blanket or two, please.'

This time she allowed him to fuss over her, the fight having gone out of her. Soon she was swaddled nicely, and Eirik had to be content with that. He could only watch from the edge of the crowd, but at least he knew she was safe now. He threw her hound a grateful glance. The dog had earned a huge reward for saving his mistress. Eirik would beg a massive bone for him tomorrow from one of the cooks. Sceadu deserved it.

As for Merewen, the sooner he could get her away from here, the better.

Chapter Nineteen

Hereford, early June, present day

Alix groaned as she stretched her spine in the break room at the back of the library. She'd been shelving books all morning and was tired from bending and lifting repetitively. Thankfully, it was lunchtime, and she was looking forward to sitting down with a cup of tea and the tuna sandwich she'd brought. Everyone else appeared to be busy still, so she had the place to herself, which suited her just fine. Apart from Eileen, she hadn't really bonded with anyone else yet, although the others were friendly enough. Just in a more superficial manner.

As she bit into her sandwich, her phone rang. She was surprised to see Noah's name flash up on the screen and hurried to answer. 'Noah? Is everything all right?'

She wondered if something had happened at Howell's End; perhaps there was a problem with the fields.

She heard a low chuckle that sent a frisson down her back. 'Hi, Alix. Yes, fine. Why did you think something was wrong?'

'Well, you don't normally call me, and it's the middle of the day. I'm at work and I assumed you'd be too.'

It sounded silly when she said it, but it was true nonetheless. So far he'd only ever contacted her via text message, and the few times they'd met up it was because he'd come over to her house in person. And he'd been fairly quiet since that strange incident at the cairn, just texted a couple of times to ask if she was OK, then nothing more.

'Ah, I see. Sorry if I'm disturbing you. Have you got a moment?' When she said yes, he continued. 'It's just . . . I've been thinking about the hoard. Is there any way I could have a quick look at it? You said you had something to do with the exhibition, didn't you, and I would really like to see it. If that's possible?'

'The hoard. Right. Yes, of course.' Alix was a little bit disappointed, if she was honest, to find that he hadn't called to ask her out. More than a little, actually, but she told herself not to be ridiculous. They were friends and neighbours, nothing else, even if he'd seemed to seek her out repeatedly. But that was before that strange kiss . . . Anyway, she'd sworn off men, hadn't she? 'I'll check with Eileen, who's in charge of it,' she told him. 'When could you come?'

'Any day that's convenient for you. I'll work around it.'

'OK, I'll let you know soon. Bye for now.'

The thought of him coming to the library, which was her domain, was exciting, even if he was only here for the treasure and not because he wanted to see her. As soon as she'd finished her lunch, she went in search of Eileen.

Noah hadn't been to a library in years. He had a Kindle and liked to read, but was usually too tired to manage more than a chapter at a time. Borrowing from the library would have merely led to huge fines for late returns, and he didn't have time to be going into town anyway.

'Hi! There you are.' Alix came striding towards the front desk, where he'd asked for her. She looked a tad flustered and he couldn't help but wonder if he had that effect on her or if she'd simply been rushing. He hoped it was the former.

He took in the prim outfit – another skirt, a pretty blouse with some sort of bow at the neck, and flat sensible shoes. Her hair was twisted into a loose knot on top of her head, seemingly held in place by a pencil. The sight made him smile. In fact, just seeing her made him want to smile, and it did other things to him as well. The nerdy look shouldn't be sexy, but it worked for him. He longed to unravel her hair, untie that smart bow and peel her out of the tight skirt, then do very naughty things to her . . .

He cleared his throat and tried to think calmer thoughts. 'Hey. I hope I'm not interrupting something?'

'No, not at all. Eileen is waiting. Come on.'

She led the way towards the back of the building, and on instinct, he reached out and grabbed her hand. She shot him a look of surprise, but didn't pull away. He noted how tiny her hand was compared to his. She wouldn't be much use around a farm; most tasks required strength. When her fingers briefly squeezed his, however, her grip was firmer than he'd thought, so perhaps he was wrong. She might be stronger than she looked. Although why was he thinking in terms of her working at the farm? He doubted she'd want to be a farmer's wife. This, here, was the life she was made for. At the library, she fitted in. It was her natural environment, no doubt about it.

'Here we are. Eileen, this is Noah, my neighbour.' Alix shot him a quick glance before adding, 'The hoard was found on his land.'

'Pleased to meet you.' Alix's colleague greeted him with a handshake. 'I wouldn't let just anyone in here, but as you were part owner of these treasures, I'm making an exception.'

'Thank you, that's very kind,' he murmured. If his sister and her boyfriend had done everything by the book, Noah would have been a rich man now. So far, he hadn't even received half the value of what had been recovered, as was his right. The authorities were still arguing about ownership, and there was the question of where the money for the sold items had gone. Reece had refused to say, and clammed up every time he was asked.

Eileen indicated a workbench behind her covered in an assortment of glittering objects. 'Here you are. All the items we've recovered so far.' Noah was thankful she didn't mention the fact that a lot of people thought he was still hiding the rest.

He walked over to study the treasure trove laid out before him. It wasn't a huge hoard by any means, and he couldn't help but wonder how much more Niamh and Reece had found. There were gold and silver coins, a gold ring, some bracelets and a silver ingot, and last but not least, the pendant Alix had mentioned. It was uncannily similar to the one she wore, presumably hidden under that silky bow.

She was holding out a pair of disposable gloves to him. 'If you put these on, you're allowed to touch.'

'Right. Thanks.' He tugged them on and bent to pick up one of the coins. It was almost the same as the one currently tucked into his wallet. The writing around the edge said *EDELRED REX*, and he guessed it had been minted for the same king. He ought to hand over the one in his possession to Eileen, but he didn't want to. Not yet. It made him feel incredibly guilty, but something told him to hold on to it for now. Besides, if he disclosed that he had it, he'd come under suspicion by the police yet again. They'd think he knew the whereabouts of the rest too, which sadly wasn't the case.

He put the coin back and had a closer look at some of the other items. 'They are all beautiful,' he said, receiving enthusiastic nods in return.

'Yes. You must come and see the exhibition when it's opened. Alix is doing a fantastic job with the displays and creating little stories for each object. She's invented this fictional young couple who are in love but having to hide it. Visitors will be following their journey.'

That sounded uncannily like some of the visions they'd both been having, and Noah briefly raised his eyebrows at Alix. She ducked her head, face flaming.

'It's going to be fab,' Eileen finished, oblivious to any undercurrents.

'I can well believe it.' Noah smiled at Alix, trying to put her at ease. He wasn't going to give her away. Whatever those strange incidents were, it was their secret. No one else needed to know about it.

'No, it's all thanks to Eileen's hard work. I'm just adding a few touches,' she protested.

The crystal pendant was the final thing Noah picked up. Unlike Alix's, which was suspended on a silver chain, this one hung on a simple leather cord. Presumably that was a modern addition, as the original leather would have rotted away in the ground. Apart from this slight difference, the two pendants could have been twins. After what had happened when he'd handled Alix's crystal, Noah was almost afraid to look more closely at this one. He told himself not to be a coward and lifted it up to catch the light, turning away from the two women.

At first he saw nothing but a clear sphere encased in silver filigree. Beautiful, but harmless. However, as a sunbeam pierced it, he suddenly caught sight of the two figures inside again, just like before. His senses swam and he drew in a sharp breath. Images flooded his mind and he closed his eyes.

He was digging in the soil, working as fast as he could. His heartbeat was pounding in his ears and he knew that time was of the essence. There was no way he'd leave without the buried treasure, though. He needed it. Not for himself, but for the woman he loved. Turning his head slightly, he scanned the area to make sure no one was watching. The leather sack appeared, and he tugged it loose, rushing over to another spot nearby. There was more there and he had to grab it now, before it was too late . . .

'Noah? It's pretty, isn't it?' Alix's voice brought him back to the present and he put the pendant back into its nest of untreated wool, still a bit disorientated.

'Yes. Very.' He tried not to let on that he'd been affected by the strange magic again, but he wondered if she could tell. Pulling off the gloves, he turned to Eileen with a smile. 'Thank you so much for letting me have a look. I really appreciate it.'

'No problem. I hope the police will be able to recover more eventually.' The woman's expression was bland, but her gaze was searching and intense.

There it was. The unspoken accusation. Noah wished he could produce some proof that he wasn't hiding the rest of the hoard. Sadly, he couldn't. Not yet, but he was hoping to change that.

He nodded, not rising to her bait. 'Me too. Unfortunately, the man who found the treasure isn't talking, and I can't make him. Not until they let him out of jail, at any rate.' If and when they did, he'd be very happy to try and persuade Reece of the error of his ways. Since the man had received a sentence of ten years, however, he wouldn't be out for quite a while.

'Do you have time for a coffee?' Alix asked, steering him purposefully away.

'Sure. Are you free?'

'I can take a half-hour break. Thanks again, Eileen.'

They found a little cosy café and ordered tea and carrot cake. Both were delicious, and Noah muttered that it was just what he needed.

Alix peered at him. 'Why? Did you see something again?'

'Yes. In the crystal. Those things are clearly jinxed. It's . . . creepy.' He shivered. 'I saw a man digging in the soil and had this unbearable feeling of urgency. The sensation that I – or he – was being hunted or maybe in danger. It was scary.'

'I avoided looking straight at it,' Alix confessed. 'And I haven't stared at my own pendant either. It seems safer that way.' She changed the subject. 'So why did you suddenly decide you wanted to see the hoard? I thought you said it had caused you nothing but trouble.'

Noah sighed. 'I needed to know what I was looking for.'

She frowned. 'How do you mean?'

'You know how I told you that my sister and her boyfriend found the treasure? Well, the police think there were a lot more items, at least twice as many as were recovered. That twat Reece had photos on his mobile of the hoard *in situ* before he dug it all up. So of course they're convinced one of us is hiding the rest. Reece isn't talking, which means their suspicions have fallen on me and Niamh.' He shook his head. 'It's definitely not me. That means it's got to be my sister. I'm going to look for it, but I have to know what I'm searching for.'

'I see. That makes sense. You really think she'd do something like that? I mean, why not come clean and claim the reward? That treasure is worth a lot.'

'It's too late for that, since they didn't do it at the beginning. If she produces the rest of the hoard now, she'll end up in jail as well. I don't want that. I figure if I can find it, maybe I can persuade the police that Reece hid it and it had nothing to do with me or Niamh. He's stupid enough to have left fingerprints on some of the objects, and I have no intention of touching anything myself.'

Alix thought about it. 'That could work. Do you want help?'

'What?' He stared at her, his fork halfway to his mouth.

'I can help you search for it if you want. I'm free Sunday and Monday.'

She sensed that he was very conflicted about this whole matter and she wanted to be there for him. He seemed an inherently honest person, and she could tell it pained him to be under suspicion by the authorities. If she'd been in his shoes, she would have wanted to clear her name too. The least she could do – as a friend and neighbour – was to assist in the search.

'Are you sure? I don't even know where to start looking.' He put the piece of cake in his mouth and chewed slowly.

'I'm sure. We could start with your house. A place that old has to have lots of great hiding places.'

'OK.' He smiled and took her hand across the table, giving it a squeeze. 'Thank you. How about Monday? Niamh has a meeting in person with one of her lecturers then, she told me. Not everything can be done online, and to be honest, I think she's about to be told off for not working hard enough. I've overheard some of her Zoom conversations and I gather she's been slacking recently. I suppose she thought she wouldn't need to study if she and Reece got rich from selling the hoard. Silly girl.'

'Yes, Monday works for me. I'll come over at about nine, does that sound good?'

'Very.' His twinkling green gaze was warm, and he didn't let go of her hand until it was time to leave the café.

'Where should we start?'

Alix had arrived punctually at 9 a.m., and they were standing in the hall. Shadow danced around them, having greeted her effusively. The dog had taken to her in a big way. They were both raring to go, although Shadow had no idea what was happening. He was just pleased to be included. Noah couldn't help but smile at their enthusiasm.

'How about Niamh's room? I don't know if she'd be stupid enough to hide anything there, but it's worth a try.'

'Good idea.'

He led the way upstairs and into the bedroom his sister had moved into as soon as Uncle Ifan died. It was the second largest one – he now had the master bedroom himself, having completely redecorated it after his uncle's passing – and she'd taken possession of it without even asking first. Not that it made any difference which room she had, but it had irked him that she'd taken it for granted she could do as she pleased. Not even a quick question to enquire if it was OK with him, even though it was his house.

But that was water under the bridge.

'Wow, she's not exactly tidy, huh?' Alix surveyed the virtual bomb site that greeted them as they opened the door. It was a much worse version of the chaos Niamh created downstairs all the time. Clothes were strewn over every surface, shoes littered the floor, and magazines and chocolate wrappers lay wherever she'd dropped them, probably because the rubbish bin was overflowing. Shadow found a half-eaten biscuit that he wolfed down. Noah hoped it wasn't so old it made the dog sick.

'Disgusting,' he muttered. 'She has no respect. I don't even know where to start!'

'Let's check for loose floorboards, then her drawers and the wardrobe,' Alix suggested. 'We'll have to leave everything as we found it, though.'

Not an easy task, but they began to search methodically. Noah checked every floorboard, including under the bed and any other furniture that moved. He looked under the mattress, behind the wardrobe, on top of it and inside, feeling the sides and bottom in case there was a hidden cavity. Alix, meanwhile, did the same to the chest of drawers and Niamh's dressing table, which sported an impressive array of perfume bottles, make-up and nail polish, some spilled and with the lids off.

'Urgh! I want to go and get a hoover so badly,' she muttered, and Noah chuckled.

'You and me both, but I'm not cleaning up her mess. I'll make her do it before she moves out.' And he was determined that she wouldn't be staying here much longer. He'd had enough of her taking the piss.

'I don't suppose you've taught Shadow to search for stuff? Other than food, I mean,' Alix asked hopefully, glancing at the dog, who had curled up on the bed after having finished his inspection of the room.

'Sadly not. I doubt he could smell metal in any case. Does it even have a scent?'

'No idea. Oh, hang on. What's this?' Alix took her house key out of her jeans pocket and prised something out from in between a couple of floorboards. 'Look, Noah, a coin just like the ones in the hoard.'

She turned it over with the tip of the key and he could see that it was similar, although with a different king's name on it. There was no doubt it was old, though, and must have belonged to the hoard. He shook his head.

'I can't believe how careless she's been. I found one downstairs as well.' Too late he realised he shouldn't have told Alix that. Now she was going to wonder why he hadn't reported his find. He rushed to defend his actions. 'I know, I should have mentioned it, but I was afraid it would cast suspicion on me again. I will hand it in, I swear.'

Alix smiled and put a hand on his arm. 'It's fine. I understand. Let's not report this one yet either. We need to find all the treasure first. As you said, hopefully there will be fingerprints on some of the rest. This one looks like it's been polished.'

'Yes. I'm afraid I caught a whiff of silver polish on the other one too. I really hope she hasn't done that to everything.'

'Eileen would have an absolute fit.'

'Just in case there are any prints left, though, I'm going to pick this one up with a plastic bag so I don't touch it myself.' He pulled a bag out of his pocket. 'I came prepared.'

Despite an exhaustive search, they found nothing further, and after a short break they carried on looking in some of the other rooms. The house was so big, it was like searching for the proverbial needle in a haystack. They tried to be methodical, doing it room by room, but halfway through the house they gave up.

'No more today,' Noah decreed. 'I've got to get back to work outside.'

'OK. I'll get out of your hair.' Alix turned to head for the front hall, but he snagged her wrist and made her turn back towards him. The momentum propelled her straight into his chest, and his arms automatically went around her to steady her.

'*Oof!* Wait. I want to thank you properly for helping me. Can I take you out for a meal sometime this week?' He looked down into her upturned face and smiled when he noticed a smudge of dirt on one cheek. Lifting a finger, he rubbed at it. 'You look very dishevelled,' he murmured. 'I like it.'

'What? Why? You want me to be dirty?'

'Mm, yes, in the best possible way.'

Her eyes widened. 'Noah!'

He didn't give her a chance to protest further. She was in his arms and she felt good. More than good. It was as if she'd been made for him, her curves the perfect match to the hard planes of his chest. Without thinking about it, he captured her mouth in a searing kiss. When she didn't move away, he did it again, exploring, tasting, teasing, the way he'd been fantasising about every day lately. He carried on kissing her until they were both thoroughly out of breath.

'Thank you,' he whispered. 'That was exactly what I needed.'

'Um, you're welcome?' She was blinking up at him with a dazed expression. 'What was that for?'

He laughed. 'I just couldn't resist. I've wanted to kiss you again for days. And no, before you ask, I don't feel any strange magic in the air today. This is me, Noah, kissing you, Alix, hopefully without interference from supernatural forces.' He did it again for good measure and to prove his point, then leaned back and looked her in the eyes. 'I've never felt like this before, you know. I want to be with you. All day, every day. Is that OK?'

'Yes. It's more than OK.' She smiled at him and stood on tiptoe to give him a soft kiss in return.

'Good. I'm glad that's settled.' He grinned at her and turned her around, giving her a gentle push towards the front door. 'But now you'd better go, or I'll be tempted to drag you upstairs and not let you leave ever again. I really do have work to do, unfortunately.'

She grinned back. 'Well, when you finish, perhaps you'd like to come to my place for dinner. I'm not the world's greatest cook, but I can rustle something up. You can treat me to a meal some other time.'

'Sounds great! Is seven thirty too late?'

'No, that's perfect. See you then.' She blew him a kiss and let herself out, and Noah had to stand in the hall for quite a while trying to calm his body down.

He couldn't wait for this evening.

Chapter Twenty

West Mercia, early June/Eggtið AD 874

With Merewen temporarily in charge of her father's settlement, she didn't have a moment to spare all day, and there was no chance to go on any foraging excursions. Eirik watched her surreptitiously as she went about her duties, but since she was surrounded by people all the time, he didn't get an opportunity to talk to her one-on-one. They had to make do with furtive glances that made him smile inwardly and feel warm all over, but to everyone else he kept up his usual bland demeanour. The only advantage was that Oslac couldn't corner her either, but Eirik was still happy to see that Sceadu was her constant shadow, never leaving her side.

He wanted to hold her in his arms again. Make plans for their escape and discuss the future. The kiss they'd shared and the way she had felt as she melted against him haunted his dreams. He wanted to do it again. Repeatedly. But several days passed and he grew impatient. There had to be a way that they could meet in secret, but how?

Luck was finally with him as he sat outside the workshop carving yet another comb. Merewen came walking from the direction of the hall, and he saw her and Sceadu hurry inside her little hut. There was no one else about, and he rushed to follow her a few moments later, knocking softly before entering. After the incident with Oslac, they had agreed on a special knock so she would know it was Eirik if he ever visited. She turned with a smile when he shut the door behind him, obviously pleased to see him.

'Eirik. Thank the Lord it's you.'

'I don't think he had anything to do with it.' Eirik put his arms around her waist and pulled her in for a kiss, but he kept it brief in case anyone came looking for her. 'I need to see you, *unnasta*, but it's too dangerous to do it here. Please can we meet at the cairn somehow?'

She kissed him back, a soft melding of mouths that didn't last nearly long enough for his liking. 'I would love to, but I can't get away at the moment. Burghild is watching me like a hawk, no doubt hoping I'll make a mistake with the running of the household. That means she would definitely notice if I went missing for a while.'

'Hmm, tricky,' he agreed, reaching up to push a strand of her unruly hair behind her ear. The dark, curly tresses were soft and he longed to bury his fingers in them. To undo her plait and spread the heavy mass out around her shoulders. 'How about at night? Can you slip away once everyone is asleep?'

'I could try. If I complain of a stomach ache after supper, it won't look odd if I go out to use the privy, then hopefully no one will notice that I haven't returned.'

'Do that. I'll be waiting by the back fence tonight. Leave Sceadu here in your hut, then he won't give you away. I'll collect him on my way out. Now I'd better leave before anyone sees me. Please can you check that there's no one about?'

'Will do. Hopefully I'll see you tonight, but I make no promises.'

He slipped out, but instead of going back to his carving, he headed for the cairn. Apart from Oslac, the inhabitants of the settlement didn't pay much attention to his comings and goings. The annoying man had gone out to inspect some fields today, however, so Eirik was free to do as he wished.

Once he reached the ancient stone monument, he made sure he was alone before going to the place where he'd buried his treasure. He quickly dug it up and rummaged in the leather sack, finally finding the object he'd been looking for. He pulled it out before reburying the rest. It was a beautiful silver and crystal pendant, the one he'd been thinking of when he was at the market. It had come from a particularly prosperous settlement in Northumbria that they had raided last year, and he'd kept it intact rather than dismantling it for the silver. His uncle owned a similar one, but Eirik thought his was slightly superior in craftsmanship. It would suit Merewen perfectly, and he wanted her to have it as a token of his love.

He hoped she would like it.

Sceadu sent his mistress a wounded look when she told him to stay put and shut him inside her hut. She hated having to confine him like that, but it was only temporary. Eirik was right in thinking it would be easier for her to slip outside without the dog. She'd be less noticeable on her own.

'I'm sorry, but Eirik will fetch you soon,' she whispered before closing the door.

She'd been busy with household duties all day and should have been exhausted, but excitement fizzed in her veins, making her jittery and unable to keep still. It had been torture having to watch Eirik from afar for days without being able to talk to him or touch him. The brief interlude earlier in the day had helped a little, but the prospect of spending longer with him at the cairn made her want to jump with joy.

Burghild's disgruntled gaze had followed her for most of the day, but fortunately her sister's priority was to catch Merewen making a mistake when it came to the running of the settlement. She wasn't watching out for secret trysts with the Norseman, thank the Lord. And come evening, she would retire to her and Oslac's chamber, and hopefully no one else would be overly interested in Merewen's whereabouts.

Supper came and went, and to Burghild's frustration, everything about the meal was handled smoothly, overseen by Merewen.

'You're doing well, daughter,' Beorthric praised her, looking well fed and content. 'I hope you're not overtaxing yourself.'

'Not at all, Father. As you know, I was trained to oversee my own household, just like my sister.' It was a pointed reminder that she should have been married by now as well. Beorthric cleared his throat, clearly uncomfortable with the subject, but he refrained from comment.

At last everyone bedded down for the night. Merewen had made sure to complain several times of severe stomach cramps, and when the time came for her to sneak outside, no one so much as looked her way. They were all busy snoring.

Eirik had slipped out earlier and was waiting for her by the back fence as he'd promised, together with Sceadu. The hound greeted her with joyful tail wags, but she quickly shushed him in case he decided to bark and give them away.

'Let's go,' Eirik whispered, lifting her over the fence as if she weighed nothing at all. Sceadu jumped, and as he had such long legs, he had no trouble sailing across. Eirik climbed after them and took Merewen's hand, plaiting their fingers together. Whoever was on guard that night must be doing his rounds, as they were able to slip away unnoticed.

Midsummer was approaching. The light was other-worldly,

making the summer night appear magical, and the scent of flowers and vegetation perfumed the air. Merewen shivered with anticipation, holding on tightly to Eirik's hand. They had no problem finding their way to the cairn, and once there, Eirik produced a blanket and they sank onto it together near one of the openings.

'Sceadu, guard,' he ordered quietly, and the hound obeyed, lying down nearby with his ears up, alert to any danger. Merewen ought to have resented the fact that her dog followed his command, but Sceadu was intelligent and had already understood that Eirik would soon be his master as well.

'I've missed you,' Eirik whispered, pulling Merewen into his arms.

'I've missed you too,' she admitted. When he put his fingers under her chin to angle it just so and kissed her deeply, she leaned into him, gripping his tunic with her fists so that she could reciprocate properly. She'd more than missed him – she craved him.

The kiss went on for a long while, but then Eirik pulled away. 'Wait,' he said, his voice deeper than usual. 'I have something for you.'

He got on his knees and crawled behind her, rummaging in his pouch. Then he pushed her long plait out of the way and slipped something over her head, holding it up in front of her eyes. Even in the semi-darkness of the summer night, Merewen could see the object clearly. A crystal orb, flashing in the faint light and encased in silver.

'Eirik!' she breathed. 'What . . . ?'

'I want you to have this,' he murmured, fastening a leather cord around her neck. He bent to nuzzle her cheek, putting his arms around her waist from behind, then placed a butterfly kiss under her ear. 'Do you like it?'

She lifted the pendant and watched as it swivelled, sending

little flashes of light into the night. 'It's beautiful. Thank you,' she said. 'But it's much too costly. You shouldn't—'

'Of course I should.' He nibbled on her ear lobe, sending shivers right down to her toes. 'I want to spoil my wife as much as I can. This crystal reminded me of your gorgeous eyes, like clear raindrops in sunlight. Wear it and think of me every time you feel it on your skin, although you'll have to keep it hidden for now.'

He reached up to tuck the pendant inside her shift, brushing the tops of her breasts with his fingers. Merewen trembled. 'Eirik,' she whispered.

'Shh, I won't do anything you don't want me to. We will take it slowly.'

She twisted round on the blanket until she was on her knees too, facing him. 'And what if I don't want to go slowly? What if I want you, all of you, right now?'

She had no idea where this boldness came from, but she was certain she couldn't wait another instant before becoming his in every way. They belonged together, and even if their escape plan came to naught, she would have this night to remember. If things went awry, it might be her only chance to experience it. Should she end up in a monastery, she'd be able to think back on this moment and relive it over and over again in her mind. Oslac had been right about that, despite the fact that he'd been the wrong man.

Eirik drew in a sharp breath, one she felt as well as heard because she'd twined her arms around his neck and shuffled forward. Their bodies were as close as two people could get, her breasts squished against his hard chest. She moved restlessly, craving some sort of friction, and he hugged her tightly to him.

'Are you sure, *ást mín*? There's no going back after this. Either way, I already consider you my wife, whether we've spoken formal vows or not.'

His hands had already found and cupped her backside, pushing her even further into him, and his mouth blazed a trail from her cheek down to the neckline of her shift before returning to her lips.

'I'm sure.'

It was all the invitation he needed, and he continued to kiss her while making swift work of removing his belt, tunic and shirt. 'Touch me any way you like,' he murmured, placing her palms on his chest.

She explored the firm contours of every hard ridge, raking her fingernails through the smattering of hair, continuing downwards. His stomach muscles jumped the way they had when she'd tended to his wound, but this time she allowed herself to trace them. He was hers, and she revelled in the fact that a mere stroke of her fingertips could affect him that much. Meanwhile, he tugged her tunic over her head, swiftly followed by her shift. The night air hit her sensitive skin, but his warm hands caressed her and seemed to be everywhere. He groaned when his palms enclosed the heavy mounds of her breasts, making her gasp as his fingers teased her nipples. They appeared to be directly connected to her most secret place, and arrows of lust speared through her.

So this is what it feels like. She couldn't believe she was finally experiencing something she'd dreamed of for a long time. And it was special because she was with Eirik, the man she loved.

'Lie down, my sweet.' He moved the blanket so that it was spread out further inside the cairn, away from the entrance. She did as he asked, crawling over to sink down on it. Soon his clever hands continued their onslaught, although he paused for a moment to remove his trousers before resuming where he'd left off.

Merewen hardly dared to look at his naked form, but she

couldn't resist. The act of procreation might not be something a Christian lady spoke about, but serving women gossiped, and she had always been a curious child. She'd wanted to know all about it and some of the older women had tried to explain, but even so, they hadn't prepared her for this. What she saw now almost made her gasp out loud. Eirik was magnificent. She'd watched the animals on the farm mating and thought she'd known what to expect, but she'd been wrong. This was entirely different. In the most exciting way.

Another shiver of anticipation shot through her.

He must have mistaken it for fear. 'We don't have to do this now, Merewen,' he told her, although his husky voice gave away the fact that he very much wanted to. 'I don't want you to be afraid, but it might hurt just a little the first time.'

'I'm not scared. I'm ... excited,' she admitted. Her cheeks heated up in a fiery blush, but thankfully the darkness didn't give her away.

He chuckled. 'Ah, I see. Well, good. I don't want you to have any regrets.' He leaned over her and began to kiss her again, his mouth moving down across her chest. He teased her nipples with his tongue before sucking on each one in turn. At the same time, his fingers moved further down, finding a place that made her moan when he touched it.

'Eirik!'

'You like that, hmm?' He continued to move his fingers, the caresses becoming more forceful, until her body was strung so tight she thought she would die. A slight pinch and the world exploded into stars, a maelstrom of sensations assailing her all at once. She cried out, but he covered her mouth with his and swallowed the sound while she crested the wave of pleasure.

Before she'd come back down to earth, he'd moved over her and was pushing inside her, slowly but firmly. 'Relax, *unnasta*, it will feel good in a moment,' he promised, sounding strained, as if he was holding himself back.

There was a brief flash of pain, but it was over quickly like he'd said, and when he began to move in and out with deep, sure strokes, the pleasurable sensations started to build once more. Merewen reacted instinctively and wrapped her legs around him, spurring him on.

'That's it, sweetling,' he whispered. 'Hold on tight.'

It wasn't long before her body spasmed yet again, the eruption inside her even stronger this time. She was vaguely aware of Eirik groaning out his own release before leaning his forehead on her shoulder, breathing heavily. He was taking most of his weight on his arms, so as not to crush her, and she reached up to caress the nape of his neck and the long, soft strands of his hair.

He lifted his head and stared down at her, a worried crease between his eyebrows. 'Are you well? Did I hurt you?'

'No.' She smiled. 'Far from it. That was . . . simply amazing.'

He grinned, brushing a kiss across her lips. 'I'm glad. If you're not too sore, we can try again in a little while.'

He retrieved his cloak from nearby and draped it across both of them, holding her close. 'Thank you, my lovely wife. That was even better than I'd imagined.'

Merewen felt exactly the same.

Chapter Twenty-One

Hereford, early June, present day

The doorbell sounded half an hour early and Alix rushed to answer it. She wondered if Noah was as impatient to meet up again as she was. So much so that he hadn't been able to wait until 7.30. The thought made her smile, and happiness bubbled up inside her. He'd just have to sit and watch while she cooked, and then perhaps they could continue where they had left off earlier. She couldn't wait for him to kiss her again. It had been magical.

She opened the door with a big smile on her face, but it died instantly.

'Autumn? What are you doing here?'

Her sister stood outside holding up a bottle of wine and a box of chocolates. 'Peace offering?' she said, her expression sheepish and slightly hopeful.

Alix stared at her. She'd fallen for that so many times in the past, but no more. Autumn was acting, as always sure that she'd be forgiven no matter what she did. Their parents would have given in immediately, and urged Alix to do the same. To be the bigger person. This time she couldn't. Autumn had crossed a line and there was no return.

'Sorry, but no. You need to leave. I don't have time for this right now.'

Autumn's demeanour changed instantly, her eyes narrowing with displeasure at having been rebuffed. 'Important date?' she taunted, sniffing the air demonstratively. 'Is that lasagne I smell? Must be someone special.'

'Go away, Autumn. I have nothing to say to you.' Alix tried to close the door, but Autumn managed to grab the edge and held it open.

'Look, I'm sorry, OK? It was all a big mistake. I've dumped Sean. He's a loser and we're both better off without him. He was only with you for your money, you know that, right? I did you a favour really.'

'A favour?' The nerve of this woman. Alix shook her head and crossed her arms, glaring at her sister. 'You're delusional. I definitely don't want a man who thinks it's all right to hook up with my sister behind my back and use me as some sort of cash cow, but that doesn't make what you did any better. You're always taking what's mine, even when you don't actually want it. It has to stop, Autumn. Now please, go back to London and find yourself some rich sugar daddy, and stop bothering me. I don't want anything to do with you and I'm not going to forgive you this time, understand? I'm done with you and this weird game of yours.'

Autumn's expression soured even further and she looked more like a petulant three-year-old than a grown woman. 'You're just being stubborn now. I have apologised. And I want to visit Grandpa while I'm here. I was hoping you'd take me, as I came by train. Dad said he lives out in the sticks somewhere. I've no idea how to get there.' She held up a hand. 'And don't say taxi. I can't afford it.'

So she was only here to use Alix as a chauffeur? Charming. Alix was about to refuse, but then a thought hit her. Did she really want Grandpa to be alone with Autumn? There was no telling what her sister might say or do. She'd been known to twist people round her little finger, and by now she must have found out about Howell's End. Grandpa had told their dad, who would have informed Autumn. She guessed Autumn was going to try and wheedle something out of Grandpa immediately. She wouldn't be content to wait for her share. That must be why she was here. It couldn't be a coincidence.

Alix made a decision. 'Fine, I'll take you, but not tonight. It's too late and he'll be tired. Come back here tomorrow at five thirty. I'll be home from work by then.'

'What, you're not even going to offer me your sofa for the night?' Autumn seemed genuinely aggrieved.

'No, I don't have one. This is a studio flat with one bed and a couple of armchairs. Go find yourself a hotel and I'll see you tomorrow.' Alix caught her sister by surprise and managed to shut the door this time. She added, 'Unfortunately,' under her breath.

Autumn kicked the door once and shouted, 'Bitch!' but soon afterwards, her steps could be heard on the ornate iron staircase leading down to the ground floor. The flat Alix was renting was situated above a shop in Church Street and could only be reached via the staircase and balcony walkway at the back of the building. She peeked out of the one window that faced in that direction and watched Autumn stomp off down the street. Relief flooded her, but the evening was ruined. Her earlier happiness had evaporated and she didn't want to see Noah while in this state. Her sister always made her feel as though she was inferior. That wasn't the right frame of mind for a date with a gorgeous man who she already considered way out of her league, if she was honest.

She quickly sent him a text message. *Sorry, something's come up. Can we make it another day please?*

He replied almost immediately. *Sure but are you OK?*

Yes fine. I'll explain when I see you.

She received a thumbs-up emoji and a heart in return, which made her smile a little. It didn't ease the tightness in her chest, though. With Autumn around, was there even any point in starting a relationship with Noah? Her sister would try to ruin that as well, and she'd probably succeed.

Swallowing down tears of anger and frustration, Alix went to retrieve the lasagne from the oven. She wasn't hungry any longer, so it would have to go in the freezer. Maybe Noah would come over some other day.

Then again, maybe he wouldn't.

Noah was extremely disappointed when Alix cancelled their date at the last minute. He'd been looking forward to it all day and had almost messed up some of his chores while dreaming about all the things he wanted to do to her after dinner. He wondered what had happened. Had Morgan taken a turn for the worse? Had a heart attack even? He sincerely hoped not, as he liked the old man and knew that he meant a lot to his granddaughter.

Not feeling in the mood to cook, he heated up a microwave meal and grabbed a beer, slumping down in front of the TV. Shadow curled up next to him, and although Noah knew he shouldn't let the dog lie on the furniture, he couldn't be bothered to chase him off. He put the news on, but didn't actually register anything the woman said. Right now he couldn't care less about the rest of the world. He was too worried about Alix.

He heard the back door slam shut and then Niamh popped her head into the living room. 'Hey. What's for dinner?'

'Whatever you make yourself.' Noah didn't even look up from

his own meal, which was some tasteless version of shepherd's pie. He took a swig of his beer to wash it down with and glanced at his sister, who was still standing in the doorway. 'What?' he said, unable to hide his irritation. 'I told you I wasn't cooking for you any longer. You can fend for yourself since you never reciprocate.'

She sighed dramatically. 'This again?'

'Yes. I meant what I said. I'm not your servant or your parent. And while we're on the subject, I happened to look into your room today. It's a pigsty. I need you to clean it up.'

She rolled her eyes. 'Jeez, if you don't like it, just shut the door. What's the big deal?'

That was the final straw. 'No, Niamh, I've had enough. In fact, I met Reece's mother at the supermarket the other day and she was saying she'd told you you'd be welcome to stay with them any time. She knows you're missing Reece, and they can take you with them when they go and visit him in prison. I think maybe it's time you took her up on that offer. Not permanently – you'll always have a home here if you really need it – but perhaps a time-out is what we both need. And living with other people for a while might teach you to treat this place, and me, with some respect.'

He knew Reece's mother genuinely liked Niamh and would treat her well. Mrs Watkins had been devastated when her son was sent to jail, but to her credit, she'd stated that if he'd done something wrong, he deserved to be punished. Of course she loved her child, but she wasn't a complete pushover. Noah knew for a fact that she'd made Reece help out at home, which was probably why the guy spent so much time at Vaughan Court, where no one nagged him. With a bit of luck, Mrs Watkins might teach Niamh a thing or two about real life. About responsibility. His sister wouldn't be pampered there, but expected to do her bit when it came to household chores. Maybe then she'd finally realise that she'd been taking Noah's kindness for granted.

'You can't be serious!' Niamh put her hands on her hips and sent him a death glare, which he ignored.

'I am. I'd like you to move over there by the end of the week, please, if that's OK with Mrs Watkins. We've had this conversation so many times, but you never listen. I honestly can't take it any more. Plus, I don't know why you were so rude to my girlfriend. That was totally uncalled for.'

Niamh sneered. 'Oh, so she's your girlfriend now, huh? I knew it! The minute she's got her foot in the door here, I'll be out on my ear. I know her type, wanting a husband and a home and grabbing every chance they get. I really didn't think you'd be stupid enough to fall for her Little Miss Perfect act.'

Noah raised his eyebrows, perplexed. 'That's why you were horrible to her? You think she'd make me kick you out of here?'

His sister crossed her arms over her chest and leaned on the door frame. 'Well, I'm right, aren't I? That's exactly what's happened. And it didn't take her long.'

'For fuck's sake, Niamh!' Noah growled and stood up, grabbing his plate and empty bottle. 'I've only just started dating the woman. She hasn't made any demands of me whatsoever, and definitely nothing to do with you.' He marched past her into the kitchen, dumping his plate in the sink before turning back to her. 'I'm your brother, and I will always love you, but there's a limit to my patience and you've exceeded it.' When she opened her mouth to protest some more, he held up a hand. 'No, I don't want to hear it. Move in with Mr and Mrs Watkins by the end of the week or I'll drive you there myself. Are we clear?'

'Fine. You're a bastard, Noah, and I hate you.' Eyes glittering with fury, she turned towards the stairs.

'Wait,' he called after her. 'Before you leave, please hand over the rest of the hoard you and Reece found. I know you have it, and if we don't give it to the authorities, you're going to end up in jail too. I really don't want that for you, no matter what you've done.'

'Why?' she snarled. 'Surely it would make you happy? That way I'd be out of your way for a long time. Anyway, what makes you think I know where it is? Reece was going to handle the sale. Nothing to do with me.'

'You're lying.' Noah ground his teeth together to stop himself from shaking her. To prove that he wasn't bluffing, he dug out his wallet and took out one of the two silver coins currently in his possession. 'You were sloppy and left this behind in the living room.'

She went pale, but quickly recovered. 'Reece must have dropped it the day we found the treasure. Like I said, it wasn't me.'

He shook his head and sighed. 'Fine, have it your way, but when they eventually arrest you, don't come crying to me.'

She didn't reply, merely stomped off up the stairs and slammed her bedroom door so hard the windows rattled.

Noah sighed and dry-washed his face. He was so tired of this constant warfare; it would be wonderful to have some peace around here for a while. Although he felt guilty for asking his sister to move out, it wasn't for ever. He knew it was time to take a tough stance. He couldn't continue to mollycoddle her. She needed to learn some basic manners and not take it for granted that everything was going to be handed to her on a plate. Once she was ready to do her fair share of the chores and help look after the place, she'd be welcome to come back.

When she'd been younger, he had cut her some slack because she had been the one most affected by their mother's passing. For a long while afterwards, she had suffered from depression, and her way of coping with grief was to lash out at everyone and misbehave. In the end, Noah had forced her to see a doctor, who had prescribed antidepressants. Things calmed down a bit after that, but the carefree girl she'd been when their mother was alive only returned when she was with Reece or her other friends. Never at home. It was as if she was punishing her brother for being the only real family member left.

Well, Noah had had enough. He couldn't continue to make excuses for her bad behaviour and sullen, entitled attitude. It was time for Niamh to grow up and take responsibility for her own actions.

If she couldn't listen to her brother, perhaps Mrs Watkins would have more luck. He hoped so, as he was done trying. It was time for a change.

Autumn was already outside Alix's flat when she returned from work the next day, sitting at the top of the iron staircase. The bottle of wine and box of chocolates could be seen peeking out of a carrier bag next to her, but this time she didn't try to give them to Alix, so she assumed they were for Grandpa now. She could have told her sister he preferred beer or a nice malt whisky, but she knew he'd never be impolite enough to refuse a gift, so it didn't matter.

'I'll be five minutes,' she said curtly, squeezing past Autumn. 'I'm just going to change out of my work clothes.'

'Good idea. They look like they're strangling you.' Autumn shot her a critical glance. 'Was it "dress like the eighties" day at the library today or something? Or do you have to look buttoned up to work there?'

Alix ignored her sister's taunts and went inside, shutting the door behind her. She took a deep breath and tried to swallow the anger that swirled in her chest. Just because she didn't dress in short skirts or tight jeans all the time didn't mean she had no fashion sense. The blouse with a bow was actually in vogue at the moment. Perhaps it was a bit conservative, but then she had no interest in flashing her cleavage at the people who visited the library.

'Let it go,' she muttered, before taking another breath and going to change.

Just to show Autumn she wasn't as fuddy-duddy as her sister thought, she put on cut-off jeans shorts over black leggings, a baggy T-shirt and Converse sneakers. A hoodie she'd bought at a concert – Valhalla Storm, her favourite rock band – completed the outfit. Worried that the chain of her pendant might show through the material of the shirt, she hastily took it off and hid it under her pillow. The last thing she wanted was for Autumn to catch a glimpse of that. She'd covet it immediately.

Outside, she led the way to the small garage where her car was parked. She'd rented a space since it was more expensive to park on the street all the time.

As they drove south out of the city, Alix didn't bother to make small talk and her sister kept quiet for once. Perhaps she'd finally realised she couldn't talk her way out of the mess she'd created this time. Good. Alix had no plans to forgive her any time soon and hoped she would leave after they'd visited Grandpa. She had called him from work to tell him they were coming, as she didn't want to surprise him. He'd seemed pleased, and she hoped he wouldn't fall for any of Autumn's tricks. It wasn't her place to remind him what her sister had done, though. Autumn was his granddaughter and he had a right to be nice to her. She knew he loved her, faults and all.

'Here we are.' She parked and headed for the old-fashioned entrance to Pentwyn Place.

'Wow, swanky,' Autumn murmured, eyeing the place speculatively. 'This must have cost him a bomb.'

'Not really,' Alix replied. It had actually been quite expensive, but Autumn didn't need to know that. 'He only has a small flat. This way.'

Grandpa greeted them with smiles and hugs, and ordered tea and cake for them all. He chatted to Autumn as if nothing was wrong, enquiring about her life, although he threw Alix a glance from time to time as if to check that she was OK with seeing her sister. When she stayed mostly silent, a small frown appeared between his bushy eyebrows, but he didn't comment.

'So I hear you're getting married,' he said to Autumn, taking a sip of his tea. 'When's the wedding?'

Autumn choked on a piece of cake. 'What? No, there's no wedding.'

Grandpa pretended bewilderment, looking between his granddaughters. 'Oh? I thought Alix said you had a fiancé. I was hoping to hear all about it.'

'That's over. I dumped him.' Autumn shot Alix a dark look, then turned back to Grandpa with a fake smile. 'I'm afraid he was a bit of a cheapskate. Didn't even get me a proper diamond ring. Who needs a man like that, right?'

'I see. Sounds like you both dodged a bullet there,' Grandpa commented, clearly indicating that he knew Sean had belonged to Alix first. This earned her another glare from her sister.

'Yes, well, it's all water under the bridge.' Autumn quickly changed the subject. 'Tell me all about you, Grandpa. How are you liking it here?'

'I'm loving my little flat, and I've made lots of friends. There's always something to do. Moving here was the best thing for me.'

Autumn studied the high ceilings with cornicing, the marble fireplace that was a leftover from the building's heyday and the huge French windows leading to the garden. 'It's very fancy. Can't have been cheap. I would have thought you'd need to sell the farm to afford something like this, not give it away.'

And there it was. Alix had been waiting for a reference to Howell's End and wondered how Grandpa would handle it.

'Not at all,' he said, calmly taking a bite of his cake before continuing. 'I invested in a good pension scheme a long time ago, as well as life insurance for your grandmother. When I cashed them in, that was enough to buy this place. I have other assets too, so don't worry, there's enough left over for me to leave you a legacy after I'm gone as well. Not to mention the proceeds from selling this place. I gave Howell's End to Alix as she's the only one who wants to live there, and I really wanted it to stay in the family. That was my condition and she accepted it, but rest assured you'll get your fair share of my estate eventually. It's just that Alix has had most of hers in advance and she's signed a statement to that effect. Or have you changed your mind and want to live out in the boring sticks? I'm sorry, I should have asked, but I was under the impression nothing would make you move here.'

That was the expression Autumn had used the last time she'd been forced to spend the summer here, and now Grandpa was throwing it back in her face. Alix silently applauded him and watched as the corners of her sister's mouth turned down.

'No, I'm afraid I can't leave London at the moment. I've just landed a new job at Selfridges on one of the make-up counters. It pays a lot more than anything I could get around here. Plus, all my friends are in London.' Autumn hesitated, then added, 'I don't suppose you'd like to give me some of my share in advance too? I could use it to make a down-payment on a flat. My savings aren't quite enough as yet, so I'm having to live with Mum and Dad until I can afford to move out.'

Alix held her breath, wondering how Grandpa would deal with this request. It was reasonable, after all, but he shook his head, pretending to look chagrined. 'I'm sorry, my dear, but all my money is tied up in investments at the moment and I can't access it for a few years yet or I'll lose the interest. You'd be welcome to stay with Alix at Howell's End, I'm sure, but I understand if you prefer the bright lights of London to this old backwater. Just like your dad.'

Annoyance flashed in Autumn's eyes, but she schooled her features and smiled at him. 'No, no, that's fine. I wouldn't want to impose on my sister. And as I said, I can't leave London at the moment.'

'Well, it was lovely that you could come for a visit.' Grandpa smiled back. 'It's been a while. I hope you'll be back soon.'

They all knew it had been years actually, but he didn't need to spell it out. Autumn's cheeks turned red, but she busied herself with pouring more tea and changed the subject yet again.

Perhaps in order to appease her slightly, Grandpa asked Alix to get out their grandmother's jewellery box and allowed them to divide up the contents. Alix let Autumn have the lion's share, as she already owned the most important piece, but she was pleased to take possession of a gold bracelet and a couple of gold rings that Autumn considered too old-fashioned. They were exactly to Alix's taste, but she didn't say that out loud. If she had, her sister would have changed her mind.

As they drove back to town, Autumn chatted as if they were friends again, but Alix only gave one-syllable answers.

'For God's sake, how long are you going to sulk?' Autumn sighed as if she was the most put-upon creature on earth. 'Let it go, will you? I didn't even make a fuss about the damned house. Not that I want to live there, but Grandpa could have sold it and split the proceeds between us. Now I've got to wait years for my share. Is that fair?'

Alix shrugged. 'He didn't want to sell it. Like he said, he wants it to stay in the family and I had to promise to live there.'

'Ridiculous,' Autumn huffed. 'Why would anyone want to live

out in the middle of nowhere? And in that old hovel. He could at least have sold the fields, or are you taking up farming now in your spare time?'

'Hardly. He's rented them out to a neighbour.' Alix decided not to mention that the fields also belonged to her and she'd be receiving the rent, although she'd decided to share it with her grandfather whether he liked it or not.

'Hmph.'

'Should I drop you at the station?' Alix asked as they drove into Hereford across the new bridge that spanned the River Wye. The old one could be seen only a stone's throw away, and the sight of it always made her smile. It was beautiful.

'No, the Green Dragon Hotel. It's too late to go back today. I'll stay another night.'

No 'please' or 'thank you', Alix noted, but then she hadn't expected it. At least Autumn hadn't demanded to sleep at her place again, so she'd take that as a win. And with any luck, she wouldn't have to see her sister again for a long time, as there were unlikely to be any further visits. With Grandpa resisting Autumn's demands for her inheritance, there was nothing more for her here.

Good.

Chapter Twenty-Two

West Mercia, early June/Eggtið AD 874

When they finally headed back towards the settlement, it was almost morning and Merewen knew she was going to be exhausted all day. It didn't matter. Thoughts of their wonderful night together would keep her going. They had talked about the future and discussed plans for their escape, but they hadn't decided on a specific day yet. She hoped it would be soon. She couldn't wait to spend every day and night with Eirik.

'Let's walk back via the river,' he suggested. 'We can freshen up a little.'

Merewen's cheeks caught fire, but the dim light hid her embarrassment. And she didn't need to feel that way with him. He had already seen every part of her. What they'd done wasn't shameful, only what was right and proper between husband and wife. Besides, she definitely needed a quick wash.

They found a secluded spot with a sliver of sandy beach and quickly shucked off their clothing once more. Sceadu joined them in the water, enjoying a swim before proceeding to shake himself off all over them. After scrubbing themselves with sand, Eirik handed Merewen his cloak to dry herself off with. It wasn't ideal, the material scratchy and not very absorbent, but it was better than nothing.

'I'll hang it up when we get back,' he said, before using it himself.

Feeling languid and sated, they slowly made their way home hand in hand. Sceadu trotted in front of them, but suddenly stopped and growled low in his throat. His ears and hackles went up and his nose lifted.

They came to a halt next to the hound. 'What is it, boy? Is there someone nearby?'

Standing still, they listened for a moment, and Merewen caught sounds floating on the night air. As they were close to the river, any noises were amplified. Eirik must have heard it too.

'Stay here with Sceadu and keep quiet,' he whispered. 'I'm going to reconnoitre. If I'm not back very soon, hurry home, please.'

Merewen nodded and grabbed Sceadu's collar so that he wouldn't follow Eirik. She and the dog moved to stand behind the nearest clump of bushes and stayed silent and watchful. Time seemed to pass excruciatingly slowly, but just as she'd started to debate whether she ought to leave, Eirik returned. He didn't say anything, just took her hand and started striding towards the settlement. She didn't protest.

Once by the back fence, he finally spoke in a hushed whisper. 'There's a boatload of men down by the river. I think they're preparing to attack your father's settlement. I need to wake him to let him know so that he and his men can be prepared.'

'Are they coming now?' Her heart raced at the thought of violence, and the possibility that Eirik might be hurt. Killed even. She didn't want to lose him now. *Please, dear Lord, don't let him be harmed!*

'I think so. Soon at any rate. There's no time to lose. Slip into the hall and lie down, and when I raise the alarm, take charge of the women and children and make them hide somewhere.' He lifted her over the fence. 'Do you have a weapon of any kind?'

'My eating knife. I'll see what else I can find.'

'Please do. I'll make sure you get there safely, then I'm going to loop around so that I arrive via the front gate as if I've been out for a walk. Let's go.'

He vaulted the fence at the same time as Sceadu jumped, and they crept back towards the hall. Merewen took the dog inside this time, and fortunately no one stirred. Before lying down on her sleeping bench, she grabbed a heavy iron poker and placed it next to her under the blanket.

Now all she could do was wait.

Eirik returned silently the way he'd come. This time he had to wait while a guard patrolled past him, doing his rounds. The poor man had no idea he'd likely be killed by a silent arrow or knife before he had time to raise the alarm. Hastein – if it was him – wouldn't take any chances; surprise was his greatest advantage.

Once on the other side of the fence again, he circled back towards the main entrance. Out of sight of the two guards posted there, he jumped up and down for a while to make himself seem out of breath, then he took off at a sprint.

'Quick! Wake Beorthric! There are raiders down by the river and I think they're heading this way,' he panted when he reached the gate.

The two guards were startled by his sudden appearance and raised their pikes instinctively. 'What are you doing out so late?' one of them asked gruffly when he recognised Eirik. He lowered his weapon but still looked uneasy.

'I was out for a swim. It was so hot in the hall and I couldn't sleep. It was as I was coming back that I saw them. They're not far away and this is the closest settlement. We need to be prepared. One of you go and tell Beorthric, please! I'll stay here.'

They regarded him with suspicion. 'Are you sure you're not helping them? You're half Norse, from what I hear,' the older of the two guards said, narrowing his eyes.

'For the last time, I'm a comb-maker, not a warrior.' Eirik tried to sound as offended and impatient as possible. 'But if you'd rather I go, then just let me through.'

'Yes, that would be best.'

They opened the gate and allowed him to pass, but their gazes were still suspicious. 'Keep an eye out. They'll approach stealthily,' Eirik warned them.

'Fine. We'll be on our guard.'

He didn't spend any more time with them. If they didn't want to heed his words, that was up to them. Instead, he sprinted towards the main hall, rushing inside and over to the back chambers. He knocked on the one that belonged to Beorthric, and one of his men came to open the door. There was always someone sleeping on a pallet in there to guard their chieftain personally.

'Yes? What do you want?' The man was sleepy and surly, clearly irritated at being woken so late. Or early, since it was almost morning.

'There are raiders down by the river. I went for a night swim and saw them. It's likely they'll be heading this way. Please can you wake Beorthric? He needs to prepare.'

'Raiders?' The man sighed. 'Why is it always you bringing these tidings?'

Eirik shrugged. 'I like going for walks and to swim at night. I don't sleep well and it was too hot this evening.' The previous day had been sultry and it was true that the hall had felt unbearably stuffy at bedtime.

'Very well. Wait there.'

Beorthric emerged surprisingly quickly, buckling on his belt and the baldric for his sword. 'Eirik? What's going on?'

He told his tale yet again, growing impatient now but trying not to show it. Dawn would be upon them very soon and Hastein would definitely strike before then. 'All the women and children should be moved to a safer place. The hay loft perhaps? And all the men woken up. It might be best for everyone to pretend to be asleep but be ready for combat, with their weapons hidden under the blankets. That way the raiders won't be the only ones with an element of surprise.'

'Good idea. You go and wake Oslac and Burghild, then find Merewen. She can take charge of the women.'

Since that was exactly what Eirik had wanted, he hurried to do as he'd been told. Oslac wasn't best pleased to be roused in what he called 'the middle of the night', and especially not by Eirik. His searching gaze was even more suspicious than that of the guards at the gate, but he reluctantly went to join Beorthric.

Merewen pretended to have been asleep when Eirik shook her and relayed her father's orders, but she was soon herding the women and children out the door with swift efficiency. Eirik watched her go and hoped the gods would protect her. He must put her out of his mind for now, though, or he wouldn't be able to concentrate on fighting.

It wasn't long before everyone was in position, and not a moment too soon. Eirik hadn't been lying on his bench for more than a few moments when the door to the hall burst open and the attack began. He guessed that the guards hadn't seen the raiders coming, as no alarm had been raised. They were probably dead, but that wasn't his fault – he had tried to warn them after all.

'Now, men!' Beorthric bellowed, his voice ringing out above the din the marauders were making.

Men erupted from under their covers, weapons in hand. These

ranged from swords and spears to knives and axes, and for the most part Beorthric's men appeared to know how to handle them. The raiders were taken aback, as Eirik had envisaged, and their steps faltered, but not for long.

Hastein, who was indeed the leader, rallied quickly. 'Attack!' he shouted. 'They're just peasants!'

He caught sight of Eirik and froze for a moment, his eyes widening in recognition. Eirik stared back defiantly, letting his uncle see his disdain clearly. Hastein must have realised the implications of his nephew being alive – the fact that he should have checked and made sure, not left him behind while saving his own skin. For an instant, a shadow of guilt flickered in his gaze, his cheeks flushing, but then he sent Eirik a look of fury. They were on opposing sides now, and that made them enemies, kin or not.

Eirik waited to see if Hastein would give away their relationship, but his uncle was too far away to say anything and had to concentrate on fighting first and foremost. It was clear he wasn't best pleased, however, but Eirik didn't care. Hastein should have listened to him. They could have been settled somewhere peacefully by now, living a good life. Instead it had come to this.

Chaos reigned in the hall and the noise of fighting was almost deafening. The clang of metal striking metal rang out, as well as thumps and crashes as men were beaten and fell down and benches were smashed. There were grunts of effort and high-pitched screams of pain, as well as curses and profanities. Beorthric must once have been a formidable fighter, but he was older now and was one of the first to die. It was Hastein who delivered the blow, and Eirik swore under his breath. He'd been too far away to help and didn't have time to mourn now. He had to concentrate on his own opponents. Luckily he knew the way these men fought and had even sparred with some of them during training sessions, so he was able to parry most of their blows. A couple of times he was nicked by a sharp blade or punched by a sudden fist, but it wasn't anything life-threatening.

As he cast a quick glance around the hall, he could see that Beorthric's men had the upper hand. Led by a grimly determined Oslac, they had managed to kill quite a few of the raiders, but there were still some skirmishes going on. Meanwhile, Hastein had worked his way towards him, and after what seemed like ages, they were eye to eye.

'So Gunnar was right. He *did* see you at that market,' he snarled. 'You'll pay for your treachery!' he hissed, raising his sword.

'*My* treachery? How about an uncle who leaves his nephew behind to be slaughtered?' Eirik shot back. He didn't raise his voice because he'd rather not advertise the fact that they were related. Fortunately everyone else was concentrating on their own battles, and the din was such that no one could hear them. 'You didn't so much as call out to see if I was still alive,' he added.

Hastein's cheeks turned dark red, but his scowl didn't let up. 'There were three men attacking you. I didn't think you stood a chance. And I saw you go down after a mortal blow. You weren't moving.'

'Well, thank you for checking. As you can see, it wasn't mortal after all.' Eirik didn't have his own sword, as that was still at the cairn, but he'd managed to grab one off one of the other raiders earlier after he'd killed the man with his Saxon *scramasax*. He raised it now and stared his uncle in the eyes. 'Are you really going to fight me? Your brother's son?'

Hastein glared back. 'Not if you're willing to help me defeat these peasants.'

Eirik shook his head. 'No. I'm done with your way of living. Leave now and we can part amicably. You will find plenty of other targets.'

'Never.'

'Fine. Have it your way.' Eirik tightened his grip on the sword and prepared to fight the man who'd raised him. Sadness that it had come to this almost overwhelmed him, but then he thought of Merewen and hardened his heart. He was fighting for their future. For the right to live his life the way he wanted. If that meant having to kill his uncle, so be it.

Before they could begin, however, there was a commotion over by the door and Eirik's eyes briefly widened in horror as he saw two of Hastein's most trusted men dragging Burghild and Merewen into the hall. The women were pale with fright, Burghild crying loudly and begging for mercy on account of being pregnant. Hastein, never slow to see an advantage, must have noticed Eirik's reaction. Quick as a flash, he barged his way through the melee and grabbed Merewen, raising his sword blade to her throat.

His eyes glittered with triumph and malice as he taunted Eirik. 'You care about these two, do you, nephew? Well, well, that's interesting. Are you willing to honour your oath and follow me again, or should I slit this one's throat? I might spare her if you want to bring her along for our amusement.' He turned briefly towards Burghild and backhanded her. 'As for you, shut your mouth, woman! I can't bear the noise.'

Burghild stilled, her eyes wild with terror as she clutched her rounded stomach. Oslac finished off his current opponent and growled at the sight. He also threw Eirik a glare of hatred. The word for nephew was similar in Norse and Mercian, and he had probably understood the gist of the rest of Hastein's words too. Now he'd had it confirmed that Eirik was a true Norseman, he'd never let him leave here alive. *Skítr!*

There was no time to think about that right now, though.

'Let her go or I swear you'll regret it,' Eirik growled at his uncle. His insides had turned to ice and he was having trouble breathing. Hastein's blade glittered in the dawn light spilling in through the door, and he couldn't bear the thought of it slicing through the neck of the woman he loved.

Merewen was frozen in place, not moving so much as a finger. Her gaze found his, pleading for help, but Eirik didn't know what to do. Slowly he moved towards them until he was close enough but out of range of Hastein's blade, should he decide to turn it his way instead. The fighting all around them had mostly died down now, and they didn't need to shout to make themselves heard any longer.

He was frantically trying to come up with a way of killing his uncle while keeping Merewen alive. A diversion was needed, but what? In that moment, he saw Sceadu slinking inside the hall on silent paws. The dog took in the scene, his intelligent eyes noting the danger to his mistress. Eirik raised his left hand, as if urging caution to his uncle, but in actual fact he was signalling to the dog. Sceadu stopped behind Hastein, staying motionless in the shadows.

Eirik glanced over his shoulder and found Oslac watching him. A look passed between them, and he could tell the other man had seen the dog as well. They both knew they'd have to attack in unison if they were to have any chance of success. To that end, they silently declared a temporary truce for the sake of the women. Their own differences could be settled later. Oslac gave Eirik a small nod to show that he was with him.

'So what will it be? I don't have all day,' Hastein spat. 'Do I kill your woman or not?'

'Not,' Eirik said. At the same time, he gave the hound the sign for attack. Sceadu launched himself at Hastein from behind, sinking his sharp teeth into the man's backside.

Hastein stumbled, his sword sliding briefly into Merewen's flesh, but thankfully it looked to be merely a nick in the shoulder and not an important vein. She took the opportunity to throw herself sideways, careening into her sister, whose captor was also taken by surprise. Merewen pulled Burghild out of the man's grasp before he had time to register what was happening and tugged her to safety behind some of the local men. At the same moment, Eirik hurled himself forward and sank his sword into his uncle's stomach, following up with a slash of the *scramasax* for good measure, while Oslac and his men rushed in to attack the other two marauders.

'Noooo!' Hastein cried out, dropping his sword to cover a deep wound in his abdomen with both hands, as if that could stop the blood from flowing. He was bleeding from a deep gash on his shoulder too and stared in disbelief at Eirik, as if he hadn't truly believed him capable of killing him. Struggling to speak, he sank to his knees. 'How . . . could you?' His breath came in gasps, pain making him grimace. 'I raised you. Gave you my all. You . . . We . . . This wasn't how . . .'

'You should have listened to me,' Eirik told him, speaking quietly so that no one else would hear. 'It need not have come to this. We had enough riches already. Besides, you abandoned me when I needed you most.'

They stared at each other for a moment, registering the reality of the situation. The finality. Eirik hadn't wanted it to end like this. All he'd wished for was the freedom to live his life on his own terms. In peace. But he could see now that Hastein would never have settled for that. Would never have let him go. It wasn't in his nature.

Hastein opened his mouth as if to say one last thing, but it was beyond him. With a final laboured breath, he fell to the floor. His chest stopped rising and falling, and he went limp.

He was gone.

'May the Valkyries take you to Valhalla so you can continue to fight and feast for the rest of time,' Eirik murmured, bending to close his uncle's eyes. 'Thank you for your care when I was young.'

Oslac and his men had successfully defeated the final raiders and stood panting as they surveyed the gruesome scene in the hall. 'Merewen, get Burghild out of here,' Oslac ordered. 'You women can come back and clean up once we've carted out the bodies.'

Merewen nodded and did as he'd asked. Sceadu threw Eirik an enquiring glance, as if to check whether he needed more assistance. That almost made him smile, but he nodded at the dog, who left with his mistress. Then he turned and readied himself for one final battle, as he was sure Oslac wanted to kill him now. Although he didn't doubt he could defeat the man one-on-one, Oslac had backup so Eirik's fate was sealed. He'd go down fighting, of course, but the outcome was not in doubt. He was glad Merewen wouldn't have to witness it. That would have been awful. Better for her to merely be told about it afterwards.

To his surprise, however, Oslac sheathed his sword and came over to where he was standing.

'Don't think I'll let you have her,' he hissed. 'You may have saved us all tonight, but that's your final act here. This is my settlement now and I want you gone as soon as you've helped clear up this mess. You knew those men, which means you were one of them. I should kill you for that, but I owe you for Merewen and Burghild's lives. And my own and everyone else's, I suppose, so I'll let you walk away. But don't ever come back, understand?'

'I'll be gone,' Eirik replied, not promising anything else, then he bent to pick up his uncle's body and walked towards the door. He was surprised at Oslac's fairness, but extremely grateful for the reprieve. And no matter what the man said, there was still a chance he could escape with Merewen.

He just had to find a way, and hoped the gods would be on his side.

Chapter Twenty-Three

Hereford, early June, present day

Noah had checked in with Alix several times to make sure she and Morgan were both OK. He still didn't know what had upset her on Monday evening, but he didn't want to push for answers so early in their relationship. He gave her space, but by Wednesday he was jittery with impatience and sent her a text.

Hey, can we meet up for a drink tonight? You don't need to cook. I just want to see you. If it's easier, I'll come into Hereford and we can find a pub near your place. Xx

She replied almost immediately.

Yes thanks, that would be lovely. Pick me up at seven? Xx

'Yesss!' He smiled and put his phone away, then went to tell Aidan that he was in charge of the farm for the evening.

He arrived at Alix's place a few minutes early, but she was already on her way down the stairs outside her flat. The smile she gave him was radiant, and something in his chest loosened. He'd been so worried that she'd developed cold feet and didn't want to pursue a relationship with him for some reason. Yet here she was, looking gorgeous and very happy to see him.

He swung her off the final step and gave her a kiss, which made her blush adorably. 'Hey, you,' he murmured. 'I've missed you.'

'Same.' She took the hand he held out to her and he plaited their fingers together.

'Let's go.'

The pub they chose was only a stone's throw away, down near the river, and it was apparently very popular, as there was quite a crowd even though it was an ordinary weekday. Noah managed to find a small table for two in a corner and held out a chair for Alix. 'Tell me what you want and I'll go and get it. You'd better stay here or we'll have to stand up for hours.'

'A glass of white wine, please.'

He made his way through the throng and went to wait his turn by the bar. The staff were very busy, so he knew it would be a while. To pass the time, he studied the menu that was listed on a large chalkboard at the back. He was hoping Alix would want to stay and eat with him, as he'd only had time to wolf down a quick sandwich before he left. A more substantial meal would be welcome.

'Well, hello there. Are you going to buy me a drink as well?' A flirtatious voice and a hand on his arm made him turn to his left with a frown.

A beautiful woman had placed her fingers on his forearm, the well-manicured talons gleaming under the bar lights. Her features looked familiar, but he was fairly sure he'd never met her before. Long, straight glossy brown hair shot through with golden highlights hung over one shoulder, and she wore a lot of make-up even though he'd guess she didn't need it. Fake eyelashes, sooty eyeshadow and deep pink lip gloss. She was dressed in figure-hugging jeans and a top that showed a lot of cleavage, with a boxy little jacket on top that screamed designer wear. Chunky jewellery completed the outfit, with a row of bracelets that tinkled when she moved.

She was exactly the sort of woman he didn't want.

He shook her off. 'No, I'm taken,' he replied curtly, and turned towards the bar, hoping he would be served soon so he could get away from her.

'Aww, don't be like that. After all, we're practically family.'

'What?' He glanced at her again and frowned. 'How do you mean?'

She laughed and grabbed his arm again, but this time with both hands. As if she was imparting a great secret, she leaned in close and gazed up at him through her lashes. 'I'm Autumn, Alix's sister,' she told him. 'Didn't she tell you I was in town?' With a smirk she added, 'I guess she wanted to keep you all to herself.' She looked him up and down with an appreciative glint in her eyes. 'I can totally see why.'

'No, she didn't mention it.' He disengaged his arm from her tenacious grip once more. 'And there was probably a reason for that.'

He could see it now, the likeness between the two sisters. It was obvious when you looked past the superficial embellishments Autumn had added. To Noah, it was like staring at a fake version of Alix, a painted doll, and one he disliked on sight. The woman didn't appear affected by his instant disdain, though.

She pouted. 'Oh dear, has she been telling tales about me again? You shouldn't listen to her. She's just jealous of me. I really don't know why.' With a practised move, she threw her hair back over her shoulder and shook her head as if to show off the shiny tresses. 'But I'm sure you're a reasonable man. You'll make up your own mind about people. We should get to know each other better, don't you think?'

'No, I don't.'

It was finally Noah's turn, and he leaned over the counter to shout his order. It was the only way to make himself heard, as the noise levels were rising. He didn't ask Autumn if she wanted anything. He figured something fishy was going on here. If Alix had wanted him to meet her sister, she would have told him. And after what she'd said about Autumn stealing her fiancé, not to mention everything else, there was clearly bad blood between them. He'd prefer to check with her before doing anything else.

Autumn was nothing if not tenacious, however, as he soon found out. While he waited for his order to be prepared, she grabbed him around the waist from behind and stood on tiptoes to lean her chin on his shoulder. 'You're not even going to buy me one teensy-eensy little drink?' she asked. 'Isn't that a bit rude? I don't know anyone here apart from you and my sister.'

'What are you doing? Let go of me!' Feeling supremely uncomfortable, he tried to unwrap her arms from his middle by grabbing her wrists and forcefully removing them. Autumn hung on for a moment longer before loosening her grip.

She giggled. 'OK, OK, I'm just messing with you. Can I at least come with you to say hi to Alix?'

He paid and grabbed the drinks. 'Do as you please,' he said, stalking back towards the table where he'd left Alix.

But she was gone.

Alix settled at the table and took off her jacket, draping it over the other chair so that people would know it was taken. Butterflies danced in her stomach. It had been so good to see Noah again, and she regretted not letting him come over on Monday. Autumn had gone back to her hotel and Alix should have just put her out of her mind and concentrated on Noah. It shouldn't matter if her sister was in the vicinity. She wasn't staying.

The pub was full of customers and very noisy. Normally she preferred quieter places, but there was something cosy and romantic about being tucked away in a corner among so many people. She and Noah would be in a little bubble of their own and she didn't mind being squashed against him one bit. She shivered with anticipation, wondering what the rest of the evening would hold. Whatever it was, she was up for it.

He seemed to be gone a long time and she guessed he was having to wait in line. She hoped he wasn't getting impatient, but so far he'd seemed very laid-back about most things. Standing up, she craned her neck to try and find out where he was and if he was anywhere near the front. At first, she couldn't see anything, but then the crowd shifted and she suddenly caught sight of him.

But not just Noah – Autumn as well.

Oh, hell no!

Alix's stomach dropped and a ball of anxiety formed instantly. Why was Autumn here? She was supposed to have left today. And not only was she here, but she was holding on to Noah's arm, gazing up at him with that look that seemed to turn most men to putty in her hands. Alix's heartbeat sped up and her lungs constricted. She couldn't believe it was happening again, and right in front of her eyes this time. Autumn was going to take Noah away from her before their relationship had even properly begun.

'Dammit!' she whispered.

She'd glanced away for a moment, but when she looked back, Autumn had her arms around Noah's waist and was leaning coquettishly over his shoulder. Her beautiful hair – which Alix knew was chemically straightened, unlike her own unruly curls – hung like a shimmering waterfall down her back and touched Noah's arm when she moved. In that moment, Autumn turned around and stared straight at her, a triumphant smirk on her face. Was this payback for not accepting her apology? Or just her sister's way of saying that it didn't matter how far Alix moved, she'd never get out from under Autumn's shadow. And she would keep on taking everything away from her, no matter what.

Something broke inside Alix at the sight, and she couldn't breathe. She had to get out of there before she made a complete fool of herself. There was no way she was watching her sister snatch yet another man away from her. It was simply too painful.

Grabbing her jacket, she pushed her way to the door and out into the cool night. She stopped for a moment to lean over with her hands on her knees, trying to suck some much-needed air into her lungs. It took a while, but finally she managed it, then she started walking. Up Bridge Street, then right into King Street, passing the cathedral, which brooded silently over its surroundings. Along Broad Street and past the Green Dragon Hotel, where Autumn was apparently still a guest.

'Damn her!' Alix hissed. Why did she always have to ruin everything? Why couldn't she be happy with what she had? Wasn't it enough for her to be the golden child, the one their parents doted on and whose every wish was fulfilled? Why was it never enough?

And how was she going to remain civil to Noah from now on? They were neighbours, and that wouldn't change. They'd have to interact occasionally, but it would be so painful. She'd have to try and appear unconcerned. It wasn't as if she hadn't had a lot of practice at that already. In fact, she'd perfected a mask of indifference, because any time she showed her true emotions, Autumn was delighted.

She stopped to catch her breath again, and as she calmed down, some measure of reason returned. Perhaps she'd overreacted. Hadn't she sworn that she wouldn't give in to Autumn so easily any longer? That she would fight for what she wanted and stop being such a doormat. And shouldn't she have stayed to at least confirm that Noah had ditched her for her sister? After all, he'd seemed so pleased to see her earlier. Was she doing him a disservice in believing him that fickle?

But he'd let Autumn hug him from behind. The image of that still burned her retinas and made her vaguely nauseous. At the same time, anger built inside her, making her stop and clench her fists. Had Noah actually allowed her sister to take liberties, or had Autumn just accosted him? Alix wouldn't put it past her. Come to think of it, she hadn't seen him reciprocate. The instinct to flee had kicked in and she'd run away before verifying what was truly happening.

She sighed and unclenched her fists, then turned to retrace her steps. If she didn't go back and find out for sure, she'd regret it. No matter how painful it turned out to be, she had to know the truth.

She was about to turn into Broad Street again when she became aware of running footsteps. As she lifted her gaze, she saw Noah sprinting towards her. He came to a halt in front of her, out of breath and with an anxious expression on his face.

'Alix! What happened?' he huffed. 'Why did you leave?' He reached out, taking her hands in his. 'Are you feeling ill?'

She almost laughed at that. She wasn't sick, but she was so far from OK it was almost stratospheric. Pulling out of his hold, she took a step back and stared up at him.

'No, I'm not, but I saw you with Autumn. It was like déjà vu, you know? I just couldn't watch.'

'Alix, what the hell?' He grabbed her shoulders and bent to look her in the eyes. 'I don't want your sister! What on earth gave you that idea?'

'You were letting her touch you, hug you,' Alix mumbled, a catch in her voice. She cleared her throat. 'And when she sets her sights on someone, that's usually it. Game over for me.'

Noah gave her a little shake. 'No! I wasn't *letting* her do anything. She accosted me and wouldn't let go even though I told her to several times. Honestly, she was like a leech or some kind of octopus. Someone needs to teach her about not crossing personal boundaries.'

The knot of anxiety inside her began to loosen and Alix felt as if she could breathe properly again. 'Oh. I was really hoping you'd say that. I, um, was on my way back to check. I realised I was a bit hasty and should have at least made sure you were a willing participant.'

'Well, thank God for that!' Noah looked both relieved and exasperated. 'Listen to me, please. I definitely wasn't willing. I don't find her attractive in the slightest, I swear to God!'

'You don't?' Alix was having trouble assimilating his words.

'No, not at all.' Noah let go of her and shoved a hand through his hair distractedly. 'I mean, objectively I can see that she's a beautiful woman, but she's not the kind I want. Alix, I want *you*, no one else. Only you.'

She swallowed hard, emotion clogging her throat. 'Are you sure? I'm nothing special. In fact, I'm plain and boring. She's the fun sister.'

'The hell you are!' Noah placed his hands either side of her face and stared at her intently. 'You're not the slightest bit boring to me. And you're not plain either. You're gorgeous. I love your crystal eyes, your sharp little nose, your freckles, your unruly hair that's just begging for me to push my fingers into it, not to mention your tempting mouth.' He added in a husky voice, 'I want you, Alix. Do you believe me?'

In a daze, she nodded. He seemed sincere, and he was here with her, not with Autumn. That had to count for something, right?

'Where's my sister?' she asked.

'Who cares? Not our problem. I ran out of the pub without checking. She's probably drinking your wine or my beer right now, flirting with some other poor schmuck. Whoever he is, he's welcome to her.'

Alix digested this and finally nodded. 'OK.'

'Yes? Are we good?' When she nodded again, he pulled her face to his and gave her a fierce kiss, as if he was branding her. 'Then let's forget about drinks so I can show you just how much I want you. Is that all right with you?'

'Mm-hmm.' Alix was completely on board with this. Who needed a drink when you could have Noah's kisses instead?

He smiled. 'So are you going to invite me to yours, or do you want to come home with me?'

'My flat is closer. This way.' She took his hand and towed him along the alley and up the stairs. She managed to retrieve her keys from her handbag and opened the front door with shaking fingers. Once inside, Noah shut it behind them and kicked off his sneakers. Alix removed her shoes as well, and as soon as she'd finished, she found herself pushed against the back of the door while Noah started to kiss her like there was no tomorrow. She put her arms around his neck and closed her eyes, revelling in the sensation of being in his embrace again.

This was what she'd wanted ever since the last time. This was bliss.

Noah's body was hard up against hers and she loved the feel of it. She could tell how aroused he was already, and it gave her a heady sense of power. *She* had done that to him. He truly wanted her. She could hardly believe it, but his body didn't lie.

His hands were roaming and he pushed warm callused fingers in underneath her shirt.

'Off,' he ordered, kissing his way down her neck and nipping the junction where it met her shoulder. She complied and let him pull the shirt over her head. 'Mm, nice,' he whispered when he caught sight of the black lace bra she was wearing. 'But that needs to go as well.'

Deft fingers undid the clasp at the back and she slipped it down her arms.

'You too,' she demanded, tugging at the hem of his T-shirt. He grinned and wrangled himself out of it faster than she'd thought possible. She drew in a sharp breath at the sight of his bare chest. He was magnificent, hard troughs and hollows accentuating the muscles. With tentative fingers, she reached out to touch him, while he did the same to her.

'So beautiful,' he murmured, palming her breasts and rubbing the taut nipples with his thumbs. 'So perfect.' Then he bent to tease them with his mouth and Alix lost herself in the delicious sensations that shot through her.

His fingers moved further down and dived inside her clothing. He found the exact right spot and began to stroke her, making her moan and breathe hard. She'd never been this turned on in her life. He had a magical touch, seemingly knowing just what she needed. But there was something missing.

'I need you. All of you. Now!' she whispered, kissing him again deeply, hungrily.

'Yes.' Somehow he got her out of her leggings and underwear, then lifted her legs and wrapped them around his waist. 'I want you right here,' he told her, his voice deep and gravelly with desire. 'I can't wait.'

'Please.'

'Do I need protection?' He was undoing his trousers while still balancing her with one hand. 'I'm clean.'

'No. We're good.' She hated having these sorts of conversations and had never allowed anyone inside her bare before, but Noah was different. She wanted to feel him properly and he wasted no time in fulfilling her wish.

He surged inside her, and she drew in a sharp breath. It felt so good, so right. He fitted her perfectly, and as he set up an even rhythm, hitting just the right spot on every thrust, she could already feel her body getting ready to combust.

'Mm, Alix, you feel incredible,' he muttered, quickening his pace.

The door behind her rattled, and her back was probably going to be sore later, but Alix didn't care. There was only the feel of him moving, the wonderful things he was doing with his mouth and fingers, and the imminent eruption. It didn't take long before they both shuddered in a pleasurable release that seemed to go on for ages.

When Alix finally came down to earth, she was sandwiched between the door on one side and Noah's body on the other, and she wanted to stay there for ever. He held her tight, keeping his hands under her thighs so she wouldn't fall, and placed a soft kiss on her shoulder before looking into her eyes.

'You OK? I'm sorry, I should have taken you to your bed.' He gave her a sheepish smile. 'I just got a bit carried away.'

She smiled back and kissed his mouth. 'I'm fine. Probably have splinters in my back, but you can dig those out later.'

'It will be my pleasure. Maybe in the shower?'

'Good idea. If you put me down, I'll show you the way.'

He nuzzled her neck again. 'Nuh-uh. Now I've finally got you in my arms, I'm not letting go of you yet. Just point.'

Chapter Twenty-Four

West Mercia, early June/Eggtið AD 874

Merewen only saw Eirik once more before he left the settlement. She'd noticed Oslac's suspicious glares and understood that he'd realised there was something going on between them. It was clear he didn't like it, and she heard whispers of how he'd ordered Eirik to leave and never come back.

They didn't have a chance to speak, but when she and the other women had finally finished cleaning up the hall and setting it to rights, she went to her hut, hoping he'd find her there. She was careful to bring Sceadu, and to leave the door open so that Eirik could slink in if the opportunity presented itself. He didn't come, and eventually she had to return to the hall.

Frustration ate away at her. She had wanted to at least say goodbye before he left and ask if he was going to find a way to return. Perhaps snatch her away in secret. He had promised not to leave her, but Oslac was apparently keeping an eye on both of them. She was forced to watch with some of the others as Eirik left carrying a small bundle.

'Thank you for your hospitality,' he said, not looking her way.

Oslac nodded, and when Eirik had disappeared through the gate she heard him mutter, 'Good riddance.'

Merewen was tired and listless, and operating on very little sleep the night before. It made her feel like weeping, but she managed to keep the tears at bay. She went to oversee the cooking of the evening meal, but when she entered the hall, Burghild was already there, clearly in charge once more. Now that their father was dead, there was no one to stop her taking up the reins, especially as her husband was the owner of this settlement henceforth.

With a look of triumph, Burghild stared Merewen up and down. 'It's a good thing you're going off to the monastery soon. Seems you have a lot of sins to atone for. I'll make sure you're sent on your way as soon as possible.'

'I've done nothing wrong,' Merewen retorted, raising her chin. She may have slept with Eirik, but in both their eyes they were married, and he'd promised to go through the formalities with her as soon as possible. She trusted that he'd keep his word.

'Don't be insolent! Now go and fetch some more grain,' Burghild ordered. 'Then grind it yourself. That should be a fitting punishment for consorting with the enemy. To begin with, at any rate. I'm sure I can find you more chores when you're done with that.'

Grinding flour was a menial task usually carried out by slave women. Merewen didn't protest, however, and went to do as she'd been bid.

When her sister was finally satisfied that she had been punished enough for one day, she went to sit on her bench to catch her breath for a moment. Her arms and shoulders ached from pushing the heavy quern stone around, but it was nothing compared to the pain in her heart. Sceadu came padding over and pushed his nose into her hand.

'I'm glad you're still here,' she whispered. 'You make me feel less alone.'

She was about to pat him, but felt something wet on her palm. At first she thought he was licking her, but when she looked down, she could see that he had deposited something slimy there. 'What on earth . . .?'

She glimpsed a piece of bark with runes scratched into the surface and quickly closed her fist around it. Her heart began to beat erratically and she tried to calm her breathing. Was this what she thought it was? To hide her reaction, she bent over Sceadu's head and leaned her cheek on the soft fur between his ears. 'Thank you,' she whispered.

After making a fuss of the hound for a little while, she stood up and headed outside and over to the privy. There, she finally allowed herself to look at the bark properly. She had been taught basic reading and writing by her mother, who had been raised in a noble household. As well as the Latin letters, she'd also learned to decipher runes, as some older texts were written using those. Eirik knew she could read, as she'd told him so when he showed her that he had carved her name in runes on the comb he'd made for her. What she saw now was a very short message from him: *Cairn. Tonight.*

She reached inside her tunic and pulled out the crystal pendant he'd given her. Grasping it in her fist, she closed her eyes and whispered, 'I'll be there.'

Somehow she'd have to find a way to escape and bring Sceadu with her. There was no way she'd leave without him.

Eirik paced impatiently outside the cairn, peering through the darkness and gradually losing hope as the hours went by and Merewen didn't appear. He'd bought a sturdy horse soon after leaving Beorthric's settlement – he couldn't stand to think of it as Oslac's – and it waited nearby, calmly grazing.

What if she couldn't get away? He guessed Oslac would be watching her like a hawk, as he had done all day. Hopefully she'd received his message, but if Sceadu had dropped it or not delivered it, all was lost. The hound had seemed to understand when Eirik urged him to give it to his mistress, but he was only a dog after all. He might have thought it was a game and spat it out somewhere.

'Aargh! This is unbearable,' he whispered, pacing some more.

The horse had come with two saddlebags and was loaded with his belongings, which he'd retrieved from the cairn. He had bought some provisions for the first part of their journey and packed those as well. And he'd dug up his treasure hoard, as well as those of Hastein's two henchmen. Hastein's own was missing, however. Eirik had thought he'd remembered the exact spots where all three men had been digging, but his uncle's loot wasn't there. The sneaky old man must have moved it, the way Eirik himself had done, not trusting anyone. It didn't matter, though. Three out of four was more than enough, and the two men would never return for theirs as they were both dead.

More time went by, and he had almost lost all hope when suddenly a shadow came loping towards him, almost knocking him off his feet. 'Sceadu!' he whispered, bending to greet the dog, who licked him enthusiastically. When he looked up, Merewen was rushing up the hill with long strides, and he ran down to meet her. 'You came!'

He caught her around her waist and swung her into his arms, joy bubbling up inside him. Without putting her down, he kissed her soundly, then finally allowed her to slide down his body to stand on her own two feet again. She smiled, hugging him tight. Sceadu was dancing around them, wagging his tail, and Eirik wanted to laugh out loud. But there was no time to lose. They needed to leave immediately.

'Did you bring anything?' he asked, taking her hand to tow her up the final stretch towards the cairn.

'No. I couldn't risk it. Only Sceadu, and Oslac did me a favour because he kicked him out of the hall before bedtime.' Merewen was slightly out of breath, but he heard the happiness in her voice at having managed to escape. 'I slipped out once everyone was asleep. Oslac had posted a guard at the door, who tried to stop me, but I said I was only going to the privy.'

'Good. Let's go then.'

He led her towards the horse, but as he was about to boost her into the saddle, Sceadu barked a warning. When he turned around, he saw Oslac and two of his men coming up the hill towards them, smirking.

'Thought you could get away with taking my sister-in-law, did you?' Oslac snarled. 'No Norse dog is having her as long as I'm here to prevent it.' He pointed at Merewen. 'And you, you'll regret trying to sneak out, mark my words. No monastery will want you when I'm through with you.'

Eirik hadn't been allowed to keep the sword he'd taken during the previous night's fighting, but he'd retrieved his own from the cairn, as well as his battleaxe. He pulled out both now and held one in each hand. Hastein might not have been the best of men, but he had spent hours training his nephew in fighting techniques. Eirik knew how to wield both weapons at once and he was about to show this Mercian cur just what kind of opponent a Norseman could make.

'You'll have to go through me first,' he said through gritted teeth. He'd fought three men before and survived. He could do it again. 'Merewen, my love, get on the horse and ride away from here, please. I'll come and find you afterwards. Go to where we were last night.' He knew she could easily find her way to the bathing place by the river from here.

'No. I'm not leaving you. We either kill them or die together,' she vowed, pulling his *scramasax* out of its sheath and taking a stance beside him. 'It would be a pleasure to gut that disgusting pig who thinks that rutting with his maiden sister-in-law is not a sin,' she added scornfully.

Eirik sent her a quick smile, pride blooming in his chest. His woman was strong and fearless, exactly as she should be.

Oslac's expression darkened. 'You won't get the chance.'

'We'll see about that,' Eirik muttered.

Without waiting for Oslac and his men to advance, he shouted a Norse war cry, then 'Sceadu, attack!' He ran down the slope at full tilt, closely followed by Merewen and her dog, and set about using every trick he'd ever learned from his devious uncle.

One man was dispatched almost instantly as Eirik's axe bit into his neck. He went down like a felled ox and lay twitching on the ground before his soul departed. Meanwhile, Eirik turned his attention to Oslac, judging him to be the more dangerous opponent. He trusted that Sceadu would help Merewen with the other man, at least for a while.

Oslac was incandescent with rage, clearly livid because he had lost one henchman already. He threw himself into the fight with the ferocity of a wild animal, reminding Eirik of the berserkers he'd seen occasionally during various battles. Despite this and Oslac's obvious strength, which was increased right now by his fury, Eirik more than held his own against him. He'd learned to deal with such men by letting them tire themselves out, and he therefore kept Oslac at arm's length, dancing out of the way time and time again after inflicting tiny cuts and the occasional blow.

'Did you really think I was going to let you rape Merewen?' he taunted. 'She's too good for a boor like you.'

'She's nothing but a Norseman's whore,' Oslac snarled. 'I don't like used goods, but I'll make an exception in this case. She's resisted me for too long.'

'Didn't you hear her? She'd rather die than have you touch her, but she welcomed me with open arms.' Eirik grinned, and ducked to avoid a particularly vicious slash from Oslac's sword.

The man was definitely tiring now, and there was sweat pouring down his brow. He swiped at it impatiently with his sleeve and went on the attack once more. Eirik raised his sword and pretended he was going to strike a blow with that, but in the next instant he swung the long-handled axe instead. It sank into the fleshy part of Oslac's upper arm, and he cried out a curse, staring at the wound in disbelief.

Blood began to run down onto his hand in a steady stream, making his grip on his sword handle slippery. 'May all the saints curse you!' he screamed. 'I . . . will *not* . . . let you . . . have her!' he panted in between thrusts.

By now, Eirik was merely toying with him. With a sword arm that was likely going numb, Oslac didn't have the power to defeat him any longer. Eirik wanted him to realise this before he finished him off, and to really grasp the fact that he couldn't have what he wanted, but a glance over at Merewen made him come to his senses. This was not the time to gloat and play games. He couldn't afford to be that vindictive.

'Go join your God, wherever that is, although I hope he punishes you for your sinful behaviour,' he hissed. After executing a swift feinting manoeuvre with the axe, he sank his sword into Oslac's heart. Then he swivelled round and rushed to aid Merewen.

She'd been valiantly holding the third man at bay, greatly helped by an almost rabid Sceadu. The dog jumped around behind the man, growling, barking and nipping wherever he could reach, while twisting out of the way of the sharp sword. Meanwhile,

Merewen was brandishing the *scramasax* and trying to use it to deflect the blows from the sword. The two weapons clashed repeatedly as the man aimed to disarm her so that he could grab hold of her and force her to return to the settlement. He had her backing up towards the cairn step by step, but she still hadn't lost her grip on the knife. Even though she was almost sobbing with the effort, and clearly terrified, she wasn't giving up.

Eirik ran after them with another war cry, which had the desired effect. The man turned his head for an instant towards this new threat, and Merewen took the chance to pounce. She slashed the long knife across the man's chest, and at the same time Sceadu hurled himself into the air and sank his teeth into his forearm. When Eirik reached them, he made short work of finishing him off. There was no point prolonging the fight and he wanted to get as far away from here as possible, quickly.

As the man sank to the ground, Eirik gathered both his weapons in one hand and put an arm around Merewen's waist, drawing her close. 'Are you hurt?' He peered at her intently. It was another light summer night, but it was still dark enough that he couldn't see every detail clearly.

'I'm fine. A few cuts, that's all. I just . . . I can't breathe. So tired.' She sank to the ground, kneeling while she tried to catch her breath.

'What about the wound my uncle inflicted on you? I didn't get a chance to ask you earlier.'

'Wasn't too deep. I've bandaged it.' She shuddered. 'I thought Oslac was going to hurt you. I . . . I couldn't bear to think it.'

'Never. He was no match for me. Shh, *ást mín*, it's over.' Eirik kneeled beside her and she sagged against him. He held her until she had calmed down. 'They can't hurt you any more. I'm here. I've got you,' he murmured soothingly, lightly kissing her forehead, nose and cheek, and finally, when she had caught her breath, her mouth. He glanced at the dog, who sat next to them licking one paw. 'Are you well, Sceadu? Did the man harm you?'

The hound gave a short bark, then shook himself. He didn't appear to have suffered more than perhaps a scratch. Eirik resolved to check him over thoroughly in the morning.

'When you're ready, we should go, *unnasta*. Best not to linger here in case anyone comes looking for them.'

She nodded and slowly let go of his tunic, which she'd been clutching. 'Yes, you're right. Let's leave now. I want to be far away from this place by morning.'

Eirik couldn't agree more. He helped her to stand, then boosted her onto the horse and mounted behind her, after securing his weapons to his belt. Taking one last look around to make sure there were no other threats, he grasped the reins and urged the horse into a canter.

'Come, Sceadu,' he called out, 'we're going to your new home.'

As they set off, with the dog loping beside them, he allowed himself to relax properly for the first time in weeks.

They were free.

Chapter Twenty-Five

Hereford, early June, present day

For the rest of the week, Alix spent the nights at Noah's place, as she knew he needed to be at home in order to get up early and do his work around the farm. It was easy enough for her to commute to the library, and she didn't mind. Vaughan Court was lovely, and he had a much bigger bed than her, so it was a win–win.

Noah had told her about his latest fight with Niamh, and the fact that she had moved out temporarily. Alix was secretly relieved, as it would have been awkward meeting up in the mornings knowing that Niamh might have heard what she and Noah had been up to at night.

On the Saturday morning, before dawn, she was woken by Shadow, who was standing by the bed whining softly and putting his wet nose on her bare arm. Noah didn't appear to have heard – he was a very deep sleeper – so Alix extricated herself from the covers.

'What's the matter? You need to go out?' she whispered to the dog, stroking his soft head. 'OK, hang on.'

She found one of Noah's T-shirts, which was like a minidress on her, and tugged it over her head. Then she tiptoed down to the kitchen, closely followed by the dog, whose tail was wagging as if he was grateful that she'd understood.

The house was silent, and it was barely light. Alix opened the back door and Shadow shot out quickly to do his business. She stepped into a pair of Niamh's wellies and followed him into the courtyard, where she stood still, breathing in the fresh air. The birds were starting their chorus, but only a few of them were awake as yet. It was as if they were practising for the day, their songs not quite complete. A few bats were still swooping around, lightning-fast as they caught whatever insects were about. Noah had shown her a whole clump of baby bats hanging in one of the old stables the previous day. They were tiny and cute, huddled together.

Shadow came trotting back towards her, but stopped a few yards away and turned to scent the air. His ears went up and his head tilted to one side, while he lifted a front paw.

'What is it?' Alix breathed, peering towards the entrance to the courtyard. She couldn't see anything, but the dog had clearly heard a noise.

There shouldn't be anyone about at this time of day. The two youths who helped out around the farm, Aidan and Pete, wouldn't be up yet, and Alix shivered, crossing her arms around her middle. Noah had told her about some recent thefts of farm equipment and quad bikes in this area, and even sheep rustling. Was there a thief about?

She had to find out.

'Come on, boy,' she urged Shadow in a whisper, then set off towards the other side of the stable yard. She felt silly walking about in nothing but an overlarge T-shirt and wellies, but there was no time to consider that.

At the corner of the last building, she stopped and peeked around it, putting a hand on Shadow's collar to stop him from venturing further until she knew whether it was safe. At first, she couldn't see anything. There were vague shapes in the burgeoning morning light, but nothing moved. The dog's ears were swivelling like antennae, but he didn't bark. Surely he would do so if there was an intruder? It was his job to guard the place, as well as help with the sheep.

'I can't see anything,' she murmured, but just then she caught a faint beam of light in one of the barns. The oldest one, which was furthest from the house and normally only used for storing odds and ends, apparently.

Shadow whined and Alix looked at him. 'Why aren't you growling?' she whispered, puzzled. 'Is it someone you know?'

Were Aidan or Pete up extra early? But she was sure Noah had said the two teenagers had this weekend off. They'd make the most of it by sleeping in. Making up her mind, she sprinted back towards the house. 'Come, Shadow. We need to get Noah.'

The dog seemed to understand and followed her, reaching the back door before she did. Together they ran up the stairs and burst into the bedroom, panting. 'Noah, wake up!' Alix shook him, and he blinked at her groggily before sitting up.

'What's the matter?' He took in the half-light and frowned. 'It's not even morning yet.'

'There's someone in one of your barns. Shadow heard them, and I saw a light. A torch maybe. Hurry! If it's a thief, we need to catch them.' She grabbed her phone from the nightstand. 'I'll take this with me so we can call the police.'

Galvanised into action, Noah swiftly pulled on a pair of jogging trousers and rushed downstairs with Alix and Shadow at his heels. She heard him mutter, 'Bastards,' and totally agreed with him. Thieves were despicable.

She hoped they weren't too late to catch them.

*

Noah slowed down when he reached the entrance to the courtyard. He didn't want to give the thieves the chance to catch sight of him and flee. He needed to catch them in the act. When Alix caught up with him, he held out his hand.

'Please can I borrow your phone? I want to film them so we have clear evidence,' he whispered.

'Sure.' She unlocked the screen and turned on the video function before handing him the mobile.

'Thanks. Follow me, but please hold on to Shadow's collar.'

Together the trio made their way towards the old barn. He couldn't see any light and wondered if they were too late. Or perhaps Alix had just imagined it. There was no sound either, although a glance at Shadow confirmed that the dog could hear something. Whoever it was must have gone further into the barn. Noah wondered what on earth they thought they'd find in there. All his more valuable equipment was stored in a different barn with double locks and an alarm. Perhaps they were looking for antique farm stuff. There might be one or two items that could fetch a good sum at a salvage yard.

As they came closer, he held up a hand to signal that Alix and Shadow should stay behind him. He tiptoed up to the wide doors, which always stood open, and peeked inside. At first he couldn't see anyone, but then he caught light and movement over in one corner. The torch beam wasn't moving now, but was pointing in one direction as if it had been put down. A shadowy figure moved across it, and he drew in a sharp breath. He recognised that shape.

Pressing the screen to start the video filming, he moved closer on silent feet. Alix and Shadow hung back, but he sensed they were still behind him. There was an old stall at the end of the barn, piled high with junk, and when he reached it, he stopped to look around the dividing wall. Niamh was leaning over an old cider barrel, her head and one arm deep inside it.

Noah held up the phone and silently filmed his sister as she extracted various plastic bags. Each one seemed to hold something different, but the one thing they all had in common was that they glittered in the light from the torch. When she straightened up and bent to pick up the bags and put them in a rucksack, he decided it was time to intervene. He passed the phone to Alix, who had come up behind him, and indicated that she should take over filming. She nodded.

Noah stepped into the stall. 'So this is where you hid it, eh?' he said, planting himself firmly in the way of any escape attempt. 'I knew it had to be here somewhere.'

Niamh jumped, and was so startled she dropped the bag she was holding. It hit the floor and split open, a pile of silver ingots spilling out. 'N-Noah? What . . .? How . . .?'

'Not pleased to see me?' He crossed his arms over his chest. 'I can't say I'm very happy with you either. You do realise I'm going to have to hand you over to the police, right? I gave you a chance to come clean, but now I've caught you red-handed. You're obviously Reece's accomplice.'

Niamh's expression darkened and she sneered. 'You weren't always such a goody two-shoes yourself. I remember what you and your friends got up to in London, although you were lucky and never got caught. This stuff is mine and Reece's. Finders, keepers. You're not taking it away from us. We didn't want to have to share with you, that's why we didn't declare it.'

'Oh yeah? And how are you going to stop me? We have proof of everything and I'm not letting you walk out of here until the police arrive.' He indicated Alix, who was now standing next to him with the video still going.

'Stupid bitch,' Niamh snarled. 'I really don't know what he sees in you.'

Noah was about to defend his girlfriend when Niamh lunged

towards Alix unexpectedly. Before he had time to react, she had pulled a knife from her pocket and grabbed Alix round the throat. She held the knife under her chin, her eyes wild as she stared at Noah in defiance.

'Let me leave with the treasure or I'll kill your precious girlfriend,' she threatened.

Alix's eyes were huge and she'd frozen in place. Noah stopped breathing for a moment as sheer terror coursed through him. His sister was clearly desperate, cornered, and would likely carry out her threat. Or at the very least, hurt Alix badly. What was he to do? He couldn't allow her to get away with this. Had to stop her from harming Alix. Another image slithered into his mind, superseding the current scene.

A middle-aged man with long grey hair holding a huge sword at a woman's throat. Another woman, clearly pregnant, her eyes bulging in terror. Two more men, dressed in knee-length tunics and trousers, also carrying swords. Fear such as he'd never felt before swept through him, almost buckling his knees, but he knew he couldn't give in to it. He had to do something . . .

He blinked and returned to the present, his heart beating furiously. The fear was real, and it was for Alix, not some shadowy woman in his mind. He had to save her, but how?

Niamh shook Alix a little. 'Throw him the phone,' she ordered. 'Delete the video, Noah. *Now!*'

He caught the mobile even though Alix's aim was unsteady. Looking down at the screen, he turned off the video but saw that it had only recorded a few seconds. Where was the rest? He almost smiled as he realised Alix must have turned it on and off surreptitiously. What was on the screen was nothing but a short snippet. The rest would still be there saved separately. Excellent. This was not the time for gloating, though, as she was still in supreme danger.

'Look, I'm deleting it now,' he said, holding up the screen briefly so that his sister could see him pushing the delete button in the right-hand corner. He quickly turned the phone away afterwards so that she wouldn't notice that there were other recordings before that one.

Niamh smiled. 'Good. Now finish putting the plastic bags in the rucksack and throw it to Alix.'

'You won't get away with this,' Noah warned. 'Even if you leave this barn today, the police will find you.'

'Shut up! I'll be long gone. We've planned it all. I'm going abroad and Reece will come and find me when they let him out.'

'You're going to spend the next ten years on your own in a foreign country?' He couldn't understand her thinking.

'It won't be that long. With good behaviour, he'll be out much sooner. Now stop stalling! Do you need a reminder of who's in charge here?' In front of Noah's horrified gaze, Niamh lowered the knife and sank it into Alix's forearm before putting it against her throat once more.

Alix cried out and gripped her arm with her other hand, trying to staunch the blood that had started to flow rapidly.

'For fuck's sake, are you crazy?' Noah shouted. 'Just hang on and I'll do it.'

He bent to gather up the remaining bags of treasure, as well as the spilled ingots, and stuffed it all in Niamh's rucksack. Straightening up, he stopped for an instant and made eye contact with Shadow, who had been watching the scene with rapt attention. 'Ready to catch?' he asked Alix. Then, as he threw the rucksack, he hissed '*Attack!*'

Shadow didn't hesitate. He launched himself at Niamh and sank his teeth into her thigh. At the same time, Alix caught the rucksack, but instead of handing it to Niamh, she used the momentum of the bag to twist around and smash it into the other woman's face. Niamh shrieked, in both pain and surprise, and fell to the ground. She lost her grip on the knife, which clattered to the floor, and Noah dived for it, throwing it into a far corner. Then he hurled himself on top of his sister, straddling her and grabbed her flailing arms, pinning her to the ground. Shadow barked and growled, putting his paws on Niamh's chest.

'Nooo! Get off me! That treasure is ours! *Let me go!*' Niamh struggled against Noah's hold, bucking and doing her utmost to dislodge him, but he was almost twice her size and held her immobile. When Shadow growled and bared his teeth at her, snapping his jaws, she finally subsided, flinching away from the dog. 'Call him off,' she hissed.

Noah did. 'Good boy, Shadow. Thank you, but that's enough. Are you OK, Alix?' He glanced over his shoulder.

'Yes. Or I will be. I think I'll need stitches.' Alix was visibly shaking, but didn't seem about to faint. He hoped she hadn't lost too much blood and could hang in there for a while longer.

'Call the police, please, then I'll take you to the hospital. Is there anything here I can tie her up with?'

'Hold on, I'll have a look.' Taking the torch, she went to rummage around the barn and returned soon after with some baling twine. 'Will this do?'

'Excellent.'

Noah got off Niamh, but didn't let go of her wrists. She bucked and twisted some more, but he held on.

'You've got nothing on me,' she shouted. 'You deleted the video, remember? So what if you have the treasure. I'll tell the police it was you who hid it here.'

He shook his head while pushing her arms behind her back. 'Tie her up for me while I hold her, please,' he said to Alix, then looked down at his sister. 'I only deleted a few seconds. The rest was saved before that. You're well and truly caught.'

'Bastard! How can you do this to your own sister? You've just always been jealous because Mum liked me best. I hate you! Do you hear me? *I fucking hate you!*' Niamh was sobbing now, although whether out of sadness or fury was unclear. Probably a combination of both. 'I wish you'd died instead of Mum.'

He ignored her rant, even though it hurt. Niamh had been only fourteen when their mother died, so it was understandable that she'd missed her the most. As the baby of the family, she'd been spoiled, but once they moved in with Uncle Ifan, that had stopped. Noah had buried his own grief in hard work, while Niamh had kept hers going. Resentment had festered inside her until she'd turned into this person he didn't know.

He couldn't help her now. It was too late. Not only had she engaged in criminal activities with Reece, but she'd tried to hurt Alix. He couldn't forgive her for that.

Not ever.

Chapter Twenty-Six

Mercia/Northumbria, late June/Sólmánuðr AD 874

They rode next to the River Trent, following its banks east and then north, making a quick stop at Hreopandune to stay a couple of nights with Eirik's friend Reidulf the silversmith.

He greeted them with a big smile. 'Eirik, my friend, I hadn't thought to see you back so soon.'

'No, but things have changed somewhat. My uncle is dead and I'm free to go wherever I please.'

'Good for you. And who is this?' Reidulf peered at Merewen, who'd been standing slightly behind Eirik.

He turned and put his arm across her shoulders, bringing her forward. 'This is my wife, Merewen. We are heading north to try and find a place to settle.'

Reidulf's eyes twinkled. 'It's a pleasure to meet you, Merewen. I hope you'll bring Eirik to see me often and persuade him to purchase my wares for you.'

She ducked her head, blushing. 'Oh, he's already been more than generous to me.' She glanced at the crystal pendant, which was now on full display since she didn't need to hide it any longer. 'It's very nice to meet you too.'

'And this is Sceadu,' Eirik added, indicating the hound, who sat with his tongue hanging out. He'd run tirelessly next to them for days and they'd had a long ride today.

Reidulf smiled. 'I see. And very important he must be too, if he merits his own introduction.'

'You have no idea. He's saved my wife several times. We owe him.'

'But what am I thinking?' Reidulf exclaimed. 'You must be famished and in need of a place to sleep. Let me introduce you to *my* wife, Winflaed. She'll have victuals for us and can arrange some extra bedding.' He ushered them towards a small building. Like some of the more permanent traders here, he'd had a proper house built for himself and his family. He did good business as a silversmith and could afford it.

'Thank you, that's most kind. We've been sleeping out in the open for the most part,' Eirik said, leading their horse behind them. 'Fortunately the weather has been sultry.'

'Indeed. Let me call someone to take care of your mount, then we'll have supper. I want to hear all about your recent adventures, since I never go anywhere myself these days.'

Merewen was delighted to discover that Winflaed was Mercian like herself. Although she'd understood the gist of Eirik and Reidulf's chat in Norse, she was relieved to have someone to talk to in her own dialect. She was surprised at being welcomed so warmly, but gathered Reidulf was someone Eirik had known and trusted for many years. From Winflaed she also gleaned a bit more about their history.

'Don't be appalled,' the woman said, 'but my husband spends

most winters melting down objects the warriors have looted in order to make the metal more portable and easier to use for trading purposes.' She shrugged. 'It is the way of war, is it not? To the victor go the spoils. It bothered me at first, but I've come to accept it, and our people would do the same to anything they captured from the men they call the Heathen Army.'

'Yes, I suppose you're right. Eirik doesn't want that life any more, though. We're going to find a place to settle down and farm the land. I gather he's never had a proper home and I can see he yearns for it.'

'He's been discontented for years, but he only confided in Reidulf, no one else. As he'd sworn an oath of loyalty to his uncle, he couldn't break it, but he did try many times to talk that stubborn old man into settling down.' Winflaed sighed. 'From what I understand, it simply wasn't in his nature. And now he's gone?'

'Yes.' Merewen told the tale of how Hastein had tried to use her as a bargaining tool.

'How awful! I'm glad he got his just deserts.' Winflaed had been baking flatbreads on a griddle while they talked, and now she placed the last one on top of a large stack. 'Right, let's eat, and then I'm sure you'd like to bed down for the night. You must be exhausted.'

'Thank you, yes. I'm looking forward to sleeping in proper bedding.'

Truth to tell, though, she wasn't as tired as Winflaed imagined. Even after days of travelling, she was still buoyed up by excitement at this new life she'd be building with Eirik. Nothing could dampen her spirits now.

Before they left, Eirik found someone to help them perform Norse marriage rites, and invited some of his and Reidulf's friends for a feast. It was a joyous occasion, and although Merewen had felt like she was his wife even before this, now it was official. She would have liked to be married according to her own beliefs, but she didn't force the issue. After what they had gone through, being with Eirik in any way, shape or form was enough for her.

As they rode out of Hreopandune the next morning, they passed the site of the former monastery, which Eirik pointed out to her. It had apparently consisted of a group of separate buildings, but the only one left now was the church. It sat on a bluff overlooking the river, surrounded by a Norse encampment.

Merewen shuddered. 'Thank the Lord I didn't end up there.' She leaned her head back onto Eirik's broad chest and turned to kiss his cheek. 'You saved me from a life of boredom, although I suppose I would have been content helping the nuns to heal people.'

He had his arms around her and squeezed her tight, kissing her back. 'That would have been a terrible waste. I'm very thankful you are my wife instead.'

At the mouth of the River Trent, where it merged with a larger body of water, they crossed the wide expanse by boat, horse and all, then carried on riding northwards. Jarl Halfdan had passed this way that spring, and some of his men had settled in the area. Eirik was acquainted with a few of them, but Merewen was relieved when he didn't stop for longer than a brief chat. Most of the men had apparently continued further north with their jarl to carry on raiding.

'Are we going anywhere specific?' she asked, as Eirik seemed to know exactly which direction he was heading.

'Yes. I was in this area last year and came across the perfect place. It might already be settled by now, but we will see.'

'You mean it was empty then?'

'It appeared so. What your people call the Heathen Army has been roaming the kingdom of Northumbria for years and there are many abandoned farmsteads for the taking. This was one such, with large areas of pasture and fields that looked perfect for cultivation. As it was slightly off the normal tracks, I'm hoping no one else has found it yet.'

Unfortunately, however, this did not appear to be the case. They arrived some days later at a cluster of tumbledown buildings situated in a lush river valley. Some were burned shells, others still standing but in disrepair. But despite the sad state of most of them, the place wasn't quite deserted. One of the better buildings had smoke coming out of the gable ends.

'This is it.' Eirik reined in the horse and they gazed at the place he said he'd been dreaming of for months. 'Isn't it beautiful? But there seems to be someone living here. Perhaps they'll be willing to sell the land. No harm in asking. Let us see if there is anyone about.'

Merewen could hear the disappointment in his voice, but he had an expression of grim determination on his face. It was clear he hadn't completely given up hope of owning this settlement.

A small group of people emerged when Eirik called out. A man of perhaps thirty winters, a couple of women – one old, one younger – two youths and a toddler. They all looked like former thralls, unkempt and wearing threadbare clothing. They were also scrawny, as if they were having trouble finding enough to eat.

'Good day.' Eirik jumped off the horse and lifted Merewen down. 'I'm Eirik and this is my wife, Merewen.' He was speaking Mercian, which appeared to confuse his audience.

'I am Leofric. You are not Norse?' the older man asked.

'I am, but my wife is not. We come in peace and were hoping to settle here. Are you the owners of this place?'

'Hardly.' The man looked down at his clothing ruefully. 'Two winters ago, a group of Norsemen came and laid waste to the settlement, killing our master and his family. We were out gathering wood at the time and managed to escape their notice. We've been trying to eke out an existence since, but the marauders left no grain for us to plant, and they took most of the livestock, so it's been a struggle. Another group came by last year, but we hid again, and as there wasn't much here for them to steal, they didn't linger.'

'I was part of that second group,' Eirik said, 'which is why I'm here now. I liked the look of this place and we wish to make it our home. Could we perhaps come to some arrangement and all live here together in peace? It's a bit late in the year to sow crops, but it's worth a try, and I can supply all that is needed from the nearest marketplace. I will provide victuals for everyone until such time as we can produce our own. So long as you swear allegiance to me and my wife, together we can work the land and rebuild this settlement. What say you?'

'Swear allegiance? You mean as freemen?' Leofric looked flabbergasted, then slowly smiled when Eirik nodded.

'Yes. I've never owned thralls and don't intend to. As far as I'm concerned, you have no owner now.'

'Then that would be more than acceptable.' Leofric shared a look of relief with the rest of his group, who all relaxed their tense stances.

'Excellent! Let us get started. Unless you have any objections, from now on, this place will be known as Wensdale, and I hope we will all prosper here.'

Chapter Twenty-Seven

Hereford, early June, present day

The police came and took Niamh away, together with the rest of the hoard. It turned out to be more extensive than anyone had guessed, and included not only the silver ingots, but lots more coins, a couple of Thor's-hammer amulets, hacksilver, Anglo-Saxon-style sword pommels set with garnets, ornate belt buckles, strap ends and brooches, as well as a couple of items that must have been looted from a church or monastery. It was truly a treasure trove.

They also confiscated Alix's phone as evidence.

'Good work, Mr Vaughan,' the officer in charge said. 'I'm satisfied that you had nothing to do with this crime. As for your sister, she'll likely be in jail for a good few years.'

Noah was sad that it had come to this, but at the same time relieved that the matter was concluded. It had been hanging over him for months now, and although he knew he wasn't at fault, he'd felt the judgement of others. No one had come out and said anything to his face, but he'd heard the rumours and speculation. *How could he not have known about the treasure that was found on his own land? He must have been getting a cut. Wasn't he in a gang in London? His uncle told us he was worried about the boy.* And so it went on.

Well, now he'd proved them wrong.

Unfortunately, his innocence had come at the expense of his sister's freedom, but she had brought this on herself. She'd had every opportunity to come clean and could have cooperated with the authorities in exchange for a more lenient sentence. She'd chosen not to. As for the grief and jealousy that had seemingly festered inside her for years, Noah hoped she would get counselling to help her work through her issues.

He had more immediate concerns, however, and drove Alix to the hospital at high speed after a policewoman had performed first aid and tied a bandage tightly around her arm. He held her hand as her wound was stitched, and sat with her in his embrace while she recovered from the ordeal in a curtained-off alcove. She looked pale, which was understandable since the wound had bled profusely at first, and she still trembled intermittently. He pulled her tight against his chest.

'Are you in pain?' he asked softly, kissing the top of her head and stroking her back with soothing motions.

'No, I'm kind of numb now,' she murmured, burrowing into him. 'Thank you for saving me. Well, you and Shadow. I'll thank him later.' The dog had been left in the care of a startled and sleepy Aidan, who had arrived home after a night out with friends to find the place in chaos and knee-deep in police vehicles.

'You saved yourself,' Noah countered. 'It was quick thinking to shove the bag at my sister instead of handing it over. But dangerous.' He shuddered. 'That knife could have nicked an artery. I don't want to even think about that!'

She lifted her face for a kiss. 'Let's not dwell on it. We're both safe and it's over. Now we can get on with our lives. I'll have sick leave for a few days, then everything will be back to normal.'

'Move in with me,' Noah blurted. 'Please?'

'What? But we've only been dating for like a week.' Alix leaned back a little to stare at him. 'And what about Howell's End?'

'You can rent it out. Or we can live there if you prefer and let someone else run Vaughan Court as a B&B. Whatever you want. I don't mind. Everything with you just feels so right. I want to be with you all the time. Have dinner with you and spend my evenings with you.'

'I'd have to talk to Grandpa and see what he says. As long as I don't sell the property, perhaps he won't mind.'

'Good. You'll need to stay with me this week anyway so I can look after you. The doctor said you shouldn't be alone in case you faint. So you might as well move in permanently. What do you say?'

Alix still looked conflicted. 'Are you really sure about this?'

'Sweetheart, I've never been more certain of anything in my life. I want to be with you for ever. I want you to be my wife when you're ready to take that step. And I want to have kids with you. Lots of kids.' He smiled and gave her a lingering kiss. 'Alix, I love you. You're it for me.'

She appeared stunned, but gave him a blinding smile. 'OK, as long as Grandpa doesn't mind, I'll move in with you. Vaughan Court is too lovely to rent out to others, and you need to be there in order to take care of the farm. But can we wait on the horde of kids for a year or so at least?'

Noah laughed. 'Fine, I'll try to be patient as long as you promise you want that too.'

'I do. And Noah?'

'Yes?'

'I love you too.'

He pulled her tight until she yelped and he remembered her injured arm, but even then she just laughed and moved it out of the way before letting him kiss her senseless. Noah was so happy he thought he would burst.

Everything was finally falling into place and going his way.

Morgan came for a visit, having been fetched by Noah. Alix was delighted to see him and had baked a proper moist Victoria sponge for the occasion.

'Mm, now that's what I call a good cake,' Morgan said approvingly after savouring his first bite. 'None of that dry sawdust I'm used to now. But you should have been resting, my dear, not baking for an old man.'

'I'm fine, Grandpa. The wound is healing really well. And Noah does all the heavy work. He barely lets me lift a finger.' She sent him a loving glance, which he returned with a more heated one.

'Did I tell you I spoke to your parents?' Morgan said. 'Gave them a stern talking-to, so I did.'

'No, you didn't mention that. Why? What have they done?' Alix was confused. Had she missed something while she'd been convalescing?

'Done? No, it's what they *haven't* done.' Morgan sounded indignant. 'I told them they need to stop spoiling Autumn, who is clearly too selfish for words.' The old man scowled. 'Noah told me how, not content with stealing your former fiancé, she tried to come between you two as well. Good thing he's a sensible boy.'

Alix almost laughed out loud at Noah's expression when he heard himself described as a 'boy'. He was far from that, but it didn't matter. She raised her eyebrows at him. He shouldn't have told her grandpa about Autumn's behaviour at the pub. They hadn't talked about it since.

Noah raised his hands in a peace gesture. 'Sorry, I just happened to mention that I was glad she'd left and wasn't trying to cause mischief around here any more. I should have told you.'

'It's fine.' She smiled at him and he looked relieved. 'So what did my parents have to say for themselves, Grandpa? I haven't heard from them except a quick message to ask if I was OK after I texted them to say I'd been injured.'

When she'd replied that she was fine, they hadn't enquired further, merely mentioned something about a crisis involving Autumn and her new job. That ought to have hurt, but she was strangely immune now and honestly didn't care. She had her own life here with Noah and Morgan, and that was all she needed.

'I think they were a bit shocked, to be honest.' Morgan chuckled. 'I've never been that blunt before, but I really let them have it this time. Told them that the way they treated you was disgraceful. Always taking Autumn's side no matter what. Your dad called me back later and said he'd realised I was right and they're going to stop mollycoddling her. He's told her she has to find somewhere else to stay and not rely on them any longer. She's got to stand on her own two feet from now on. I gather she wasn't best pleased, but he stood his ground.'

'They're kicking her out? I don't believe it!' Alix murmured.

'Oh yes. I think my rant was a wake-up call. In fact, I suspect they'll come and visit you soon. And me. Your dad's been calling me quite regularly, actually. It's nice chatting to him more. I'll admit I was feeling a bit lonely and neglected, although not since you arrived in these parts, obviously. I know I can see you whenever I want to.'

'Aww, of course you can.' Alix gave him a one-armed hug. 'But are you sure you don't mind about me not living at Howell's End? I can let you have it back if you prefer. I feel like I'm cheating you.'

Morgan shook his head. 'No, it's fine. You said you'd keep it for one of your children and that's enough for me. I like the thought that it won't be sold to outsiders and there'll be a Howell descendant living there. Even if he or she is a Vaughan,' he added with a twinkle at Noah.

Noah grinned. 'How about we give him or her Howell as a middle name – would that be good?'

'Great idea!' Alix beamed at him. 'In fact, I'd like all our children to have Howell as their middle name. They'll be just as much a part of me as of you.'

'True. OK, that's decided then. Now all we have to do is start making them.' Noah winked at her.

Alix felt her cheeks turn beet red and punched him in the shoulder. 'Honestly!' she hissed, glancing at her grandfather to see if he was scandalised, but he merely laughed.

'I like how you think, boy. The sooner the better, so I can enjoy a few years with my great-grandchildren. But maybe spend some time just the two of you first, eh?'

Noah nodded. 'Yes, don't worry. And thank you, I'm glad you don't mind Alix living here with me. Trust me, we'll always look after Howell's End as well.'

One year later

'Want to come for a walk?' It was Midsummer Eve and a beautiful balmy evening. Noah and Alix had just finished clearing up after dinner, and he wrapped his arms around her from behind, leaning his cheek against hers. 'It's too nice to stay indoors.'

'Sounds good. I'm sure Shadow won't mind either.'

'He's always up for a walk, you know that. Let's go.'

He took her hand and headed towards the nearest field. The ground was dry at the moment, thirsty for rain, but it meant they didn't need to wear wellies or tromp through mud. Instead, they strolled along the edges of the fields, soaking in the quietness of the summer evening.

Alix walked beside him and didn't seem to realise the direction he'd taken until they reached the bottom of the hill the Neolithic monument stood on. She blinked, as if suddenly waking up to her surroundings, and glanced at him. 'What are we doing here?'

Since their visit the previous year, they'd avoided the place, and they hadn't had any strange visions or hallucinations either. Noah held out his hand and captured the crystal pendant that Alix wore openly at home. He lifted it up to the evening light. 'I wanted to see if we're still being influenced by the past. Are you game?'

She hesitated. 'I guess. I mean, it's not like it can hurt us, right?'

'No, I don't think so. I haven't felt anything evil.' He'd had the odd vivid dream, but the ones with bloodshed had stopped. Instead they'd all been filled with passion and a deep, abiding love that made him wake up feeling happy and contented.

They walked up the hill and crawled in underneath the stones. 'Hold on to your pendant, and I'll keep this in my hand.' He took out one of the two silver coins he still hadn't returned to the authorities. And he had no intention of doing so either. It felt as though they belonged with him. 'Now close your eyes.'

Immediately the images came swarming into his brain. *The woman he loved, her hair in a thick plait, smiling at him with a toddler balanced on her hip. Sounds of revelry going on all around them, people singing, laughing, chatting, and the smell of woodsmoke, food and warm bodies. The woman only had eyes for him, though, and he leaned forward to take her and their child in his embrace. They were a family, and he was flooded with gratitude for what the gods had granted him. He had everything he'd ever wanted, right here . . .*

'Noah?'

He blinked and realised he was hugging Alix in a strange way, as though there was someone in between them. A child. He shook his head and smiled. 'Sorry. I guess those spirits had one more scene to show us, but I think that's it. They're content now.'

'Yes, I agree. I think I saw the same thing. A feast? And . . . our child.'

'Their child, but yes. Hopefully we will have our own in due course.' He took a deep breath and let go of her, then dug something out of his pocket. He backed up a little and shifted so that he was on one knee. 'Alix, will you marry me? I love you more than I can say, and you're the woman I want to spend the rest of my life with.'

He held out a little box with a ring whose diamonds glittered even in the half-light under the stones. He'd bought a diamond eternity ring because the flawless stones reminded him of Alix's eyes – clear, bright and beautiful.

'Yes,' she whispered, holding out her hand. 'Yes, please.'

He slipped the ring onto her finger and kissed her tenderly. A wet nose pushed into his arm, and Shadow gave both of them a lick. They laughed, and Noah ruffled the dog's ears. 'I see. You felt left out, did you? Don't worry, you're part of the family. In fact, maybe it's time we got you a wife too. What do you think, love?'

Alix smiled. 'I think that's an excellent idea. You wanted a large family, so let's have lots of dogs too. Sounds perfect!'

Shadow barked, as if he agreed, and Noah took Alix in his arms again. It sounded more than perfect. He was the luckiest man in the world.

Chapter Twenty-Eight

Mercia/Northumbria, late August/Kornskurðarmánuðr AD 875

In just one year, Wensdale had been transformed from a neglected wasteland to a relatively prosperous settlement. There was still some way to go, but there were new buildings – a timber hall, a couple of barns and several workshops – and the population had increased. Leofric had known of others in the same position as him and his family who were willing to join them. They'd been welcomed with open arms. A couple of former Norse warriors and their women had also arrived and asked to stay. Their jarl had been defeated and they were as tired of warfare as Eirik was.

'The more people we have working together, the faster we will grow,' he said.

Merewen and the other women had also worked hard to make the hall a home for all the inhabitants. She was proud of what they had achieved in such a short space of time, and tonight they would be celebrating the rich harvest that had just been brought in safely. There would also be two baptisms and a Christian wedding ceremony. Eirik had invited a priest for the occasion, and now everyone waited in the hall next to a makeshift font.

'Are you ready, my love?'

Merewen finished putting on the new tunic she'd made for the occasion and looked up as Eirik came striding in. He wore a matching garment, as did the little boy in his arms. She smiled at the sight, her love for them both almost overwhelming.

'I am. How about you? It's not too late to back out.'

Eirik had agreed to be baptised at the same time as his son, even though Merewen knew he wasn't convinced about the teachings of the White Christ.

He smiled at her. 'It can't hurt, can it? As far as I'm concerned, I'm adding one more god to the ones I believe in already. If he is as magnanimous as you say, he'll not take offence. As long as you don't mind me sticking to some of my own rituals as well.'

'No, that is up to you.' In truth, she had been influenced by him as well, and recently had found herself calling on his gods at times. She hoped that didn't mean she'd burn in the flames of hell when the time came.

'Besides, I promised you a Christian marriage ceremony.' Eirik put one arm around her and hugged her and their son close. 'We've not had time until now, but today I will fulfil your wish. I doubt the priest would do it if he still considered me a heathen.'

She smiled at him and stood on tiptoes to give him a soft kiss. 'Then let's do it before little Einar gets hungry again. I don't want him grizzling all through Mass.' She looked into her husband's gorgeous green eyes. 'And Eirik? Thank you. I love you with all my heart and I always will.'

He smiled at her, bending to nuzzle her neck. 'My pleasure, and you know I love you too, more than I can ever say. Mm, you smell good. How about we cut the celebrations short later and retire early? We need to give Einar a sibling as soon as possible.'

Merewen laughed and placed a hand on her stomach. 'I think you'll find we've already taken care of that, but if it means being alone with you, I'm happy to leave the celebrating to everyone else.'

'What? Really?' An even wider smile spread across Eirik's features. 'Thank you, *ást mín*, that is the best wedding gift you could have given me. I shall thank your god later.' He added with an irrepressible twinkle, 'And mine. Come, wife, they're waiting for us.'

As she took his hand, Merewen sent up a prayer of thanks to any god who was listening. She had everything she'd ever wished for, and more, and she was looking forward to the rest of her life with this wonderful man, Sceadu and their family. It was perfect.

Epilogue

Hereford, August, two years later

'Triplets? *Triplets?* You've got to be joking!'

Alix shook her head, trying to suppress the laughter that wanted to bubble out of her at the sight of Noah's shocked expression. She'd probably looked the same when the ultrasound technician had told her an hour ago, but she'd had time to digest the news while Noah had only just been hit with it.

'Triplets?' he said again, his eyes wide.

'Mm-hmm.' It wasn't a laughing matter really, as multiple births could be risky, but she felt strangely calm. They'd wanted a large family and it would seem they'd be given one more or less immediately.

'Bloody hell.' Noah gripped her hands. 'Are you OK? Are the babies fine? I mean, wow! I can't take this in.'

'Everything looks normal, they said. You'll have to come to the next appointment so you can see for yourself.'

'Yes, I definitely will. I'm so sorry I couldn't be with you today.'

He'd wanted to come, but one of the ewes had been run over after escaping from the field and the vet had had to be called in.

Noah had been forced to stay as Aidan was off sick and Pete couldn't cope on his own. Alix didn't mind. She was used to the life of a farmer's wife now and knew that these things happened. But she definitely wanted Noah present for the next check-up.

'Here, you can see the ultrasound pictures.' She handed him the three photos. 'They're still tiny, but you can make out their heads at least.'

Noah took them and muttered, 'Triplets. Jesus!'

Alix couldn't hold it in any longer and burst out laughing. 'It's a shock, that's for sure. We might need some help at first, and they're bound to be extra tiny when they're born, so they'll probably have to stay in the hospital for a while. Hopefully all will be well, though.'

Noah pulled her into his arms, holding her gently as if she was made of glass. 'For sure. Now that we've had the payment from the hoard, we can afford as many nannies as you want. One for each kid.'

'No, no, let's not go overboard. One will be fine. And you're right, we don't need to worry about that. I guess we owe your sister and Reece our gratitude after all.'

Noah nodded. 'In a weird way, yes. Are you still sure about splitting the money?'

'Yes, it seems fair.'

They'd put aside a third of the amount they'd been awarded as owners of the land where the treasure was found. They planned to keep it for Niamh and Reece, to be given to them when they eventually came out of jail. Despite everything, they had been the ones who'd found the hoard. Both Noah and Alix felt they should have some compensation, even though they had gone about everything in such a selfish and stupid way. Hopefully they'd learned their lesson, and they would need funds to start their lives over when they regained their freedom.

Alix looked up at the man she loved. 'We have more than enough anyway. And we have each other.'

'True.' Noah kissed her. 'And three kids.' He shook his head again, mumbling, 'Triplets. Wow!'

He picked her up and carried her into the living room, depositing her on the sofa. 'Stay there and rest. I'm going to do all the cooking from now on until they're born. You just concentrate on growing them.'

'I'm not that fragile,' she protested, but he just smiled.

'To me, you and those little ones are the most important things in the world.'

Alix sank down into the cushions. If he wanted to spoil her a little, where was the harm? She'd need all her strength in six months' time and then some. But she knew that Noah would be there for her every step of the way, and once the babies were born, they'd be a team.

She couldn't wait.

Author's Note

This book is actually loosely based on a true story. In June 2015, two Welsh detectorists found a hoard in a field near Leominster in Herefordshire and dug it up in secret without telling the landowner or the authorities. The treasure was apparently quite large and consisted of similar things to the hoard I describe in my book, including a rock crystal pendant. It is thought to have been hidden by a Viking around AD 878/9, when the Great Heathen Army was in the area. (See https://herefordshiremuseumsupport.org.uk/the-herefordshire-hoard/.)

If the detectorists had declared their find, as they should have done, it might have been worth over £3 million, and they would have been allowed to share 50 per cent of that value with the landowner. They didn't. Instead they decided to sell the items clandestinely (presumably so they could keep all the proceeds for themselves) and contacted some coin dealers. They in turn tried to sell some of the coins to an auctioneer in London, who became suspicious and alerted the authorities.

At first the detectorists denied everything, but eventually they declared a small part of the hoard – the items that are now in Hereford. The police got involved and the men were arrested. There were deleted photos on one of their phones showing the hoard being dug up, so the authorities knew it consisted of a lot more than they had declared. One of the men was convicted of theft and concealment and jailed for ten years, the other just of concealment, with a sentence of eight and a half years. The coin dealers they'd first contacted were also jailed. Sadly, the rest of the treasure has never been recovered, and it's thought that about three hundred coins are still missing. The search for them is ongoing, as they are of immense historical value.

My characters are of course entirely fictitious. In my story, it's the landowner's sister and her boyfriend who find a Viking hoard and decide not to tell him or the authorities. In real life, however, the landowner and his family had no involvement in finding the hoard and have never been accused of any wrongdoing. My fictional characters decide to offer their treasure for sale online, unlike the real detectorists, who tried to sell their find via dealers. Also, the real treasure wasn't found anywhere near a cairn south of Hereford as in my story, but in a field north of the city.

In my novel, I have the hoard being displayed in the new Hereford library, where my fictitious heroine works. In real life, this is still being built (or rather redeveloped) in the so-called Shirehall, and is not scheduled to open until autumn 2026. The library is in a temporary location until then.

The real hoard (what was left of it) was eventually acquired by Hereford Museum Service. It won't go on display in the library but is supposed to become a permanent exhibition in the Hereford Museum and Art Gallery, which is also currently being redeveloped/refurbished and is not expected to open until 2027. I look forward to hopefully seeing the hoard then!

Just for clarification, please note that apparently the Anglo-Saxons referred to religious institutions for both men and women as monasteries, which is why I haven't used the words 'convent' or 'nunnery' at all in this book.

Acknowledgements

With this story I'm returning to Viking times, but unlike some of the others I've written, I didn't have to go far to do the research as it's set in Britain (Viking age Mercia to be precise). I had already visited Hreopandune (present-day Repton in Derbyshire) where my Viking hero's story begins, and Northumberland where he wants to end up. And the farm my present-day hero lives on is somewhere south of Hereford, an area I know well. Very fortunately there is also a stone monument nearby – the so-called Arthur's Stone – which served as the inspiration for what I call the cairn in my story. It's really a Neolithic chambered tomb over 5,000 years old, not far from Hay-on-Wye, and it seemed the perfect place for someone to hide out. As always, I brought along my husband Richard to have a closer look, and I crawled underneath the massive stone slab to see what it felt like. Awe-inspiring, as it turned out, and a great place to shelter from the elements! Richard also came with me to the Avalon Marshes Centre near Glastonbury to check out the reconstructed Saxon longhall (like the one my Mercian heroine lives in), so many thanks to him for his continued patience and company!

Thank you so much to my lovely editor Sophie Keefe and her team at Headline – it's such a great pleasure to work with you!

Thanks also to the cover designer Sarah Whittaker for the beautiful cover, and to the narrator of all my books, Eilidh Beaton. She has once again had to grapple with some Old Norse pronunciations (and a few Anglo-Saxon ones as well!), and she always does a wonderful job. And huge thanks also to Lina Langlee, my fantastic agent, who is always there for me!

As ever, thank you to my amazing friends – Henriette Gyland, Sue Moorcroft, Myra Kersner, Gill Stewart, Tina Brown, Carol Dahlén, Nicola Cornick and the other Word Wenches: Anne Gracie, Andrea Penrose, Patricia Rice, Mary Jo Putney and Susan Fraser King. I so appreciate your support and friendship!

Most importantly, I want to thank the lovely readers, reviewers and book bloggers for buying my stories – without you I wouldn't be able to continue to do this job! Writing can be a very lonely occupation, but thanks to your kind reviews and comments on social media, I feel connected to you all. I hope you enjoy *Ripples Through Time*!

Christina x

PS If you want to keep up with news about my books, behind-the-scenes information and special deals, please sign up for my monthly newsletter – you'll find the details here: **https://tinyurl.com/mr3fu9ch**

Don't miss Christina Courtenay's
sweepingly romantic standalones!

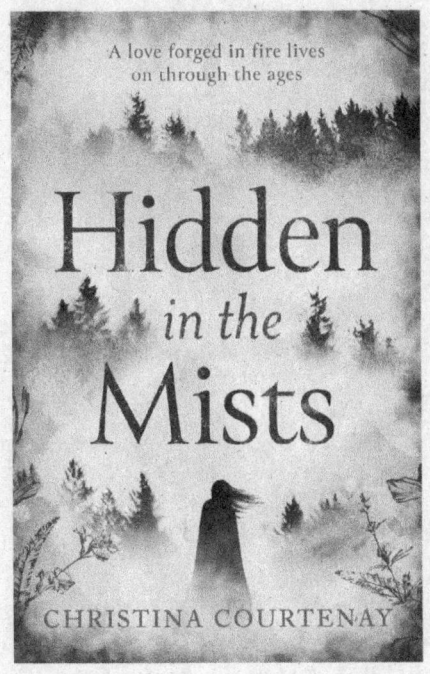

A love forged in fire lives on through the ages . . .

Available now from

Travel from the present day to Roman Britannia in this gripping dual-time novel!

Two souls bound together for eternity but lost in time. Until now.

Available now from

'A vivid picture of life in two very different time frames and . . . how the themes of life and love change little with the centuries. Fast-paced and thrilling!'
SARAH MAINE

She must forge a new path from the ashes of her old life . . .

Available now from

'Once again, Christina Courtenay has transported me through time to a world that feels more than real . . . I can only recommend that you read this absorbing, energising novel for yourself'
SUE MOORCROFT

Brimming with romance, adventure and vivid historical detail, Christina Courtenay brings the Viking era to life in her epic Runes series!

Available now from

REVIEW

RAISING READERS
Books Build Bright Futures

Dear Reader,

We'd love your attention for one more page to tell you about the crisis in children's reading, and what we can all do.

Studies have shown that reading for fun is the **single biggest predictor of a child's future success** – more than family circumstance, parents' educational background or income. It improves academic results, mental health, wealth, communication skills and ambition.

The number of children reading for fun is in rapid decline. Young people have a lot of competition for their time, and a worryingly high number do not have a single book at home.

Our business works extensively with schools, libraries and literacy charities, but here are some ways we can all raise more readers:

- Reading to children for just 10 minutes a day makes a difference
- Don't give up if your children aren't regular readers – there will be books for them!
- Visit bookshops and libraries to get recommendations
- Encourage them to listen to audiobooks
- Support school libraries
- Give books as gifts

Thank you for reading.
www.JoinRaisingReaders.com